MW01516121

To Alicy
Happy Reading
Dae Huth
Sept. 13/2011

Radioman

Radioman

Dave Nichols

To order additional copies of this book, contact:
Xlibris Corporation
1-888-795-4274
www.Xlibris.com
Orders@Xlibris.com
88123

CONTENTS

This book is dedicated to my children,
Andrew, Leslie and Graham.

No man can justly censure or condemn another, because indeed, no man truly knows another.

—Thomas Brown, English physician and writer.
From Religio Medici.

Nature's Way

Part 1

I'd read numerous accounts of adopted children and the search for their birth parents. There were startling similarities to the stories and the emotional hangover that appeared to be never ending. Unless of course, the natural parents were found. Then, it was practically a given that a happy ending ensued.

My own search began in my mid thirties, although when I think about it now, it began long before, and was surely hard wired to my evolving personality.

"Just like water off a duck's back," my mother would remark when it appeared that my reaction to an unpleasant situation would be lacking in bravery. She knew my weaknesses and was damned if she was going to let them get to me. She was a brick . . . if not an entire brick wall . . . placed strategically in front of her children. A kind of oracle. Scottish though, not Greek.

Visiting with relatives was always an awkward experience that left me feeling lonely and confused. I simply couldn't understand why I was the only one in any family gathering that didn't look remotely like anyone else. Even my sister didn't belong to me. She was adopted from another family. My strongest feeling was one of disconnection, practically from the human race.

My day dreams were dominated by thoughts of freedom, control, "perfectly-in-touch-with-my self"—isims. Everyone in my *sleeping* dreams wanted to simply either ignore me or kill me.

Being distressed usually means having to deal with that which threatens one's balance. My balance teetered on the abyss more often than not. I turned on the radio. Ten seconds before, *Lionel Ritchie's* song *Hello* smashed me in the face, and had me reeling from an impending anxiety attack. *Who was I?* The romantic "song guru" of the 1980s spoke to me at exactly 5:05 p.m.

A cold sweat, then—*who was I? where am I? where the hell are you?*

It was obvious where song guru was. He was in the radio. And I was rounding the bend.

"You're in the file, Mr. Nevis," she said, with copious amounts of indifference and condescension.

"That's very interesting," I replied.

The person in charge of information for the Department of Social Services was an efficient bastion of civil servileness.

"Could you possibly give me just some basic information about my parents . . . their last known whereabouts . . . anything at all?"

"No, I'm sorry. That's classified."

"Well, could you please tell me how I might find something or someone who might be willing . . . ."

"This is classified information. You will have to talk to the Director of Family Services or perhaps the Chief Justice of the Family Court. Or you might try your Member of Parliament . . . ."

I had already turned her off. I'd heard it all before.

I am a person, but the system does not think it in my or society's best interest that I be fully trusted with privileged information. They, of course, complete strangers, have complete access and know all there is to know about me. Perhaps they see me as a threat to their archaic bureaucracy. Perhaps they are right.

The government building that held my birth records and the people who worked there symbolized the supreme injustice that led to my identity crisis . . . a viral worm that expertly eroded my soul and parlayed my obsession into hellish deliverance.

I can barely describe the intensity of my pursuit. I phoned, wrote, badgered and provoked every potential source that might lead to me finding at least one of my birth parents or relatives. Fits and starts. Rest and regroup.

"I am wounded, but not slain. I'll lay me down and rest awhile, and then I'll fight again." *John Diefenbaker* said it and did it. So would I!

The *Parent Finders* group that I had joined nearly 10 years into my search, reached me one evening while I was in New York on business. How appropriate, I thought, that I should be given vital information on my origins, in a city where everyone is looking for the Holy Grail.

Both of my natural parents were alive. I gave the kind and resourceful people at Parent Finders the go-ahead to make contact and attempt to bridge the gap. And I waited. I was used to that.

Fear, hurt, anger. These were my constituents and the only real emotions I understood. Emboldened at first with the promise of resolution, the tidal bore delivered me once again to the mud flats and the curse. The refusal for reunion from the female was unequivocal. No response from the male.

Part 2

My childhood

"He was a son-of-a-bitch spy . . . her too probably." I overheard this type of conversation by the next door neighbors all the time. "Both of them were up to no good, that's for Goddamn sure!" "God help that boy, if it's ever proven!"

They said it loudly, just to make sure I heard from the other side of the fence. The ears of an eight year old. My parents, who'd adopted me at birth, weren't able to explain. They said it was outrageous.

Always lingering doubts, questions, and I'd heard the rumours, even if I was never quite sure what it all meant. That was over thirty years ago.

My Adulthood

I've read a lot about explosives. Literature on this subject is comprehensive. My bomb would have character and represent truth, freedom, justice. I decided to move.

Movieland, California. Most of the people who live here are obsessively trying to adjust the minor defects of their terribly fucking successful lives. It would seem like a perfect place to live. I chose to attend UCLA *Berkeley*. Say it. *Berkeley*. It resonates. I took "Environmental Studies" as a lark, perhaps to fortify my sneering cynicism.

The hangover was of unusual intensity, each particle of protoplasm inexorably linked to pain, and each cranial composite, leaden with the requisite dose of remorse.

The landscape before me revealed a scene straight out of *Dante's "Inferno"*. Beasts of all shapes and sizes exploded into view, the consequences of plundered synapses brought on by the proliferation of infusible ordinance. I was wasted.

My rehabilitation this time appeared to be a success . . . technically anyway. I was told in no uncertain terms, that another relapse would probably be my last.

It was six months before I saw the true light of day. The imprisonment to which I voluntarily submitted, allowed me to indulge in my favorite pastime: John LeCarre, Robert Ludlum, Ken Follett and other lesser lights, whisked me daily through the nether-world of espionage and murder. I was fascinated by the monumental research they had done, and the skillful unfolding of the plot lines. The technical details and complex surreptitiousness of the characters was amazing; a pathological talent for lying, their most salient feature. I thought of my birth parents often, and imagined them engaged in these life and death situations, which evidently had been their stock and trade. Knowledge and respect paralleled and sped along in sync. Tracking. Irrevocable.

The *L.A. Times* was my beacon. Honing in on a daily basis was my raison d'être. I was free. I was clean. Thirty days in the tank did it. And the *L.A. Times*. Love it and/or hate it, a comfort zone.

During the second month of drug freeness, the heat seeking missile found its mark. Page six carried a small story that caught my eye;

"Several years of investigation has revealed a spy network in Canada that goes back to World War II. The Minister for External Affairs, Robert Denby, has disclosed the identities of several key public figures that played a major role in Russian counter intelligence which began during the war and continued through to the present day. An alarming number of prominent Canadian figures and others are alleged to be involved." *And others.*

Not long after, I received first ever contact from one of the others. The letter was postmarked from somewhere in Germany:

Dear Jake:

By now you may have put the pieces together—in any case you now deserve to know the truth. Unfortunately, most of the rumours are accurate, and this of coursel has left m no other choice but to vacate and run. You can guess where my only choice of asylum lies. The famous traitors Philby, MacLean, Burgess and many others ran long before me. God only knows what lies ahead in Russia, but for me it seems the only recourse. Many lives including yours have been left in ruins because of your father and me and trust me when I say that it would have been better if none of us had been born. We had a choice in the direction our lives took but you really had none. Everything and everybody was sacrificed to our cause. And to what end?

Please don't try to contact me. The authorities know of you and will follow the trail. They take treason and spying very seriously. My name and appearance have been altered, but they know I am in Germany. It's just a matter of time.

Your father is dead. He took his own life rather than face the horror of capture and disgrace. He was a decent man. You are his image.

There is a large sum of money being deposited in your account. At least you will never suffer that way. Perhaps you will use your wealth to create a new and productive life for yourself. God bless you. I'm sorry.

Love,

your first Mother.
(her name)

Part 3

My new life

It was supposed to be just a one night stand, but uncharacteristically, I quickly became enchanted. My new girlfriend Wendy was almost overqualified for the position, but with infinite patience I knew I could harmonize her to my life directions.

Wendy and I decided to spend a few days tooling around the Finger Lakes in upstate New York. I liked her a lot. She was from a normal, decent family and provided me with normal, decent etiquette and great sex. She had a Masters degree in political science, but didn't flaunt it. She knew a lot about me. Enough anyway. The search for self, involving drugs, sex and rock and roll, she took in stride, as a predictable occurrence of modern life. She didn't know anything about my parental inheritance and I had no intention of telling her.

The BMW 740i cost $85,000. I paid for it in cash. It was a dream of high tech orgasmic rush, and I loved it. Wendy decorated the new condo we had acquired that fall with natural flare. She appreciated beauty, had great taste, and brought off the details of upscale interior decorating with such élan. We were a team.

The car and the condo represented pay back for me. Right? I'd suffered, I'd fought. This was my reward. The balance in my account, from all sources, was close to five million, and I knew that I could "grow" that to much more, quickly. I suppose I was relatively rich, but demons haunted me and pushed me away from the dock every time and true destiny was finally taking hold.

Pushing the plunger was the biggest kick. Boom! Fucking boom! The old shed just expanded in every direction and flew apart. We jumped and squealed and fell down and rolled and laughed and screamed some more. I'd rceived an explosives liscense through "special dispensation," greased with considerable cash and other connections from my Los Angeles days. God Bless America!

Wendy's teeth were perfect . . . even more so when she laughed. I loved her, I think. Even though she seemed to be changing.

There was lots of literature on how to make explosive devices. It was a great hobby, studying all this stuff.

The farm we (I) bought in Vermont consisted of a farm house, several barns, three paddocks and several hundred acres. It was expensive, but I loved to lay out the big cash.

While we experimented with explosives (at one point, we brought in a Hollywood explosives expert), the world continued to turn. For the life of me, I couldn't understand how my bank account continued to diminish, and with such speed.

Wendy said goodbye, good luck, and good riddance, although the latter was not verbal. Wendy had changed. Was it the Prozac? Hell, I'd given up drugs long ago. Did I seem completely cracked to her? Maybe she sensed that our offspring, assuming we had any, would inherit my (our) predisposition and leave the world an even worse place to live. Funny, but I got over her pretty quickly. Concentrating on ones work usually does the trick.

There was still about two hundred thousand left, (where did it all go!) but I had lost my desire for money. I went to Vegas for a four day junket and blew it. But I still had my beloved Beemer.

The BMW weighed over 2.5 tons. It's top speed on the autobahn was, I'm told, about 190 mph. Speed didn't matter for my purposes, but trunk size did. It took nearly a month to modify and load the car. I did it alone. It didn't seem fair to involve anybody else in my cause any longer. Half a ton of plastics and chemicals, many of which were agriculturally based.

My education at Berkeley was paying off. The super-hydraulic suspension levelers with which the car was fitted flexed its Teutonic muscles and finally permitted the conveyance of superb German engineering to move forward into destiny and history . . . once again, I might ad.

Not long after *my* manifest destiny unfolded, more details about my mother's *Mata Hari* falderal came to light. The new *"Freedom of Information Act"* forced the government to reveal to the public all kinds of ortherwise guarded secrets. It was all quite juicy. It seems that the Russians weren't comfortable with my mother's attempt to integrate into their society. She was no more Russian than I was, notwithstanding her clandestine activities for politics and country of choice. She was shuffled away in the fashion of British spy and defector Kim Philby and company, to a marginalized existence as a social outcast. They said she died of natural causes.

Her story exploded in the media. Much was made of her treason, the ultimate deception. This blueprint for creating social and moral havoc had undoubtedly etched itself into my psyche. A twelve gauge shotgun shell of querulous genes taunting a hair trigger. That was me alright.

I did not suffer from the Crime and Punishment syndrome of guilt, as did Dostoyevsky's hero Raskalnikov. I have no need to reveal my identity, and will never be apprehended.

With armaments the equivalent of a WW2 B29 Superfortress, the Beemer morphed into a hugh conventional bomb. The main bridge over the Rideau Canal in the Nation's capitol was delivered spectacularly heavenward. Ten vehicles and 15 people went along for the ride.

Wendy had a change of heart and medication, thus allowing her for forgive my childish shenanigans and become once again the kindred spirit I knew her to be. No questions or chastisements. Just the purposeful task of providing new "fruit of the womb." (her phrase, notwithstanding the biblical credit)

My financial fortunes have turned around, and I am once again in clover. (I seem to have a penchant for the investment banking game.)

Wendy and I and our two small children live comfortably in elaborate rural digs about 50 miles northeast of London. Someone else was arrested and convicted of my crime, but I sleep well. I am living out my life with the tools given me, and those tools are ever at the ready. Aren't we simply pawns in this temporal accident called life? *Thy rod and thy staff, they comfort me.*

p.s. these personal notes shall remain sealed until 100 years after my death. Maybe I can cheat that too, if I really concentrate . . . . see you in hell?

Balls of Steel

Curiouser and curiouser
as any homely swain can see
a preemptive strike
with the sword of Damocles
rushes judgment to the
bowels.

Pity not the poor fool
who fails to see the viper hiding in the weeds.

Parry and thrust and a day well spent
reward is to feel the selfish end of things

Oh waylay the pesky bite of conscience
placing itself well behind the line of fire
and brimstone
drumming innocence
into defeat
                    with abundant faith in deceit.

A blackened stump of what was a limb
now a gruesome symbol of the covering storm
                    to allow entry
                              of the Philistine.

Goose stepping jack boots arc weld the point
and the black ice forgives only them
lighting the way to quantum physics
                    a place so dense
                              it collapses into
                                        itself

so hard to conceive such godlessness
unless you are

    the Creator . . .

SEPTEMBER '97

On the edge
on the verge
on the mountain looking at
the big wide empty.

when the man is found
the other man is found and all the children
of the man are found.

He is so elusive
and silently effusive
and the children wait
for a sign.

Breathless and silent
looking near and far
and the man is silent
and the past is still
and the hum of tedium
rests its hungry head
on the shoulder of the children
who wait.

We are patient,
hopeful
penitent
silent
angry
and armed.

MIDDLEMAN

Middleman for middle times
Moving for a middle space
Sloth a thing to see
A recompense of eye to be
Short term lot of good room thoughts
And long term plots
A circumspect and then some above to say:

Who fuckin' cares
And boast no longer counts
It's me to who no longer lies
Lies
Seeking sonnets aftermarket
Wankers
A nationlot of good flankers
Catch the ball
Running
Groaning
Stuff of making withal a taking
Lowered expection
And true to tradition
Hopes of the picked off
Ripped off mutations
And screaming libations
Go find a creation
And get some serene asshole
perfect and rhythmical
Scrambled cranial spiritual.
Stupid
Cloudy and messy
Awake from the dream
Jean Paul Sartre
More, by the intellect awake than
Smart and supreme.
Terrorism before it was supported
He is revealed . . . . middleman

PRAISE THE LORD

Find the muse
Go on a cruise
And heaven help the redeemer
The hidden power doth devour
A slimy mendacious schemer.

Seek protection of the flowers
Spending many happy hours
A hungry dagger rips and slices
like Julia Childs in cuisine crisis
Low and behold the cattle
The Jesus child death rattle.

And gives us hope and the Pope
Has more with which to prattle.

MICROSOFT

Watch how slippery the slope it bend
Not to correct uphold or mend
Only treachery it pushes
The agenda
Microsoft to the end.

Pterodactyl to the sky it raises
Our hopes and all we birds it praises
We flop and bust our flimsy landing
The interloper a triumphal branding
No soft field to absorb.

So What

Long limbed harbingers of despair are flying over my territory
and I don't like it.
But given an option that thing would quickly and maybe even
quietly
dispatch itself and leave the air space and make way for more
important objectives
hardly a time to objectify the spiritual stuff and diminish it
to mere idealism whose heartfelt dogma takes far too much
advantage of the human condition.
Only a beach, coarse, is the place and replacement for interference
but it must be hot and breezy and whimsical and forgiving
of its own nature of vast misunderstanding and forgiveness,
(only the bipolar type gets the drift) a rebel of one's own that
is totally understood but unforgiving and always protected
with no reward and no glimmering intro-intrusion to the nut
center of untenured mind female—my seed has taken a road
less traveled and surprising.
Manufacturing because anything can be made including
mindlessness
which is
very very important
to the human condition
and nobody gets it.

Amen

the
only way
you can understand
the mystery of the pyramid
is to understand the . . . why . . . of the
stone blocks that built the mystery of
the engineering feat that neither man nor successor
fully understands and cannot collect within the walls of
a place that worships deities and symbols of extreme vacuum
and aging notions of superior gestation through evolution and
spot checking
to make sure we all understand that which is for now is not for
always and ever or
forever amen . . . . but the base must remain secure . . . . and
final.

Simon's Bath

Several days had passed since the image in the mirror had revealed an interloper. Simon had always known the principle of *bending infinite images*, an occurrence, when two mirrors face each other.

The bath was the one place where cares of the day evaporated, obediently finding their way down the tiny whirlpool at the conclusion of one's ablutions.

Marny, Simon's current squeeze and long suffering sounding board, was not known for her tact when dealing with his paranormal speculations.

"You're taking way too many beta blocker's, Simon. They can cause hallucinations even in well adjusted people!"

"You are as cruel as that guy that beckoned to me while I was having a bath the other day."

"Maybe you should signal back. Ask for an email address. Facebook? Do some internet boy bonding!"

That's the way it had gone ever since Simon had his experience with a simple fact of physics. Look into a mirror that is facing another mirror behind you, and the reflection causes the image to bend and repeat itself, ad-infinitum.

"I am no longer introducing chemical substances of any nature into my body and have never suffered the dreaded "flash-back," Simon replied to Marny's typical rebuke.

"Simon, you are a decent person at heart. Why do you have to be so bloody "old" and crazy all the time?" She was relentless.

It had only happened the one time. How many baths had Simon taken, blissfully naked and alone, immersed in the decadent blending of bath bubbles and near boiling water—allowing his own personal brand of reverie to consume him.

Abstract musing had been his dotty but adorable mother's distinguishing trait and it had led to some bizarre reasoning.

"My god mother, what were you thinking when you torched the boathouse?"

"It was old and needed expensive repairs, Simon dear." she had answered sympathetically. "Besides, it obscured the view of Mr. Wrigley's vegetable garden."

She had died a contented woman and her aphorisms continued to imbue the souls of those left behind. Simon's favourite was "Replace facts with lots and lots of fiction, and life will be ever so grand."

She would have thought Simon's experience in the bathroom to be a "manifestation of a fertile imagination finding a new way to beat the odds of succumbing to convention, dear."

Perhaps if I put in more bath time, my uninvited guest in the mirror will give an encore, Simon thought to himself.

By Sunday evening, his skin had become so prune-like and Marny's horrified mute expressions so unnerving, Simon relented by retiring to a dry place in the house and drowning his dismay in a large bottle of 100 proof body lotion.

Two weeks since this last horrendous attempt at reaching out to the stranger in the mirror. Simon's refusal to enter the large bathtub fortunately did not preclude daily showers in a stall safely removed from bath and mirrors. His compulsion to peek into the reflecting glass was at times overwhelming, but common sense, combined with basic cowardice, prevailed.

Things were not going well at work. Any attempt at concentration beyond 30 seconds at a stretch was completely out of Simon's grasp. He overheard colleagues speculating. Was it depression that was setting in? God, I am not by nature a depressive type, am I? thought Simon. Obtuse at times, perhaps, but not the big "D" word. Worming itself into the recesses of his cranium, the recurring image of this perverse apparition chipped away at his ever diminishing sanity.

"To hell with it, I'm going to take a bath," Simon said to no one in particular as he sprang from his desk and escaped the accursed bondage surrounding him. Now, stock brokers are a cynical, unpredictable lot as a whole, having been professionally weaned in an atmosphere of rollercoaster emotions formulated on greed and one-upmanship, but their looks of dismay and sympathy at Simon's frantic departure appeared heartfelt.

The drive home was a blur—quickly, the tearing off of garments, as Simon prepared to take the plunge once again. Not until his numbed fanny touched the steaming liquid, did Simon awaken to his actions and the accompanying reverie that settled in.

"Alice would understand precisely what I'm going through," Simon chuckled to himself as he imagined Alice and her cat before the looking glass. Did *Lewis Caroll* know something that he didn't? Simon pictured himself sitting fully clothed in the bath wearing a gingham dress, patent leather shoes and blond wig, waiting for the big move as Kitty debates whether or not to take the leap. Overcome with hysterical laughter, as hot, sudsy water invaded his windpipe and his mental state, Simon suddenly thought that he might expire in his own bathwater, leaving a legacy of whispers and innuendo.

But Simon was no longer alone. There, in the mirror he was facing, appeared the human form seen only once before. Now, it was much closer, and as Simon slowly focused on the impossible, it became clear that his life was about to change forever.

It was Marny's fear for Simon's collapsing mind that led her to discover the inestimable Dr. Beresford M. Beecher. A shingle hanger extrodinaire. Having spent several sessions with this "mind in motion" magician, Simon sensed that Dr.Beecher was bored. So often, he imagined, the good Dr. B. had listened to the rantings of seriously unbalanced individuals who probably just needed a healthy dose of self esteem and cuddles.

Since Simon was lying on the couch with the good doctor just behind him, there was no way of knowing for sure if Beecher was sleeping, smirking or sneering. Anyway, his aftershave was noxious, but helpful in keeping Simon distracted from the very serious implications of why he was there. "You said that this 'person' was standing in the long corridor of the repeating mirrors, abutting each end of the tub," Beecher said.

"Yes."

"Any distinguishing features . . . moles, scars, tattoos?"

"No, it was just a . . . you know . . . form . . . silhouette." Simon began to think that perhaps Dr.Beeacher was just a tad too much of a literalist. He envisioned Beeacher and him sitting in the bath together, both dressed in Alice's clothes and the good "shrinker" taking notes. He just wanted to scream.

"Why do you have mirrors at each end of your bathtub, Mr.Roe?" Simon could feel the doc's right eyebrow raising in a dramatic and arrogant fashion.

"It was my mother's idea."

"I see."

Suddenly, Simon began to feel a little better about his relationship with Dr. Beecher, for here was a man who just might buy a simple, visual presentation. "Try it some time doctor. Stand between two mirrors facing each other, and lean in and take a look. You probably won't see anything other than a dozen or so repetitions of the reflected mirrors, diminishing in size as they quickly seem to bend and disappear around a corner. Simple physics. But my mirrors are different, Doc. I've got something humanlike living in there. I think it wants me for something."

Simon quickly turned to try and catch the Doctor's reaction to this outrageous and terrifying experience, only to catch Beecher seriously examining something he had just excavated from his nose.

In a melancholy mood and despite the luminous introspection that reading "Alice Through the Looking Glass" had given him since childhood, the funk clung to Simon like some repacious leech. The "Phantom of the Bath Glass" as he referred to it in private, had appeared twice again to him in the past week. Each time, Simon was struck dumb in his tracks.

Oh, Kitty, how nice it would be
if we could only get through into the
Looking—glass House! I'm sure it's got
Oh! such beautiful things in it! Let's pretend
there's a way of getting through into
it, somehow, Kitty. Let's pretend the
glass has got all soft like gauze, so that we
can get through.

Marny had been gone nearly three days, and she had removed all traces and acknowledgements that she had once shared the same abode with "Mr. Mental," as she so lovingly referred to him.

> *"Beware the Jabberwock, my son!*
> *The Jaws that bite, the claws that catch*
> *Beware the Jubjub bird, and shun*
> *The frumious Bandersnatch!"*

Now that he had been granted his request for a leave of absence from work, Simon could devote his full attention to the task at hand. His considerable powers of deduction told him that given the increase in the frequency of the "encounters," before long, some sort of real contact would be made.

His mother Rose had known *The Walrus and the Carpenter* by heart, which was no mean feat. But then, Rose could quote chapter and verse, practically the whole of *Through the Looking Glass:*

> *"I know what you're thinking about," said*
> *Tweedledum; but it isn't so, nohow."*
> *"Contrarywise," continued Tweedledee, if*
> *it was so, it might be;and if it were*
> *so, it would be; but as it isn't, it ain't.*
> *That's logic."*

Acceptance of mystical forces was something that Simon had less and less problem with, as his strange circumstances intensified.

Since most of his waking hours were spent in the bath, Simon felt it expedient to move most of his eating provisions into the bathroom, along with the tv, (which proved pretty tame entertainment by comprison) all of his mother's volumes of Lewis Carroll's books, as well as dishes, microwave and fridge. Constant immersion in water had changed Simon's appearance dramatically. He saw someone quite different in the mirror, now. But it wasn't just the water that was changing his demeanor. Self-imposed imprisonment had given him a remarkable sense of freedom to explore a new dimension with which he was becoming one. His metamorphosis allowed him to explore the thoughts and actions, not only of Alice, but of all the characters she encountered on her journey. He'd almost forgotten that Rose had taken him on these journeys many times before:

> *The Walrus and the Carpenter*
> *Were walking close at hand:*
> *They wept like anything to see*
> *Such quantities of sand:*
> *'If this were only cleared away,'*
> *They said, 'it would be grand!'*

With a sense of well-being he had never experienced before, Simon rose from the bath and looked squarely at the vision before him. The long corridor of repeating images was now full. The next step was the easiest and most joyful he had ever taken.

When Simon didn't answer the phone after repeated calls, Marny alerted the police. Except for the peculiar rearrangement in the bathroom, there was no indication that a robbery or any foul play had taken place. Only Marny noticed that a mirror was missing from the wall at one end of the tub. The police were curious to know why someone had written where the mirror had been:

"ALICE DOESN'T LIVE HERE ANYMORE."

ACKNOWLEDGEMENTS:

MacMillan Children's Books: Excerpts from: Through The Looking Glass, And What Alice Found There by Lewis Carroll, with fifty illustrations by John Tenniel.
London: MacMillan Children's Books,1980.
ISBN 0 333 29037 2.
With permission of MacMillan Publishing Ltd., London, England.

CHILDISH

A white shirt
pale blue shorts
a field of clover and timothy grass
I am a boy of seven

a sweet summer day
hues abound
a field of clover and timothy grass
a boy of seven

sky so clear
air so fresh
absent—one to share with
a field of clover and timothy grass
a boy of seven

beauty and fragrance
beyond level 10
in a field of clover and timothy grass
and I am a boy of seven

longing to be that boy again
aching to find that place

A new white shirt
new pale blue shorts
could only be heaven.

CHANGES

When the air changes tone
Leaden skies look for home.
Tired leaves lay to rest,
that's the time I like best,
But I've never felt New York in Winter.

When the park's a lively hive
and the city seems to strive
to ensure there is no place of indifference,
That's the top of everything,
But I've never seen New York in the Winter.

Reaching, soaring, never ending,
a crush of power, glory, all is bending.
The machine that waits for nobody
still waits for me,
But I've never felt New York in the Winter.

The soldiers of the streets push on
beyond the call of duty
Quick pulse denies the tired eyes,
strangely close at hand with beauty
Ah, to finally feel New York in Winter.

1. Islaand Mentality

weight forward
easing upward to new season
close and yet so far as to beckon
and the promise of islaand(sic)mentality
is nearly a typographical error.

the sword allows the pen freedom
it is not mightier—only
newer.

restraint
disallowing Darwin his due
blasting civility
over to innocence
a baby's hand or breath
resistance foremost of bestiality
see it in films
see it in life.

look up
purity
skies of infinite reality
earthbound sensibility
an anchor imposed by god and his helpers.
an option for the seafarer,
only an option.

bright, easy travel in mind for
wherever.
a sky so perfect it becomes
suspicious and guilty of beauty we
are denied

landscape/bedrock/soundtracks/visceral
interference/interference
correction to impede creativity
a daemon truly dedicated to its mission—a-regulator.

2. Art

through hell
to twelve noon
forgive time the host
molecules micro and magna
make no difference
all is small
a breath so timeless
an interpretation waiting
small/big
no difference
earth
small/big
no difference,

islaand indifferent
controlling big and small
is nothing but all of those who define it.

we are not arrogant
alas, there is no word . . . .

islaandness?(sic)

DAUGHTER

daughter gone
her own alarms are not loud enough
mine scream.

stay close so i can tell you
whispered hello i'm here
screamed hello i'm here

time limits
out of time and now
a final pronouncement

smarten the f up
take it from an old guy who would like to know
who knows enough to know
enough

love yourself more
take more for yourself from the trough
the system
which permits choice only.

give something back to the source
of your conflict

wise be
not always safe.

My Children

watching
the time moving towards my rest
return to birth and grave
making focus clearer
love for blood of self
Intensify
to give spirit a rational
to give
with hope for their peace

strength comes
as past is revisited to an anachronistic
space
and anachronism lives well
in space without contemporary definition
squeezing through the black hole
at speed of unknown proportions
a speck of dust emerges
as a speck of dust.

will by nature
of god unknown
and control at ready
the foe has flown

. . . .

. . . .

rhyming couplet
a fighter's stance
for natural objecting
and calculated chance.

lessons to them who want to
know
keep not the faith of the new driven
snow.

washing gently
and infinite hope
sands of ancient persuasion
protect them
to cope.

STRAIGHT AND NARROW

miter boards to direct the straight
ouija boards to direct the obtuse
bored boards to direct no one

Sharing thoughts with strangers
contemporary fascism
and the means to revolution

get on board
to get bored and face the boar

allabored (sic)and avoid
the hydro wires

RADIOMAN

From where I sit, the outside world is not strictly visible, although the odd shard of light struggles through from time to time.

Ten years have passed since my scuffle with the law, and I am, as always, optimistic that the parole review board will consider releasing me. I have been a model inmate and played the game to a tee. I'm also drug-free. Completely in control. The laws regarding the release of dangerous offenders are laughable, and decidedly a piece of good fortune for yours truly.

Incarceration of the type I am obliged to endure, does have its advantages, though. Like compelling the imagination to work diligently, either in overdrive or in a stunningly neutral mode. As I am yet another victim of an unjust system, I chose introspective rage as a means of daily propulsion. I guess you'd call it overdrive.

The radio show I hosted, had the highest ratings in "talk" radioland. Management, staff, listeners and callers had great praise for my style. It was said that I had a knack for drawing out the callers with just the right mix of empathy and chastisement, crying with them on one hand, eviscerating their views and their souls on the other. A hired gun; a saint; a mentor; a prick.

Being loved was not my thing but the sweet taste of respect powered my ego and allowed me to take my wisdom to the masses. I mean, what sort of pathetic individual spills his guts and pushes his fallacious views to some bogus guru of the airways like me? I gave not a fiddler's fuck about any of them.

Oh, I'd had more than my share of death threats. Most public figures live, to some degree, in peril, so I took it in stride. However, my unique method of manipulating my callers was altogether too precise for some, and with few exceptions, I won the con game in spades. Yes, I had more than my share of death threats.

My addiction to intellectual control was only surpassed by my addiction to mood altering substances. My injestation of cocaine, (power thoughts) booze, (balancer) and xanax (downer) was relentless. A few lines of the white stuff before and during my "therapy of the air," eventually led me down the path of my own customised disaster. No surprises there, I guess.

Like a novice theologian or politician, I was ripe with idealistic fervour. There was no subject that this gold-plated radio jock couldn't or wouldn't handle. Nor was there any listener that couldn't be subdued and mentally swindled. Knowing that my prolific nature wasn't everyone's cup of tea, I decided way back when that packing a "piece" was a prerequisite for the job. One never knew when a dilettante might get too close. (You can see that I am not entirely without humour.) But yes, the weapon was real and of great comfort. In fact, it had a special romantic appeal unto itself and shared its lust with my lady friends.

The first time I spoke with Tanya, she seemed determined to crash and burn. A typical caller. Over-amplified, simple minded hang-ups. I offered wisdom from my treasure trove of learning and arranged to meet her after the show. Why her? Because she seemed uniquely hopeless and lost. That characteristic always made me feel more empowered. She was a feast of blonde perfection. About 27 or 28. Five-eight, 120 pounds. Skin, eyes, legs, ass, breasts. All immaculate and a mind that proved God was often unkind with his creations. There, on the roof, next to the 50,000 watt transmitter that powered my mutating ego, we met and made love. I also shot her to death with my 9 millimeter semi-automatic. I felt she might be a dilettante. You were special number one.

I always sleep well here in the lock-up, knowing that whatever crimes I am accused of committing, nothing for me could be more heinous than the crime of blind faith. The callers sought my superior wisdom. I offered it freely. They cried out for help, for peace. I provided that too.

Sylvia provided more temptation. More potential danger. Easy. A total fuck-up. Beautiful physically. Revolting mentally. A total turn-on. She seemed a special caller and because she excited and emboldened me in that certain way, I knew we had to meet. She confessed she had an abnormal fear of dying violently. We met on my rooftop and she would have jumped if I'd told her to. She was very surprised when she saw the 9 millimeter. But not so surprised when the noise and fire exploded from it into her face. Strange, that. I'll never forget you, number two. A definite dilettante.

I've learned lots and lots in prison. For instance, it is total enlightenment to discover that the obdurate mind of those considered dangerous offenders follows an unwavering pattern of behaviour that circumvents societal tenets. It is revelations like this that keeps me drawing water and hewing wood. But no one ever said that the criminally insane are stupid. Or uncooperative. It is with great interest and relief that so many of my fellow guests are truly individuals, in a collective sort of way and ever so garrulous. The fact that I am somewhat celebrated for accomplishments other than my so-called crimes, (no, let's just call them crimes) does not seem to impress my cohorts, for they too, in their minds and deeds, are also unique as well.

Mavis was not so easy for me. A person with real potential. Satisfying however, because of her deep knowledge of the specious nature of man. Her last words were, "This can't be happening." Almost certainly a potential dilettante. I'll never forget you number three.

"You consider yourself an anarchist, James?" My guidance counsellor, (it's less clinical than the other word) is Dr. Headley. He is definitely not a dilettante. He's seen and heard so much strange shit and is nearly as fucked-up as the rest of us, though he disguises it well.

"More," I reply.

"More than an anarchist?"

"I am a freedom fighter and an iconoclast with real purpose."

"So that's why you murdered those innocent women?"

"Yes." I enjoy the parry and thrust of a good chin-wag, and delight in my witty replies to his fairly predictable questions and observations. "Give me liberty, or give me death!" I often use this famous phrase to drive home a point.

He pretends to be even and patient.

"But liberty and death go hand in hand, according to your version of . . . ." He trails off, fearful of engaging me in a serious headbanger, which he knows he is sure to lose.

"Progressive lifestyle," I offer, with a quiet chuckle, knowing full-well the good doctor's secret discomfort with psychos, despite his professional training.

Today, I am most excited at the thought of sitting before this group of incompetent social workers, for this will be the most important account I have ever handled. A sell job "par excellence" is required, and I am ecstatic at the challenge. Watch out world, I've got more goodwill and good intentions about how I'll fit in with society than you can shake a stick at! So I take my script with me to the parole board and play it for all it was worth.

They don't buy it for a second. The hearing takes no time at all. Am I imagining it, or are board members Smith and Kline actually smirking at me? It is unanimous that I continue my penal visitation a while longer. I'd have plenty of time to analyse what went wrong with the pitch.

I have fashioned my script along the lines of the Charles Manson girls, Leslie Van Houten and Susan Krenwinkle, the killers of actress Sharon Tate and several others, way back in 1969. Swinging L.A.! The television revealing their lives from crime time to the present was fascinating and supremely informational. Here were these now middlaged women pouring out their lives to some filmmaker and displaying considerable intellect at times, as well as media savvy. They'd had lots of exposure to the media before and during the trial. In contrast, was the irascible and incorrigible Charlie Manson doing his usual "evil incarnate" number. Van Houten sought personal absolution through candidly admitting, in vivid detail, her involvement in the murders. Krenwinkle sought public forgiveness through her own journey of enlightenment while serving her life sentence. Van Huten and Krenwinkle had also struck out with the parole board on each occasion. Why?

They seemed genuinely remorseful and pleaded their case sensitively and professionally. That was it. Too professional, too sensitive. That the public would have been extremely unhappy with their release hadn't occurred to me. Neither did the public's possible take on my release ever enter my headscape.

How time flies when you're havng fun! My next hearing 3 years later is a smashing success. Based on my thorough analysis of the Manson girl's failure to convince the parole board halfwits of their reliability, I rewrite my script brilliantly convey sincerity, contrition and my best sell job ever. My research of the transcripts of dozens of successful parolee hearings gives me a new power punch credo: *Look. Learn. Imitiate.* Three days later I am released into the custody of a halfway house, compliments of the John Birch Society. Fourteen months later, I am a free man.

Radio listeners love me! Not that I really care for that sort of thing. (I believe I made that clear earlier on.) A small but well placed town takes me in and thrusts me to its bosom. The listeners in this community are very observant and at times opinionated. A perfect breeding ground for dilettantes.

Luba. Oh, Luba! She is quite drunk and offensive, at times insecure. But oddly, I find her agreeable. In the fractured light of 3 a.m my pitching and rolling Mustang 5.0 litre GT becomes my diamond studded playpen. Thank you Mr. Ford. Luba, despite here natural gifts, looks somehow grotesque and projects a potential for . . . what was it? Ah yes by God, it is anarchy! She is drenched in it! It flows from her in torrents! Audacious. Determined. Courageous. Not like the others. She is no dilettante. I can spare her. Perhaps even love her!

I am never into playing the part of the submissive. Don't care for being tied to the bed, but I'm going along with it anyway. There is time now. Time to give myself to my new love!

"Pray for death, cock sucker!" she says. "You'll wish you were dead, I guarantee!"

I am without speech, thought or feeling. Numbness. This can't be happening.

"I know who you are, you sick fuck. Well kiss 'em bye, bye, radioman!"

She is found guilty by reason of temporary insanity, and given six years. She will be out in two and a half. I'll never forget you number four.

The healing is slow, and I may be less of a man in one sense, but my physical depreciation has in no way diminished my creative, free thinking nature. On the contrary, I have expanded considerably my treatise on the singular make-up of the dilettante personality, and am anxious to proceed with more tactile research. There seems to be more of them around than ever, and I fear that they can only serve to disrupt the lives of productive free thinkers, as we like to call ourselves.

Thankfully, a new challenge beckons, and I look forward with renewed excitement and purpose to the day when, once again, I can sit before my studio microphone and announce:

"Don't go away, troubled listeners out there in Radioland. I'll be back soon with more of the same."

BIG BANG

Celestial moons and silly tunes
enforce the tattered space
of time and thought and circumspect
a somewhat crowded place.
microcosms at best define
such tiny particles and yet devine
or no more up than down
or no more smile than frown.
A word or two placed upside down
makes lots of sense if they don't drown
and running out of couplets
works wonders all aroun(d)
there is no getting away from sexuality
it is the tenant of all places
an interloper whose whisper is louder than
any scream ever heard
and a scream as silent as
the creationary big bang
ears need event
event needs recognition
the big bang was
God's orgasm
lucky God.

BONFIRE

bonfire of vanities
a cause for celebration
a loosened banner
a wakening from incarceration
a fire brand/ an oxen
a book of importance
a dead romance buried
lest wistfullness reorients
and makes smoke of pensive
nonsensical protractions.

white light hums blandly
amid screeching reflection
a boardroom where always the meek
get rejection
a mendacity of valueless stony conjecture
impaled upon motherless son's apoplexy

earth and seed do what *they* do
so well
amazing in their simplicity
and impeccable design
while the bonfire of vanities
smiles
and waits.

TASTING AIR

once a purpose
all ascending
rushing full, in thrall
amending

finding naught— a pall descending
ripping thus a major ending

over twice and little sizzle
watch another life unfizzle

check the time it doesn't matter
folks are feeling somewhat fatter

feed the dogs of war
their appitite unending
no aftertaste of doing
only vagueness of mending

the stitch not taking
appropriate measures
faking
denial till seeing things remembered
and falling numb, bending

no parachute
for a small plane pilot-
never has been

small planes
denied principal
large cough
control
no more metaphors
only taste fading

SUPREME BEING

reflection does no good
it is wavy and fraught with deceptive science
illumination which was always so handy
disperses ultraviolet light and harm's way
intellectual pundits have lost their prized virginity
and the rapist kicks and bashes his way to being supreme as
judge and jury all want blood and now there is not enough for
everyone

god is in cape cod
for a rest like his images and creations
and the shores that brought the good pilgrims and holy men of
virtue
accepts blood over the stones of eternity washed forever
and the view of perfect human nature to kill and be killed
for the love of god
a flimsy fabric by any measure and completely misunderstood

be afraid of god who creates in his own image
the product of evolution is just a plaything
for strangeness never to be fathomed
or begot
men are only created as equal as they so choose
and god waxes and wanes at leisure.

OUTSIDE

to abstract—to remove oneself
from the demands of
recrimination/abortion

madrigal songs

i hear them on the cd
reminding of a more simplistic time
a standard bearer to calm the savage.(beast)

only a naked swain
watching weakness and beauty and saying I knew it,
I knew it.

flutes from somebody—I don't know-
fiddles, the same-
together.

voices
suddenly,
interruption.
silence is currency but too expensive
don't call the broker

a quiet penetration-
only traces of being there-forever.

SHIT AND SHOES
(military expression for aftermath of plane crash)

Shit and shoes
I guess you lose
and god is just a metaphor

with spit and polish
attempt to abolish
the cursor

leaving hot and dying
young
a questionable cuckold

only just a spot of blood
feeble badge of courage

god as just a metaphor
hopeful blind repose
a quaint and jumped up interlope
a silly silent pose

explain clandestine nature
unwilling to reveal
tiny witless destiny
for whom, the bell doth peal.

GHOSTS OF PORT HOOD

Early 1700s

It had been 300 years since the ferocious crash and bang of exploding gun powder and splintered rock resounded for miles. Sometimes, if the workers weren't agile enough the sandstone peeling off the side of the cliff would come smashing down upon them—as many as 25 men dying a horrible but quick death. Raymond could identify with his surroundings and the bounteous ghosts of history. His ancestors were from around here and probably participated in the mining of the material that would become the great fortress. Port Hood was on the wrong side of Cape Breton (Nova Scotia) in the 1700's. Louisbourg was a long and hazardous journey around the northern tip of the island and then 3 days travel south along the coast. The French ships were strong and heavy laden with the rock that would give the remote town and military guardian called Louisbourg it's distinctive place in history.

Present

Jenny figured that she was in love with Raymond. After all, why had she been coming back to Cape Breton and in particular Port Hood for all these summers? July through August to the first whisper of autumn for 5 years now. Roanoke Virginia to Nova Scotia with her parents. Relatives all over the place from the Canso Causeway to Pleasant Bay on the north west coast.

It was love at first sight. Not with Raymond. That came later. It was the place. The same old mystical allure that hooked most people that visited here. Especially if numbers by the Rankins or Natalie MacMaster or bad boy fiddler Ashley MacIssac reached out from the car cd player and grabbed you by the senses. Feeding on the myth and allowing an idealized fantasy to take over sensibilities was like free falling through time and history. All the clichés applied. Time lapse cameras rewinding.

1720's

The French vessel held 20 tons of ballast in her hold. But this was more than ballast. It was the stone that would define the fortress of the North Atlantic. At six knots in five meter seas, this would be a voyage of some danger but great reward. The Treaty of Utrecht in 1713 had spared the relinquishing of Cape Breton. It was, along with Prince Edward Island, a strategic and economic stronghold for the French in North America and was moving from simply a cod fishery town, to a mighty guardian of French protectionism in the new world.

Jean LeClair had come to colonial Louisbourg in 1715 aboard the Semslack, the same ship that brought the first settlers to Havre a L'Angloise, it's original name. Jean was drawn to this place and the adventure that it promised. His life in St. Malo France was one of religious persecution and spiritual confinement. The roiling sea and the cargo of stone bound for Louisbourg around the northern tip of Isle Royale awakened new danger worth every second of imposed risk. A young man free to live or die in glory and purpose. The defense of North America against the ever increasing British menace.

2005/Montreal

Sylvie LeBlanc was drunk. Probably stoned as well. The Montreal clubs that were becoming her raison d'etre, left her high and anything but dry— Night after night. She had recently talked with her uncle Claude. He had legally adopted Sylvie when her father was killed in a gang war involving the Hells Angles several years before. Sylvie was grateful but never got out of the rut. Uncle Claude moved from Montreal back to Cape Breton soon after Sylvie's fourth or fifth drug addled desertion. There was always an open invitation for her to come and live or at least visit. She declined and vanished—or so it would seem.

Present

This all seems to be leading to the conventional idea of "new age" meeting "old", in some kind of accidental or intentioned ancestral collaboration. It is. But I can tell you this. Since my recent visit to Cape Breton, there have been hugh questions occupying my little mind concerning the ebbing and flowing of water and stones upon the shores of this place— stones washed by the Gulf of St. Lawrence—the same water that propelled and dispensed with hundreds of ships and their cargoes, bound for the utopian land we now inhabit.

I have lived next to the waters of Lake Ontario in Canada and sailed its waters. I have flown the skies of this region and experienced its broad expanses. But the mythical call of Louisbourg always demands a massive sense of history and obligation.

I now live in its domaine. Well, actually on an island, a couple of miles off the mainland. Guess I must keep moving away. At 1200 noon today, my friends from "away", Raymond, Jenny and Sylvie will arrive at the dock near my home. They have come to absorb their collective destiny and learn more about my obedience to Jean Le Claire.

Guts

structure and design
great place to define limitation of
imagination.

line up the parts and
there examine the universe in a
drop of H2O.

braille to all those who
can truly see before
braille.

guts
there to redefine
intellect, intuition, sensitivity
competition through ignorance through
distant unknowing.

good reproduction comes
through pleasure.

SQUADRONS

souls of the dead
alive
swooping to get attention
famous flight maneuvers
recognition
carrying the dead forever in poetry
and design

my line of vision
birds
perfect aviation design
wishing to be with them
or
maybe they wish to be with me

easy to see them here
perfect angle of attack
instinct how fortunate

instructional
in the air comfortable
can't find a a way to get down
science
great loud noise of greece and rome and ancient
frequency tuned to same
here is nothing much

fast and incomplete
old and death
birds with no radar
here we are.

THE LOT

another comes to fill up the space
watching the space that fills up
a small place another person

daughter friend
a comfort for me
fill up the space
the place
fill up my
vacant lot

a long line is beginning
and i can only find comfort in the
association in one room where
we are sharing distant space
inhabitation of time that is totally
different for all of us
but ok and resilient

reflection of bright lights
in and out
kind and empirical i hope

sounds like old
it is
its seeks a vacant lot

GREAT WAR?

All this time I mused and loudly wondered
In a time I mistook
That rained and thundered
The war was right but the time was wrong
It was the Great War I fought
And where I belong.

Each time I fly
I think of the men
Who flew and knew
There was only again
Another chance to maim the Hun
And make it swift and let it be done.

The gentlemen's war
Or so it was said
Took men to their death
But not quite so dead
For all was honor through bloodshed upheld
And in our souls was the god that dwelled
And still does.

For all the men and women who believe in freedom
And genetic flight to the stars.

FALLING

falling towards a better/worse place
puppetry and manipulation
gentle and rough cadences
all the woman
all the life

my love stirs
and breathes and renews vows unknown
strength where none was known
understanding where none was sown
but true to itself
ignites

current and flow correct
riverbed dug
as life old and new pass and commingle
white water souling
perfect and consistent
tailoring dimensions too fine to see
and knowing texture sublime

simple wedding
truth and comfort bridesmaid and groom
knowing eternal soul older and
sensitive waves/vibes/god
to be here and now
is enough for all.

FRENCH FOREIGN LEGION

fog and mist and no resist
a man must go and still insist
that nowhere is as good or bad as the french foreign legion

no desert no plain no threat of of a noble death
a heart too holed to respond any longer
to holes, moles or incursions into the psyche

gunbelts absent, horses a myth?
hostilities of a warring nature
out of sight of might and battered will

just a silent blowing of tons of burning sand
not grand
not even hard
a search for truth
the bard

he lives on a ghostly caravan long gone
a helmet to protect a fawn
imaginary camel droppings
and imagery lost

on the would be heroes
sliced and rendered
no where to go but back
history is not so glorious
and comfort comes
from saddles domain.

STRANGE YEARNINGS

There is so much more to us
than the mere fact of our mirror

there are so many fictions of us
like the small lights of our actions

and the rantings of reality
are there to draw the bile
a consequence of fear
a harbinger of present

off to light and destiny
down to dark and suffering

the remainder of ourselves is everywhere
and slow to disappear

geometric in design
oblique of necessity

to do is to dissolve
strange yearnings.

GIFT

Only through the product that is self
Can the embrace of inner secrets
be revealed,
Aptitude, the honest force that drives
beyond assumption;
so blood will spill on the firmament
of the psyche . . .
The table is set, the nourishment waits;
And the apogee of reality
that speaks to our antiquity
is the focused fire of the flash that is
Creation's perfection . . . and gift.

A Dying Breed

Around 7 o'clock in the summer evenings, we would begin scratching around in the damp, peat-ridden turf for semi dry sticks and wild grass to get the bon fire going. Tonight, like every Saturday night on the Bras D'or lakes of Cape Breton, our little cottage by the water hosted a feast of roasted hot dogs and fresh caught lobster. The hot dogs we bought. The lobster we commandeered in our very own traps. Occasionally a hugh cod or some other fishy delicacy would make its way into one of our low-tech lobster pots and we, being the good sports that we were, would then release it to its environment or chop it up as bait for the next lobster slaughter. It never got tiresome or any less worthy. It made life what it was supposed to be—tasty.

His cigarette could last for over an hour and for the umteenth time, I watched in fascination as my father prepared his "smoke". At 10 years of age, skills of deduction are still a bit embryonic. Then, the lights begin to come on. The small red packet with the rooster on it, emerged from his shirt pocket and he carefully removed two tiny white pieces of tissue paper. I'd seen this before so often, but the cause and effect was always taken for granted. Suddenly it made sense. Yes, the second extra "roll your own" paper from the tiny packet was the key to the mysterious, long life of Dad's poison. It restricted the intensity of the burn, and immediately went out if not attended to constantly. I'm sure he spent more on matches, just relighting the damn things, than he did on the actual cigarettes. What a discovery! It was celestial enlightenment! The universe was unfolding as it should.

Perhaps it was because he didn't suck greedily on the weed like true nicotine addicts. Or maybe, he simply knew the harsh economic realities of making things last. People like him had a strong sense of survival. However, had he known that these famous little tissues would become the vessel used to contain the simple drug of choice for the sex, drugs and rock and roll crowd, his bones would have done a few revolutions in the grave. Purist sensibilities and all that.

The hunt for the perfect weiner roasting sticks provided both excitement and appetite for my big sister and me. On one particular evening, I arrived back at our outdoor cook site to find my father foraging doggedly in a clump of brush. He found what he was looking for and reached for his fancy hunting knife. I watched, as he began to create, what I hoped would be, the perfect weiner stick. He walked over to me, both hands behind his back. "Pick one," he said. I indicated the left hand. "You guessed right Donald!" he replied excitedly; grinning. He didn't often grin in my direction. There, in his left hand, was the result of his toiling just minutes before. It was the crookedest, shortest and worst wiener roasting stick I had ever seen. I took it, thanked him, and suddenly, buried in sadness never before experienced in my young life, I turned and wept silently.

The summer passed with characteristec haste and my life was becoming more and more in tune with the persistent, but not unusual sensitivities of youthful confusion.

In the early 1900's my grandfather, Fredrick C. Warton, owned and operated a successful ship brokerage firm in the northeast of England. Before the advent of the new industrial age of steam and steel, the family built world famous wooden sailing ships to take people and cargo to the four corners. My father was the 3rd son to be born into the *Fredrick Warton and Sons* regime.

Much later in his life I occaionally would get him to revisit his memories of growing up with privelege. His ingenuosity was remarkable and a bit endearing:

"Father never talked about money and I never actually saw any that I remember. We always seemed comfortable and had lots of help with maids and such in the house, but I never felt we were much different than anyone else, and certainly not rich. It was considered distastful and boastful to mention money and possessions. In those days people were as one under the eyes of God." Those were the times.

I was also to learn that *his* father Fred, my grandfather, subscribed to the Victorian notion that "children should be seen and not heard." Seriously. Understandably. I believe that he secretly missed the style to which he was accustomed, although as we shall soon see, in many ways he was an advocate of collective human rights and scorned lofty born English "class inheritors."

Telling a child that they are adopted would seem a daunting task for any parent. I learned of my adoption at 11 years of age, not long after the crooked weiner stick became the lightening rod for my angst and confounding disconnect from the familial norm. I found the loose change for bus money, along with an official looking document proclaiming my *adoption order.* Even at my young age, there was no mistaking what it all meant. My birth name was not Donald Herbert Warton. It was Robert _____ and my mother's date of birth indicated she was 16 when she laboured forth. She named me and then gave it and me away, directly after my arrival.

My time at school that year was challenging for everyone. My mother despertely tried to explain that she and father had always planned to tell me the big news later on. When I was more mature. As a kindness.

My father, in his own special version of kindness, had often said to me, "Do you have any idea how lucky you are to be with us?" Or, "We are all adrift my boy, and don't you ever forget it." My father was a man of very subtle ways.

From a very early age, I wiggled my head back and forth and sang. It was the only way I could get to sleep. This lasted until I was 12. I would often do it when I awoke too, much to the frustration of the rest of the family, who were still interested in slumber. No one seemed to think that this was at all peculiar, and I was never discouraged from the practice, with the exception just mentioned. As the music picked up tempo so would my corresponding head rotation on the pillow. John Philip Sousa marches were a favourite, and these of course, being absent of lyrics, would be vocalised with interesting attempts at duplicating the various instruments. Waltzes were also up there on the musical charts. I knew all the words to the popular songs of the day and these were belted out with great conviction and joy. One of the side effects of all this head movement, was the premature development of much larger than usual neck muscles.

"Donald, would you please sing that new song you learned this week?" It was worth 25 cents and who was I to object? My mother loved music, although not particularly gifted that way herself. She would often have me conduct the symphony orchestra playing on the radio each Saturday afternoon from New York. The music of Edward Greig and Tchikowsky were favourites. My father was never part of this. His demons of workaholism consumed him in his office. But I understood. Being 8 or 9 years of age gave one a feeling of confidence and sturdiness. However, a man driven by the fear of failure and humiliation is not one to trifle with.

"Look son, it is the horrible fear of failing that leads us all to seek success." How does a child argue with that? How does a child argue with anything coming straight from the horse's mouth? It all sticks like glue. More kindness from my father.

He was sent to India in his early twenties to run the family brokerage office. Three years there, had a profound affect on how my father's life would unfold. The pictures of him from the late twenties sporting the full dress regalia of the Calcutta Light Horse were truly impressive. A confident young man in the company of the English elite. He "did his time" in Delhi and Calcutta helping to run the family firm, and left in a state of anguish. He was not of the Oxford or Eaton tribe, as so many of his colleagues were, and was treated accordingly. But, from what I can gather, he was an outsider before he ever left the family fold in Britain.

Being the second youngest in a family of three boys and two girls, his position in the male hierarchy was tenuous, at best. And I believe that his growing sense of apartness from the others, moved his feelings of self esteem further down the ladder. Shy, and not particularly attractive, with a total absence of guile, he would help design his own undoing that would lead to his flight from family and country.

Before he died at ninety, my father entrusted me with his worldly goods and chattels.That is to say, I inherited all when he passed on. Among the memorabilia, were three diaries:

April 19, 1917: Dear Diary: I turned thirteen today. I don't know what that means, except I just get more and more confused. Father paid more attention to Billy and and Robert and it was my b'day. Mother made a nice cake. I feel lonely. I'm not happy now.

Many of the entries were illegible due to age and smeared ink and perhaps rage and frustration.

June 1, 1917: Dear Diary: Mother is gone again. She goes away a lot now. To her friends place. Father is gloomy and mad most of the time. I don't think I did anything bad. I want to go away.

Physical clumsiness and social ineptness would haunt my father throughout his whole life. Sporting events totally eluded him. I had to explain baseball, hockey and you name it. I dwelled in a perpetual state of mortification. He was such an outsider.

He took me around to all my athletic activities and never let me forget it. But he did it, and that's the important thing. He told me once that when he was in the *reserve infantry,* his sergeant said that he was the worst soldier he had ever seen. "Can't march worth a damn. If you can't march, you sure as hell can't fight!" he was told.

October 2, 1917: Dear Diary: Father saw Mother with Mr. Simms. I did too. I don't understand what is happening. I just want to go away. God bless Mother and Father. Please don't let them leave me alone. Billy and Robert are stupid. They don't see or know anything. Maybe that's good. What am I going to do?

All this, during the first World War, when children along the east coast of England saw the true manifestations of war. Dirigibles hung in the North Sea skies; a flotilla of balloon fortresses, thrown up against the German aerial advance. As little boys, they were made to run into the blisteringly frigid waters of the North Sea each Saturday morning. Soon, they would become rightful Englishmen.

January 5, 1918: Dear Diary: The funeral for Mr. Simms was held today. My mother has left our house. My father acts very strangely. Maybe he's sorry for hurting Mr. Simms so badly. He was bleeding before he died. I saw him. Father said I wasn't to tell anyone.

"Yes what?"

"Yes father," I said. It seemed strange that I should have to call him "father" but he insisted persuasively. He was always angry when he came to the table. Business. Always going wrong. Or, at least, not the way he liked it.

Married people were supposed to love each other. Weren't they? Mother loved everyone, especially me. She administered to the less fortunate and where I lived, there were plenty of them. They smelled. Poor. Unwashed. Disgusting. She may have loved them, but I barely tolerated that particular whim of hers.

June 15, 1927, Calcutta: Dear Diary: I am happy to be here, in a way, but god, I miss England. The local people here are nice so far. The Fred Warton & Sons empire has expanded and here I am. Snotty Cambridge and Eaton types are everywhere. Maybe in time.

November. 14, 1927, Calcutta: Dear Diary: I feel like an outsider. They won't let me in because I'm just a chartered accountant from the northeast. The bastards are so stupid and arrogant. Father would have fixed them quick! Will I ever find the love that Mother found in Simms. Miserable sh—s.

I was the Head Prefect at my high school. That's as far as you can go in this field. My mother had high hopes and had connections from her past that would propel me through the usual formalities. She died at fifty eight. I was twenty three.

March 20, 1928: Dear Diary: Despair. Twenty four years old now, and feel eighty. No acceptance. They are INCORRIGIBLE! Spurned, is that the term?? I'm not sure. Don't give a shite anyway. Father felt it and acted upon it. I cannot do what my father did to eradicate the enemy. He was strong. His secret is safe with me at least for now. Goodbye for a while diary.

The son of Fredrick C. Warton screamed, "Fuck you!" It was not the thing any well bred Englishman would say. He said it all the time when I was a teenager. Maybe it was the times. Maybe he got it from the clients he dealt with. It never sounded right coming from him. He was an English gentleman. He destroyed all of the important furniture. Most of the walls were bashed in. I stayed in my room. He didn't go there.

August 13, 1928: Dear Diary: Time to go. Those bloody bastards hate me. Well guess what?! I hate them!!!!!!!!!!!!!! Shite eaters.

"Is it three balls or three strikes Donald ? Hockey is a bloody rough game. Not like cricket, is it? Do you really understand what's going on?"

Strange looks from those within earshot. His cigaretts still burned long but gave little pleasure. He hardly bothered to light them anymore.

February 16, '29, Dear Diary: Reading E.M. Forester's "Passage to India." Jolly good read. Am composing this entry just outside the famous Jain temple in centre of town. Many Brit visitors saying how wonderful everything is. They can go home. It wouldn't be so "marvellous" (silly snobs) if they were doing real time here. The bloody Raj. The whole lot will be kicked out before long. We Brits are experts on the class and caste system. Even our architecture is imposing itself into the lives and mosaic of this ancient culture. We presume too damn much on the whole world! Must go to Delhi soon. I will never belong here. Bullocks on the whole sodding lot!!

At first, he was fascinated with the people and the land where over two hundred languages are spoken. He studied with keen interest the diverse populations and the fascinating results of so much racial, ethnic and cultural intermingling; the seeding

of a pluralistic society, which would become more evident as
India struggled towards the modern world. He related to that
struggle, as his own discord began compounding—something
that he found harder and harder to endure.

He told me the story of the Black Hole of Calcutta, where
the nawab of Bengal captured the city in 1756. The British
defenders were locked up in that infamous room, where most
of them died a horrible death. He said he could relate to that.
He told me of the Hindu's belief that bathing in the Ganges
would cleanse them of all their sins. He told me about the
corpses floating in great abundance there at the time. It was the
great paradox of the river, and this did not escape my father's
acutely painful observations of his own wretchedness. He
learned some Hindustani and Bengali and predicted the bloody
independence movement of the 40s. The last few pages of his
"Indian Campaign" diary were torn out. What he may have
recorded might have well been too painful or incriminating:

*April 2, 1929, Dear Diary: The trip to Delhi: Six long months of
hell. Despair that just amplifies my own. Rot, stench, filth, death
and horror of all descriptions meet me at every turn. Bloated
corpses floating in the "sacred" Ganges . . . . people dying,
starving—hopelessness unlike I have ever seen or experienced. I
will die here myself if I do not leave at once. I am hungry but I dare
not eat—it would no doubt be my "last supper." I will haul myself
back to Calcutta where I shall continue to play my "untouchable"
role for those insufferable bastards. I am so tired and despairing of
everything. I even miss Father. If I think of Mother too much, there
will be no hope for me. And the meek shall inherit the earth!? God
help me.*

Back when, paved roads were by far the exception in Nova
Scotia. Automobiles lasted a couple of years at the most. And
if you travelled these modified cattle paths for business, then
God help you and the vehicle. We always had a new car right
around the time the odometer was clocking up 20,000 miles or
so. That took, at best, two years to accomplish, what with all
the time my father spent on the road. A salesman starting out

in the early 40s had a tough row to hoe anywhere. But add to that, the back roads of Cape Breton Island and the relatively basic technology of the automobile at that time, and you've got a challenge.

"Blow any tires?" I'd ask after he returned from a typical five day road trip.

"No tires this time, but the gear box jammed ever 20 miles." Any annoyance that this type of query would normally cause, was assuaged, at least in his mind, by the remarkable fact, that another gruelling trip had been survived.

July 22, 1930, Dear Diary: India has never looked so good as it does at this very moment, as we push out into the Sea of Bengal, with the squalid coastal shanties disappearing behind. To hell with all this! Give me cleansing sea air and bright tropic sun. I may find peace yet. I'm free, thank God. Sentence served!

It was a new diary. It would be a new life.

This new biographical journal was made of beautiful Indian leather with a gold clasp to secure the pages between the covers. A multicoloured engraving of the Taj Mahal had been exhaustively produced on the front cover with the initials H.H.W. just underneath. Harold Hillford Warton. It would be one of only a few entries in the entire diary.

Perhaps one of the most exotic and historically important parts of the world were unfolding before my father's maturing sensibilities. The maps of the area show a southward passage down the Bay of Bengal rounding the tip of Ceylon, eastward through the Indian Ocean through the Maldives and northwestward across the Arabian Sea:

Aug. 5, 1930, Dear Diary: A very rough passage these last couple of weeks. What am I doing here anyway? Life's unpredictable journey. Just left port of Oman. More and more squalor and strange culture. Tomorrow on to Yemen and then northward to the Red Sea and Suez—mercifully more familiar surroundings in Med. and Cyprus.

*p.s. back to England and maybe? Confront Father? Mother?
Did they get my letters? Do they know I'm alive? My family has
forgotten me, I believe. I will not return to England. Ever.*

With the northeast coast of Africa to port and the Arabian
peninsula to starboard, my father passed by and through
ancient lands and seas with no friendship and little comfort of
any kind. The past held only bitterness and fear and the future
yielded little better. When steering problems forced the *Bristol
Sea* into the yards at Aqaba in Jordan, the troubling metaphor
of the "rudderless ship" blended well into his deepening woe.

A workaholic, who never sat through a meal without making
at least three phone calls, my father did not suffer fools lightly.

"That bloody order is two days late. Have it here by three
tomorrow, or we lose the customer, and you lose the best
salesman you've got!" Slam. He worked hard to the detriment
of his family and general quality of life. "The thing that drives
a man to success, is the fear of failure. Always remember that."
Indisputable.

"I was the youngest, and thought of as the fool of the family. I
had to prove that I could make something of myself," he ranted
when under duress, preferring to recall the past in a kinder and
gentler light and calling up a much more positive assemblage
of images from his youth. "Mother and Father were wonderful!"
he would say.

The Mediterranean Sea was awash with wealth and fame. It
was a special time for those fortunate enough enough to imbibe
such exotic fare. Celebrities of all denominations cruised the
idyllic waters of "The Med," and among them was my father.

"I talked with the actor, John Mills, for Christ's sake!"

He had now travelled nearly 6,000 miles by sea, and the
rugged coastline of the tiny island of Malta loomed due west.

The *Bristol Sea* pitched and heaved through jagged seas
and made this British colony look awfully inviting to our ever
seasoning traveller. Dad had read about Malta. His father's
brokerage firm had maintained a small office there for several
years. He would have gazed upon one of the finest harbours in

southern Europe then and now. Most of the people, who are an ethnic mix of Arab, Italian and British, lived in the capital city of Valletta. Two other islands that comprise the balance of the Maltese geography, lay to the north. In 1932, when my father passed through, it is unlikely that he could have guessed that this strange and wonderful land mass between Sicily and North Africa, would be subjected to bombing by both German and Italian forces during World War Two. His famous, and too often repeated line, "I once sang on the opera stage at Malta," derived from his visit to the theatre during renovations. I remember him saying that the there were one or two excerpts from *Pagliaci* sung with gusto, but to an empty house.

"There was no one in the house at the time of course."

Even when inside, he remained outside. There never seemed to be listeners anywhere, but his smokes still lasted longer than anyones. *Puff gently and don't inhale. Thicken the skin and stop the burn. Anyway you can.*

With Malta just two days away, he received an urgent message on the ship's wireless. "Harold. Go directly Cable and Wireless office in port. *stop.* Grievous news from home.*stop.* Urgent.*stop.* Robert."

He was to expect the worst. That he knew. Just how bad the news would be was beyond imagining.The message from home, which he later transcribed in the diary, reads as follows: *"Come home at once. Such shock and sadness. A tragedy befallen us. Mother and Father are both dead. Take fastest conveyance. Robert."*

A smaller, faster vessel, landed my father in Portsmouth, four days later. Another day by train, and he was home.

Sept 3, 1930, Dear Diary: *Mother's illness was brief. The disease swallowed her up in a matter of days. I am overcome with grief. That Father would take his own life out of impossible heartache is beyond my comprehension. Could he have loved her so much? . . . . why was it not apparent to me? Such misery . . . such failure. I am a completely shamed. I am so stupid. My life seems worthless.*

Opportunity for a new beginning, presented itself. Still stricken and in mild shock several months after the tragedy, he boarded a large passenger liner out of Cardiff, in Wales, and fixed his compass on what would be his last and most important migration.

Always the practical man, my father firmly believed, as did his father, that children should be "seen and not heard." He told me the children never ate with their parents in his household, and when they did on rare occasion, they were to be as silent as possible. Children were to obey. Children were to respect their parents under all circumstances. Children were to be grateful to be alive under the auspices of their care givers.

"Oh Harold, shut up!" My mother would say this, in a fully contained and deliberate voice. Then she would go into a coughing fit and nearly choke.

"You're too bloody emotional," he would say. But he usually did shut up.

My Mother wanted him to start a lumber company. Or maybe own a sawmill. Then there was the time she decided that all the land on which our humble summer cottage existed should be mined for the white clay that lay just below the surface.

"What in God's name would be done with it once extracted?" he asked.

"Why, we can sell it to the provincial government and they can use it to make figurines and tourist bobbles to sell to . . . . well anyone who wants them! I'm sure artists and scientists will see the merit in this natural wonder!"

An ethereal person, I suppose, my mother was extremely imaginative. He never liked her ideas. Too nutty for him. The sick, the poor, the mentally challenged were all part of the revolving fixtures in my mother's house. The smell that the really poor gave off didn't bother her in the least. I often had to leave the table when the presence of *b.o.* was at the danger level.

"Donald, you love this meal. You always gobble it up like there was no tomorrow."

"I don't feel well, Mom."

I never remember my father ever being at the table when "noon-time guests" graced our table. He was always out making money. The antidote to failure.

Music was becoming the prominent issue in my young life. My mother was convinced I could become the new *Caruso,* even though *Mario Lanza* presently had a corner on that market.

I sang all the time; Concerts, music festivals, at home for an easy quarter. (big money in those days.) Remember, I directed the New York Philharmonic Orchestra from a stool in our living room when I was but eight years old. Rudolph Bing was "king" at that time, and I was soon to join his illustrious fold.

"Donald, do-as-you-are-told! Always remember, the fear of failure drives a man to success!" I was eight.

"You don't always have to come first, Donald," my mother would insist when I became morose about not being at the top of the class in school every time. However, she, like my father, expected me to be at the top of the class (no pressure to perform, you understand) and I knew this. Naturally, I deferred.

"I know I don't *have* to, but I do *want* to."

We had just retrieved the last lobster pot, when the wind and sea suddenly came up. The five h.p. motor on the transom of the tiny dory was useless, and I was on the verge of peeing my pants. Swells like I'd never seen before, came rolling in on the stern. Terror read loud and clear.

"Don't look!"

Dad was referring to the black, threatening waves that kept pounding the life out of our tiny boat, as it ran down on this ferocious watery ride to god knows where.

We made it to the lagoon, wet and weary, but somehow, alive. A similar account:

Aug 4, 1930, Dear Diary: I have never been so sick. The seas are boiling at about six or seven metres and I feel we could be in serious danger of swamping. Wind howling at around sixty knots, I'm told. Bristol Sea is of small tonnage and labours against its natural enemies. Must enter notes to my dairy and think positively. I do feel brave and hopeful. What would Father say?

1400 hours same day: *The sea has become kinder. There has been damage to the vessel (helm problems again) but we are safe and proceeding to next port. Yemen or is it Oman? The Arabian Sea is a worthy adversary. What would Father think of it? I am becoming a man, perhaps! Relief would best describe my feelings. It does transform one.*

The pictures of the Halifax Theatre Guild Productions of 1933 are priceless.

"It takes a clever man to play the fool," father would say, after regaling everyone with lame and silly jokes that none among us really understood. But he seemed to be in his element when on stage. I often wondered why he didn't make it a career. Of course, becoming a mere actor was tantamount to becoming a gypsy, or worse. *Men were made and respected through the type of commerce they practised, not the unregulated and undisciplined vocations of the theatre. Never.*

He became a salesman. A good one. Always delivered on time and with respect. He owned the territory. Many of the travelling salesmen of the time were just "a bloody bunch of drunks." And misfits. But not him. He knew how to win. Promise. Deliver. Simple as that. The fact that he was English, would have been a handicap for most of his ilk. But in his case, it was an advantage. The accent, the mannerisms . . . all a handicap to most, signified British dependability, less the swagger and superiority.

I think he was a virgin, or nearly, when he married my mother. She definitely was. Several generations of decorous Prespyterianism precluded any notions of physical intimacy. I remember the day I found the condoms in his dresser drawer. I could not imagine at 13 or 14 years of age, the possibility of any kind of union between my mother and father. This, of course, is not unusual among children of a certain age. That there appeared to be not the slightest sliver of love between them, reinforced this estimation, and when my mother died, with her, died any possibility of my continuing a relationship with my father. She had loved me in a special way. I believe he was jealous of us.

That extra layer of skin on the cigarette kept it, and my father, burning too long. Maybe it was time for me to start carrying the torch. *"We are all adrift, my boy, and don't you ever forget it."* *"Do you have any idea how lucky you are to be here with us Donald?"*

I never knew what he meant. Up until I discovered the truth at 11 years of age, being adopted was something that had never entered my mind. How come, I wonder, since we were never anything alike? My father was a man of very strange ways.

Maybe now, I have come to understand his demons from the diaries. Perhaps, the fact that he didn't have a son of his own flesh and blood, took him completely off track from my mother and me. I was feeling the weight of his and my wreckage and knew it would never get much lighter. If only the wiener stick had been more symmetrical. If only the burn of his cigarette had been brighter. Not just longer.

Three diaries were mentioned in this narrative. Some of the contents of the first two have been described. The third had all but the last page ripped out. It said:

THE END

OLD PAINT

awakened by a pulse hitherto forgotten
confluence and chop
navigation only possible through the brute force
of nature
unseeing.

magnanimity
selfish introspection
tempered steel in lambskin
impulse and correction
a fiend
an angel
a proposition
a supposition
a waste
a taste
a life of haste

like light years
time warp
a chance to
plumb the line for the fit
or blind design

a kick at the can/can—make a difference.
but even layer cake gets stale

perhaps old age
is a blessing in disguise

at least hormones are finally given
a break and laid to—?

peeling paint is about as unsexy
as it comes.

eyes fail
nature is sort of kind.

The Moth

the moth has the math
for living in strange surroundings
chewing on cloth but gently
an enviable trait and gift

not much of a future has he
but much in the present.
to be
is to be.

more importance seeks he not
just infinity before he rot
and be no more
the whore of bugs

find me the passion
and the moth who seeks
masterful strategy awaiting reward
survival of fittest and no rosy cheeks

Humble retreat
a dull jaded sword
the wings are the same
as an angel of mercy
one a cannibal; one a giver
one a thief; one a lover
perfect each in detail
homicidal both in the end
new life
regeneration and reintegration
small and nothing
and all

Mr. Moth
whereforeartthou
when i need you.

AGNOSTIC

to many signs of other intrusions
instinct goes a different way
moving force a constant push to
the place not compatible with

horizons leave a static rhythm
abstract to theology
too much discipline
too hard
too much weight

light is given after
what?

from another
different mode and
different compromises?

cosmic from whence it came
an involvement with nascent power open to all
william blake needs to be here
he is

asking questions from the grave so long
cold
to bring simplicity back
when and where it hovers
pieces of origin are waiting to explode
as they are
and as they will in their own good time

ONCE A JOLLY SWAG MAN

I watched a strange creature
more stranger than I
look for I know not what
pie in the sky?
with each movement forward
to the **de**sired perch
it found strange occurrences
all squalid with lurch
and lurch it did thus—and so it did
so
a serious quest to get out of the row
escape it could not
for fate had deemed—boom!
wake up you strange creature
and whither not under gloom
search out your lost kingdom
and never say die
for the die that is cast
is
not pie in the sky

quaintly and saintly
the images blur
finding rest only
amid the big stir
mincing and wincing
a terrible discord
more than the average creature
can afford!
and **so** it **is** thus
and thus it **is so**
a candlestick maker
with taste for the roe
the creature that slideth
and slitherith might
just consider the options
of flying a kite.

VIGILANCE

watch out for the thing that
seems quiet

It is only a precursor of
the event

stirrings and stillness
can lead only to musings
and tomfoolery of inwardlookingness
watch out for the thing that says
watch out for the thing

it is maybe the best place to be.
spread the word
fluidity smoothes the way

to
the way that goes to the top
of it
and there . . . . it is
not really very much.

the power of the soul
releases the need to let
words die.

SCOREBOARD

Smooth stone on still water
always a winner

granite was strong
no good on still water
sinks too quickly
is never flat or symmetrical

round stone sinks quickly
finds the bottom
and stays
on the bottom.

floating (wood type) is vulnerable
and hardly ever sinks
for good
except
when it wants to become
waterlogged
then it is awash usually

. . . .

. . . .

flotation and propulsion
gets the job done
but the north Atlantic is cold and . . .
very forgiving actually

the pool awaits
it is small
but
has the same expectation

sink or swim . . . or
be awash
like almost all
chronologically
living things.

final score:
sink-0
swim: might as well (1)

MORPHEUS STROLLS NYC 1996

the scene is dead,
wish i had gods knack for recreation
i'd recreate the street:
powerful and pedestrian
lock it in with wolves
and the fired straits of epsilon.

a gun or a bat
to break this glass to empty out the fumes
this great city has cast
but manhattan will sadly sink before i cross the bloodied
Rubicon
to ride the subway tracer veins
searching for new patron saints.

the powered phases of the clock
pulls at the cities mortified chains
and ancient rome spills her taunted ghosts into the streets

Romulus returns to his father and Morpheus strolls
briefly.

GOOD DOG

weaving a fine thread
with no tools
coarse fibre the ingredient
bothersome
stroking ineptitude the lingerer
making way for easy virtue
no one can beat the enemy

singular
not alone
defining principal of the
wretched

words hiding under rocks
if only I'd the strength to roll
them away as from the tomb
of Christ
revealing nothing much
corpus delecti not
available at this time
please check your listing.

biblical proclamations
of biblical proportions
insist
the living embodiment of
naiveté
releasing pressure to seek the stars
and i don't mean hollywood

a good dog can conquer the absurdity
of knowing stuff
maybe the dog knows all
before and during the fall
he sees the tail end.

Happy Land

Lost in Time

Sitting. Waiting. White paint, yellowed and flaking off the ceiling. Eyes fixed but not focused, straight ahead. Walls institutional green. Floors of hardwood. Old. A school probably. It feels quiet for a change—there is never any actual noise— and although the waiting seems endless, I am not bored or despairing. Sometimes, there are others waiting in the corridor with me. We are all the same age, but I don't really know what age is and have no actual sense of time—I wonder if the others do. No one is sad and no one is particularly happy. Waiting.

Present Time

I kiss my young daughter good night. Since I am home most of the time, I nearly always have that splendid paternal pleasure. There are no words to describe that visceral feeling that washes over the soul and momentarily softens from hairline to toes. Connection. Transferal of immutable genetic memory from one being to another. Strong feelings of hope. Of mercy. Sublime, yet incomplete and a burning need to understand more; these feelings. Waiting.

Lost in Time

A few children shuffle along the hallway, looking down without commitment. Some are familiar, others not. No one speaks. We are not friends and we are not enemies. It is neither depressing nor comforting. I know that it will not go on forever and am vaguely restless to leave this corridor

and move into one with more colour and more light. Are the people outside waiting for me to make a move or do I wait for them?

Present Time

A miscarriage is not quite as rough as the early death of a child who has already been delivered to its new family. We have had two miscarriages and one successful, healthy birth but the scars from those dark spots in our lives linger to fuel familial eruptions that otherwise would likely have been avoided. There is little comfort to be gained from the fact that it was just a fetus. To the awaiting parents and family, fetal life is just a short step removed from fully formed life. Not being sufficiently skilled in quantum cosmology which basically purports that what goes around comes around, I traditionally view death or the interruption of fetal life as being absolute termination. But the nagging question **has** always remains.What if I'm wrong?

Lost in Time

I am intellectually advanced even though I look and feel, in many ways, very young. Not that I think profound thoughts or engage in any sort of creative activity. In fact, there is nothing of importance that can be said for me, other than that. I simply exist. I sleep but there is no sensation or dreaming. The waiting in the same corridor is not represented by time in the usual sense. If I were older and more educated I might describe this state as one of suspended animation-whatever that means.

The light and shadows never change although I feel it is never nighttime. The windows lining the hallway where I live are very high and begin too far from the floor for me to see outside. A persistent flat light completely devoid of any subtlety or design, pervades everything. (I barely know what such words mean anyway.) I do not speak nor am I ever spoken to. Most people that enter my line of vision convey no impression of thought or feeling and are in fact hardly real to me. Somehow, I know that it is believed that most animals can barely read expression in the faces of humans and react more to sound, smell and body language. But then I have never actually seen any type of animal. My sexuality is a puzzle. Am I fish or fowl? This knowledge or lack of it, is not a negative in my domain. I feel the answer will be forthcoming.

Some days I find myself going from door to door in my habitat, and each time I open one, I find a room full of what would have to be grownups. I am not invited in, nor is anything said to me. They scrutinize me with mild curiosity, but quickly lose interest. These are not pleasant times for me, and the monotony of my fruitless wandering causes me no end of frustration. The odd occasion has me observing a smile on the face of one of these strange automatons, but as always, the mood dissolves and I am again alone.

Present Time

I often think back to the times when we were eagerly following the signs of life in the womb. Kicks and somersaults and then the desolation. Since neither of us are religious— more agnostic than anything else— we are not inclined to accept the will of some mythical god who arbitrarily decides whether and when our children should or should not be born. Our feeling is, that if a controlling force is out there in the universe, then it displays all the traits of a pathological tyrant.

My wife is a brick. Her wounds are deep and the double tragedy of two miscarriages has left her bruised, but completely without malice. For a virtual atheist, a kinder more optimistic soul would be hard to find. And all this from a broken home where parental leadership was seldom practised.

Now is the winter of our discontent
Made glorious summer by this sun of York.

She has always taken comfort in Shakespeare and his four hundred year old musings that are as inviolable today as ever.

Though patience be a tired mare
yet she will plod.

Neither of us has ever read Richard 111 or Henry V in their entireties, but these excerpted speeches tend to find their way into the hearts and minds of all those who have endured.

But even the well honed psyche can be blunted and the second loss was followed by what can only be described as the "abyss." While there was never any mention of suicide, the thought had clearly crossed her mind, and left me terrified that the balance was being tipped too far the other way. It is better now, but the demons occasionally dance and it is not a minuet.

Lost in Time

This adult looks at me in a way that I interpret as kindly, and takes me by the hand. I sit on my haunches staring at the green walls. The heat is making me uncomfortable. Is it winter and they've turned the heat up? Or is it summer? I have a vague notion of the seasons, but nothing to truly relate to, as I have never been outside the institution. I am obliged to call it *home*. Still, I remember one time or was it more, that for a moment I felt that the waiting was over. My perambulations have yielded results, at least of sorts.

In my usual tentative manner, I open the door to one of the countless rooms and for the umteenth time subject myself to the inordinate stares of its inhabitants.

To my utter shock, a lady gets up from her seat and approaches me. We walk down the long corridor at a good pace, but there is no sound from our shoes on the weathered hardwood floors. When is there ever sound anyway? We round the corner at the end of the hall. I have never been here before. Now, just ahead of us, two enormous doors begin to open. The sun. Glorious, smiling sunlight washing over us in torrents. The wait looking as though it might soon be over. A sound. From me. From the lady beside me. A laugh, a sigh, trembling. All senses alive, luminous. Ready to breath. Dazzling. Another step towards the feast.

Calamity. The sun, engulfed in a soundless wind storm of leadenness. The doors snarling, slamming shut. Running back to my spot in the hallway. The lady is gone. Soundless whimpering, tearless and dry. The heart stops but I am still present. Darkness finally. Just another sub atomic particle to an indifferent god.

Present Time

My wife has expressed a desire for another child. I am skeptical for reasons that have been expressed. That either of us could bear another loss would be improbable as the healing from previous damage is not yet complete. We have been advised by the best in modern medicine that any further attempts at pregnancy could be disastrous for both my wife and the unborn child.

Now, as I have said, neither of us are religious. Our loses have decidedly hardened our resolve to reject any and all forms of organised religion that has as its standard bearer, a compassionate god. Yet the forces of faith, or is it biology, are doubtless leading to a decision, that by any rational way of thinking, is reckless in the extreme.

It is decided. We will make another attempt, despite dire warnings to the contrary. Oddly, we feel no fear.

Changing Time

I remember now. The same lady as before takes me by the hand and leads me down the hall to the giant doors around the corner. Only this time, the doors don't open. But it is different because she holds my hand and leads me back to my spot in the long hallway. She looks down at me and smiles and although she never speaks any words that I can hear, she motions me to stay where I am and wait for a while. I have the feeling that the next time she returns and fetchs me, it will be allright.

. . . .

Could there be a charitable God after all? We are both confused over this issue, now that we have been "blessed" with Peter. Old expressions die hard. But didn't my wife say that this time it would be different? Somehow, we know that Peter was as ready for us as we were for him.

> *There is a happy land,*
> *Far, far away,*
> *Where saints in glory stand,*
> *Bright, bright as day.*

*   Andrew John Young— Scottish Poet—from "There is a Happy Land."

FOAL

When we take the time to learn
the promise of the soul;
ingenuous and trembling,
the will about to foal;
Ignition from a spark so small,
the children speak and break the fall.
With care they proclaim for all of us
and guide the way that leads;
our sentinels seeing attitudes
a conscience for better deeds.
And as chariots of fire
urging hope for another time,
They will tolerate no impurities;
only love, close to sublime.

SHORT AND SWEET

looking up to a bright empty space
a work in progress
a piece of clear time
gestation with luck and will
delivering the goods
after the bads
and returning to a weight bearable
a small piece of possibility

Port Hood, Cape Breton

Satellite
Mother who travels around
the lives of those close to her

of no particular ambition
and no particular import
in the grand overall

but a duchess in her own orthodox—where stones waited to be
taken

to the French fortress
Empress who demanded only
the best that nature
had to offer

in the days when Cape Breton awaited
her destiny

now
only a fantasy
where warm gulf waters
and venerable sands
challenge presence

Tourists touch and feel
her
patience for those who
are not;
were not there
at the start

but the stones
ask
and ask again
for repatriation
and watch patiently
till one comes forth
to tell tales volcanic
the tempest
that bore darwinian discharge for better and for worse
in stone.

(TO PILOT IS) NO ACCIDENT

to pilot is no accident
or casual mode of incident
genetic memory wins the day
and keeps us locked in memory

for sooner or for later
our history repeats
the values of our fathers
remove us from retreat.

and there in front enlightenment
a testament and firmament
between the wars
a holy grail
to soar and win
to plunge and fail.

no negative impediment
to slash and burn omnipotent
just silence and a steady hand
a place above the earth.

COOKING FOR ONE

slow spin, fast spin
hard to watch
but interestin'
made to test our fabric in
the worm hole of the mind.

slow time, fast time
exponential super fine
back time or front time
blurring, clear or intertwine.
all is here finite to behold
just more rosemary
and
tyme.

Comfort

as much noise and humanity
as is possible
as long as it is my own doing it . . . .
the progeny are loud and spoiled
and independent
as long as i am here:
without me they are no better or worse-
i am not really a factor.

am I kidding myself?
they feel secure in their noise
and they trust me to respect that
and I feel them around me and this enclosed place
they feel free with me
they are . . . .

comfort.

a free space where the guitar lives
the phone lives
as does the tv
the computer
the father
all selves
live

a unit familial
blood and trailing genetic microorganisims
it will never be an old or used or complacent
mutation of life;
or extension of a boxed-in embryo
always trying to be born
never wanting to be

good sense says
don't be delivered.
seek comfort
and tunnel visions
comfort.

xmas was designed
by very observant somethings
just for a moment
comfort . . . .

GOD

one ear one voice one conscience
consciousness
a new host with a new toast to recycle
never gone just transferred
infinite existence seems to work
new host, new toast
the brain feels to pain, it's true
perfect objectivity nest ce pas?

the lineal is never broken
transferal all

simple
get a life!
it's easy—a new one

can't see the air waves (electronic)
can only see towers to receive signals
ancestral past is idiot savant
the other there to take over
alive blueprint of genes
looking for a home

living is always with all things forever
one does not have to be aware
just insightful, as religious accepts God.
he's way ahead of us, of course
and he's smart.

DREAMSHOOT THE MOVIE

There were many dreams where Frank experienced the sensation of flying, but never with someone else attached to him. Often he had been at the controls of some kind of airborn craft, with very little knowledge of how the whole thing worked. Sometimes, he came close to crashing. But for the most part, he managed to wake up and gather together some of the highlights. Nobody ever died on these trips, but people and things did get mixed up. That was ok, because to try and truly understand these phenomena was futile. Now, he was dreaming on a whole new level.

FADE IN:

The dream:

His son was astride his back, holding on to his neck. There was no stress or other complications to interfere with the sensation of swooping and soaring, until it became a bit scarry. The landscape looked foreign but was the most beautiful colour of green imaginable. Father and son glided back down to earth, no longer able to sustain the thrill overload.

FADE OUT.

He had been waiting years for the lucid dreaming to include his son, and now the boy was his constant flight companion.

CUT TO:

the dream:

He watched himself pull the trigger—the sound resonating everywhere. Only one shot was needed to bring the running form down, as the bullet from the nickle-plated 44 magnum revolver slammed into him. The fence stopped the form from going any further, and it fell screaming and writhing in pain.

He'd never fired a weapon like this before. Why was he so good at it? He was in complete control, as the others started to move away. Dark blue suits and aviator sunglasses suggested who they might be. They beckoned him to follow them. He didn't want anything to do with that crowd.

CUT TO:

The dream cont'd:

Jack Lemon was waiting for him in the restaurant. The upstairs was crowded; vaguely familiar. Mr. Lemon seemed stressed and anxious to explain why they were both there in this place.

FADE OUT:

Frank woke to the sounds of the clock radio spewing its blather of news, weather and sports.

Mental circuitry firing dangerously hot.

Oh no. Not another one of those lucid dreams. Jack Lemon. The suits. The sunglasses. Shooting the 44 magnum. Flying with his son on his back. Too strange. Too real. Too much. The dream experts notwithstanding, Frank had his own theories. He figured that part of his life was lived in this dimension, and part of it somewhere else. This other dimension was the result of special cranial receptors— genetic annomalies. You had it, or you didn't. He no longer wanted it, but drifted off to sleep again anyway.

CUT TO:

The dream:

Frank wished desperately to be somwhere else. He didn't feel the safety that usually accompanied his adventures.

The open stadium was packed with people, but just why they were there was uncertain. And where was it? New York City, Sao Paulo, Athens? There was tension in the air and this gathering of thousands of people did not seem to be in a happy mood. A sporting event or perhaps a political rally.

The man with the gun stood, not 20 feet from where Frank was sitting. He took his time, looking for someone. He fired. The first victim went down, then another and another. Everything in the dream slowed down as the crowd made their way to the exits, trying desparately to avoid the slaughteer. Frank was unfamiliar with this place, but found an escape route, the reality of what was happeniing just too real. Would he wake from this nightmare, and if he did . . . .

FADE OUT.

FADE IN:

Frank's bedroom

The streetlight gradually found its way into his retina; the staggering fear releasing its hold on him, Frank returned to the tangibles of his bedroom. His heartrate told him that any more nocturnal trips, and he'd need someone good with CPR.

Scouting locations for the film industry gave Frank a pretty good living. He had trained himself to see surroundings in a certain way. His instinct was to "dress the set," and call for "lights, camera, action!" Yes, Frank, the frustrated director.

Lucid dreaming no doubt enchanced his ability to find these choice filming locations, although he never consciously put the two together. Often, he wished he could go further and scour the earth for that signature spot that had everything. But Frank didn't need this or any other Hollywood trickery, to get the mental molocules excited. That happened nearly every night.

Filming was about to begin and Frank spent most of his time helping with scheduling for cast and crew. The stars were arriving that night, and a production meeting was planned for the next morning. He checked the cast list one more time. Missing from the list was the actor for the starring role. Everything was pretty much in order, and Frank figured he could take a few hours of quality time to relax.

Usually, the transport guys got to pick up the stars at the airport, but someone had called in sick. Frank agreed to take up the slack. Besides, he'd heard that Jack Lemon was the main guy and Frank had always been a big fan.

"How's the weather been?" asked Mr. Lemon.

"We've been lucky. Not much of anything lately, and we're starting with exteriors."

Polite small talk, as Frank directed the limo to the Four Seasons.

The doorman and bell boy fussed around, suitably impressed with Jack Lemon's arrival and his status as a big draw movie star. Lemon thanked Frank for the ride in, and for just a tiny moment, Frank imagined that Mr. Lemon looked at him in a funny way and Frank began to experience the uneasiness that comes with knowing something different is underway.

Back at his apartment that night, Frank was growing more and more restless; no, not really restless. Fearful.

The phone rang at 9.35 p.m. It was Jack Lemon calling from the hotel. He asked if Frank could meet him for a drink. There was something he needed to talk to him about and it couldn't wait.

Jack was sitting in a corner booth at the back of the bar. It was a peaceful, elegant place. Frank sat down uneasily and Jack began . . .

"Haven't we met before, Frank?"

Frank hesitated. "Ah, no . . . . no we haven't, Mr. Lemon."

"Please, call me Jack," the actor replied. Jack said nothing more, for what seemed an eternity. Then he continued,

"Have you read the script, Frank?"

Frank was taken aback. He said,

"Just a rough read, nothing in detail. I've been busy finishing up details of the last shoot and haven't really had . . . . ,"

Jack cut him off. "It's ok, honest. I'm not checking up on you or anything like that . . . that's not what this is about."

Oh god, thought Frank, his fear swelling.

"Then I guess you don't know that I wrote the screenplay," Jack continued. "I got the idea for the story from someone I met under rather strange circumstances. Here's how it Happened:

Film style Flashback: visuals of the event, voice over :

Lemon

"I awoke from a very disturbing dream some months ago. I dreamt that there was an altercation outside the hotel where I was staying while filming in Seattle. Suddenly there was a gunshot. I heard the noise and went to the window. Just below, I saw the person who had just been shot, clutching his leg. A group of menacing types were shouting at another man who was holding a gun. I could see the lights from the parking lot reflecting off it. It appeared to be nickle or chrome plated. The guy holding the gun didn't want to go with the men in the dark suits who were becoming hysterical and threatening.The situation was becoming more explosive and I knew that the guy who had done the shooting would be seriously hurt if he didn't obey the others. It seemed irrational, but I instinctively felt I had to protect him. I ran downstairs and out to the lot, hollering at the gunman to run to where I was standing and that I'd help him. By now, the guys in the suits had given up on their man, and started to tear off in their cars. The man with the gun followed me into a restaurant across the street and we went upstairs."

Jack Lemon waited and in a voice that seemed to be coming from light years away said,

"You were that man with the gun, Frank. You were the terrified man in my dream."

FADE OUT . . . .

Epilogues

All the world's a stage
And all the men and women merely players;
They have their exits and their entrances;
And one man in his time plays many parts,
his acts being seven ages.

Shakespeare: *As You Like It.*

They are ill discoverers that think there is no land, when they can see nothing but sea.

Francis Bacon: *The Advancement of Learning*

ANTOINE

read flight to arras
read night flight
read any and all of Saint Exupery
and fly with him in time
in france
in south america
free fall
with the master
and poignant until death
that seems even bliss.
he flys with us now
a mind unfettered
unclaimed
a hero
unwilling prosaic master
above ground and
depths unknown
pure collectivism unencumbered-
not ayn rand-
an aberrant individualism though.
A little prince.
Alas, I look within my hollow vessel
and am despairing.
.

SMOKE

to screen the toxic waste of
all flowing down to the comfort
spot
a well deep enough to hold the pieces of
eternity and then some
the glacier moving and carrying all the
detritus of ages to appear and reappear
and never disappear
to recreate is all and nature
unspecial and determined without end
only its own and sacred trust
to be observed from afar
a star

WATCHING WALES

eternity was water
replete with swimmers and divers
no watchers no matter
divers and swimmers

small hunters with great determination
drive the swell and fading images of
beasts from a different nature
the new smell of forces foreign

no bias is
as no bias does and the misunderstanding
walks as always towards less and lethal
only to satisfy out of control evolution of
human avarice.

dexterity limited
and guile nonexistent
a fine time with fine life bows to
tiny but purposeful
destructive nature
more of an accident than a meaning
and beauty slowly dies with its master
of beauty and death.

ISMS

orbs and entities
imploding truth through tech

a new truth
similar but different from Plutarch
Plato and platypus

now fiction
standard isms up the spout
looking for al purdy to express
but he's dead now
and hope he hasn't dragged us all down with him
the perfectly prosaic bastard.
a free fall life tempering the
loose among us
and giving us hope
for an impossible expression
of simplicity

listening is very internal
and inside the internal
eternal?

the spawn of prose is prose
and isms are the offspring.

Circle

i do not miss the mirrors
for no self image
casts no imprint

is it death or distillation
is it war or is it peace

must all disembark
and seek incantation
flight of fantasy
venal soul

broken wing
challenge to reason
to release all
commit to treason

gyroscopic precession
through wear and tear
a broken psyche
in ill repair

grasp at straws
nature's laws
to mutilate and confiscate
bear down upon pontificate

a reed too limp to strike honest note
a boat too narrow of beam
a life discordant played by rote
planks lined poorly, insulting of seam

slowly turning
passion yearning
black ice known and feared
a crack of diffuse morning light

Radiant and Teared
a road less taken
broken shaken
smart and all severe
a grain of truth like any grain
willing, grows in truth to steer

No More Funky Dreams

Disinformation.
perpetration from the holders of the torch
and get to misguidance

only to hold
power
because there is nothing known about consciousness
that allows a rendering of truth without getting in the way of fact
which is not known because
consciousness is Euclidian or
wants to be.

elaborate structures that
always relate, or try to, can reverse primitivism and
release concept

to proportionate beyond the ooze

row your boat gently down the stream
merrily.

A Novel Affair

Another day, another dollar. Well, not exactly. Myles Blainey did not collect a smattering of money here and there for his labour. Last week, he had earned over seventeen thousand dollars while barely moving a cranial muscle. It was these muscles that worked for Myles, although with ongoing public appearances, he was just vain enough to also keep the body toned and fit too.

It wasn't just women who read his books. The cornerstone of his talent was his uncanny and omniscient understanding of love and the other basic human conditions, which significantly opened up the pages to many of his own gender. As far as Myles could tell, this was not attributable to any particular life experience, but more likely to his idealistic and somewhat naive nature.

The classical romance genre safely removed him from dealing with the more complex issues of the present, and he quite liked the protection of manners and mores from yesteryear.

His own abode was anything but a Regency drawing room, and the enchanting "bon mots" uttered constantly by his stable of "lords and ladies" never ventured beyond his highly respected quill.

"Jesus, Myles! You haven't given me anything on paper for ten months!" Reg Bolton had been his publisher for 12 years, and was used to an endless stream of purple prose from his star client.

"It eludes me Reg. That little bugger that sits on my shoulder and invades my every waking moment has left town," Myles replied.

That his muse was nowhere to be found was perplexing, to say nothing of his fearful notion that this irreplaceable source of inspiration was gone forever. The fact was, Myles had become incapable of rendering one full sentence, and the blinking cursor on his computer became a cruel taunt for his paralysis: "Gotcha, Gotcha, Gotcha . . . ."

To make matters worse, it was February, traditionally a time when Myles' erstwhile sunny disposition nose dived into a very dark hole the size of Saturn where the collective angst of the ages descended upon him— one dimensional, grey, flat surfaces constituted the decor of this Neanderthal cave, where all the dank, putrid gasses of devolution left little room for optimism. He normally used these imageries to advantage, in constructing the more despairing moments in his plot lines. But now, there was only impotence.

The Saturday night dinner party was a monumental effort. Yes, he was "profoundly" interested in getting his new story moving. No, he had no idea when it would be finished, "but soon, hopefully," he kept saying to those who asked.

Zero. Nada. Nothing. Evidently, a pox had been placed upon his house, and no antidote was in sight. Until much later, after everyone had left.

It was 2 a.m. Slumped over the computer. Tap, tap, tap, tap. The sound woke him. His hands were primed, the screen was lit and alive. Fingers danced over the keys with the agility of a young gymnast, but strangely, the actions did not seem to be his own. Edgar Alan Poe came to mind:

> Once upon a midnight dreary, while I pondered
> Weak and weary,
> Over many a quaint and curious volume of
> forgotten lore,
>
> While I nodded, nearly napping, suddenly there came a
> tapping,
> As of someone gently rapping, rapping on my
> chamber door."

But it was not fear that Myles was experiencing. If indeed, the Raven wished to enter his time and space, then "Welcome Raven!"

In the days following, a lingering aftertaste of these sensations dominated his waking and sleeping. He was consumed by a kind of reverie, allowing him more thoughtfullness, but most important, infused him with feelings very much like being in love.

Unquestionably, the bloom was back on the rose, and one evening, as Myles researched the work of a long deceased and favourite author of his, he began to notice the similarity in their personal writing styles—plot lines, language, character development. Fascinating and eerie. She had been a major influence on Myles Blainey, both for her compelling style and profound insight into society of the early 1800's. Also, Kathrine Morris had been dead for over 150 years.

The days and nights of frantic writing mounted, and the toll was evident. Any kind of contact with the outside world was out of the question, and those who knew and cared for Myles began to wonder if he had taken leave of his place and his senses. Indeed, he wondered as much himself. Notwithstanding his compulsion and fatigue, he was ecstatic. 3 a.m. and another marathon of words complete.

An essence of unseen female presence permeated the atmosphere of his lair. The general absence of reality had taken a determined hold on Myles and he thought he might be reaching down into another hallucinogenic state. Not altogether unpleasant, but decidedly unsettling.

She stood there before him, radiant. The most beautiful woman he had ever seen. He said nothing, waiting nervously for what he already knew.

Her visitations became more and more frequent. He had never attempted to actually touch this sublime vision, nor she to touch him. It was something that at first seemed unnecessary, but in any event, impossible.

"I believe you are the most beautiful living thing," Myles said.

The fact that she was likely not a "living" thing, was not a deterrent.

Time became irrelevant, as Myles and the object of his complete mental and physical desire, travelled the uncharted course of their co-dependence. Natural law crept quietly away, and a new universe emerged.

Early spring. New life. A new novel, perhaps the best he had ever written, according to his publisher.

"God dammit, Myles," said Reg. "For quite a while I thought you'd really lost the touch. But this latest book! How does it feel to be number one again, eh?"

"Great. Just great!" Myles replied with convincing enthusiasm. In fact, he couldn't remember a time when he felt more depressed. The finest of the grape had brought forth the most hideous of plonk. Myles had come back to earth, crashing, burning.

It had come to a head just as the final chapter of the book was being completed. Now, every thought, every word was being rendered through the constant presence of Katherine Morris, her beauty and talent the driving force. Myles felt more and more to be merely the conduit . . . the messenger boy. Katherine, of course, never spoke. Nor did she touch or move. She was simply the personification of nature's highest form of pure energy.

But now, something else was happening; a vast, pulsing entity of impossible dimension, spreading its being to embrace his captured soul. Raw nerves exposed to searing heat, then suddenly jettisoned upward into a sea of perfect blue . . . . time slowing down from the speed of light, to rhythmic perfection. Wagner, Beethoven, Liszt, scoring the symphonic masterpiece. Her retreat from him causing a wrenching unlike anything he had ever known. Her face, a mask now . . . stone-like and indecipherable. Then, just as the sun disappears into the tropical sea at dusk, in a flash, she was gone.

And, so it seemed, was Myles. The specter of melancholy broke from its tether, redirecting Myles to his erstwhile state of gloom.

She had broken down the physical barriers between them and crossed over; given herself to him tangibly, thus eliminating the possibility of any further union.

When forced to leave his hellhole for provisions, mostly of the liquid variety, he went incognito. Writing was, in any sense, completely out of the question,with the annihilation of his computer and all other writing devices and symbols.

T.S. Eliot and Milton accompanied Myles into the black holes, and continuous infusions of brandy aggravated his growing despair.

Reg Bolton was at his wits end, and just one of many people who were seriously concerned for Myles Blainey's welfare. And so it was, on that fateful day, clearly a stroke of luck that Reg broke through the lines of Myle's final stand.

"Myles, open the bloody door for Christ's sake, and stop this god-damned foolishness!" Myles hears but is to weak to respond.

The front yard was in a state of neglect; mail piled up at the front door; remnants of unrescued newspapers clinging stubbornly to the shrubbery. Reg shuddered to think how the inside of the house must look.

"Myles, answer the door now, or I'm coming in the hard way!"

The French doors around the side of the house proved the easiest access. A bold poke at one of the panes, a deft twist of the inside handle and Reg was in. He steeled himself for the worst, as he sprinted frantically from room to room, finding what could have been the work of a small neutron bomb. The two cats came to greet him; they seemed starved for attention and nourishment. He was right about his premonition on the state of affairs inside Myles' house. A small bomb couldn't have done a better job.

The ambulance arrived in minutes. Myles, on the stretcher, oxygen and iv hooked; life-giving tentacles flailing; attendants proving their considerable talents at pickup and delivery of the damaged goods.

Barbiturates, booze, and a diet befitting an annorexic, had blasted Myles to within millimetres of permanent brain and liver damage, and likely, oblivion.

Recovery was nasty. It seemed the permeating gloom might never be shaken; a personal hell, that Myles had never before even come close to exploring.

He had entered hospital April 1st. It was now the middle of May, and Myles' first week at home was proving positive. He had almost "bought the store," and this, upon reflection, gave him a completely different stance on the virtues of simply being alive. It began to feel good, and the quill dived hungrily into the cleansing ink of his imagination. The presses began rolling again.

A rejuvenated social life was among the many joys of being "reborn," as Myles referred to his catharsis.

"Ah, music to inspire even the gods," Myles thought, as the strains of a Mozart violin concerto embraced a bucholic New York Central Park and captured all those who dared to venture close.

But it was not just the music that held him. She was a vision. Not since his seemingly "surrealistic" affair with Katherine Morris, had Myles been moved by such beauty.

Her playing was extraordinary; her serenity the kind that could exorcise demons from the most blackened of souls. But most important, was her striking resemblance to the famous 19th century writer.

Her name was Andrea and she did not hesitate in accepting Myles' offer of getting acquainted. She had been a fan for years, but moreover, Andrea had read everything Katherine Morris had ever written.

He never missed one of her concerts during those first heady weeks together. And she never missed an opportunity to compliment and encourage this man, recently back from the brink.

"It's all so strange, Myles. It's as if someone else is guiding my fingers. Have you noticed how much my playing has improved? My God, is this really me making these perfect sounds?" Incredulous, bubbling.

Katherine Morris had only taken a dramatic leave of absence. Just enough time to regroup and plot an even better ending to her latest saga.

"And they are gone: aye, ages long ago
These lovers fled away into the storm."
+ *John Keats:The Eve of St. Agnes.*

INVERNESS STONES

new and different pearls of wisdom
alone and singular
only a clean surface can tell
their lightness of spirit
always slighted returned to their function
of being and mystery
and a history that only is taught by
the sun moon air water continuum
waiting to be heard and touched by
their other human partners.
perfect representatives of the invitation
from nature and washed with unspoken
knowledge and beauty.
crying to be snatched up and looked at
formitive creatures of patience and endurance
so much to teach us in their silence.

10 BILLION MEN

the snow at night in all its glory
casts light finally, the winter story
sharp and clear it well defines
and covers dreary, worn out lines

why sky so clear and full of scope
sharp contrast to the tired hope that feeds
a worn out soul.

bereft of much of everything
another death to mourn
the specter waits and always comes
but no new life is born
only shrunken folds of well pressed nerves
the kind that never spares/preserves.

to think that just scant moments ago
so much endured amid the blow
a thousand years has passed since then
and bears the weight of 10 billion men
all different all the same
chasms of unrelenting failure/ blame

normal rhythms within the heart
afraid to think or jump or start
anxious time and broken holes
left behind from worn out souls

heart and head seem almost one
perhaps the way intended
heavy and light at the very same time
if only they are mended.

the snow at night makes clear and bright
the gray dark spots beneath
a blanket for the tired earth
and time to heal and thank it.

whatever then was said in haste
however much was battered
my love goes on and searches through
the ruins of what mattered.

STRIFE

the shadow boxing
the mirror image
a heavy stance of
unremitting retrospection

watching from
(a distant shore)
a major vision
always the same

the demanding despot
takes all, knows all,
gives all but nothing.

only theory with haste
and chaste
the virtual
force of will
leads and bleeds

caring metaphysical
doing empirical
high above and far beyond

finally warmth
and only clear bright eyed
visceral
counting down.

You Only

All the things you think are corny and trite
won't go away when the heart is ailing
Simple truths bang away at the front
of sadness
and make the human look clearly human.

trying to find a fancy way to say
i love you
weakened and impoverished of spirit
will in decline
hope in retreat
a late discovery that transforms
and transgresses
new metabolism of old ideas
a rupture of tears and pain
pay back from those others
wounded
now me
invasions from particles of
our reason to be
joined places we mostly
don't allow to be subjected.
protons massive taunting
opposite of composition
just to show who's boss
as beauty and despair unite
tiny hills that feel like mountains

take leave of senses
and enjoin no more.

Arsepain

ripping up the contract
leaves room for new statements
a balance sheet
with more positive forecasts
and screaming bloody hell the vagaries of existence.

the business mind of co-existence
resting, waiting for some genius or at least
an original idea
where people speak the same language
where people like the same things.

flooding the lowlands with droplets
and migraines
systematic reduction of reason
and molecular constructs of inner being
redoubt to whining and vascialting
female armageddon.

no more ruin
no more pain
one more chance
to maybe live again.

Snakeskin

rich, thick
more dimensional than the lightness of summer
frivolity wanes and serious import of things roused by
the cooler of nature's venues
the not yet furrowed brow of Fall
worldly and paternalistic
the deepness of tone impresses from
stratosphere down
weightiness born again to relieve and test
new mettle against recycled

laughter distills to knowing smile
and preludes thoughtfulness of consummate color
and renaissance
and hope for the living

someone has died
no seasons were there for her
and now family will only feel destitute
denied cherished fantasies
of beauty and truth of imagination
with no sweet seasons for a long time.

as the change arrives resplendent
so death leaves unrepentant
a memory magnifies far greater than mundane
daily visitation
and only drastic measures cast new nets
to capture those conscious tid-bits of here and now.

the gift of life cannot be impugned
but only death of others can relieve
the great weight that shadows a requirement
where little margin for error exists
and all manner of humanity thrives.

cannibalism
a final taboo that defines
all of us.

READY

too hard and painfull
easy and tranquil neither
for here lies desperate truth
begging release
avoiding the word that has determined
all that we are and
would like to be

better alone
solitude and internal
protective
now with the other
and alone and afraid
of loss
never enough
unequal and fortress of emotions
imagined or real

understanding hardly important
another soull fighting to survive
within another
lighter and more resiliant
perhaps

natural movements amid the stars
and totally not understood.
love.

BLIND (LYRICS)

It shouldn't make a whole lot of difference
if our love is painted in the dark
And it shouldn't be whole lot of trouble
to find its centre
even as if blind.

But the blind lead the blind
and it all but disappears
on the crest of a wave
that crashes into tears,
and the centre find it s place in an
unrelenting sea
of the parts that are creation
of you and of me.

But it shouldn't make a whole lot of difference
any more
for the centre is the centre
though it bounds from door to door
and the nudge of truth that reaches in
amid the harsh and reckless din
embraces, as a mother would a child.

And the child will see the place,
the exquisite maternal lace
in an instant and with the truth of the moment we call love.

So it shouldn't make a whole lot of difference
if our love is painted in the dark,
and it shouldn't be a whole lot of trouble
to find its centre, even as if blind.

Restructuring for Mission

The Journey to Families of Parishes in the Archdiocese of Detroit

Deacon Mike Houghton

Chapter 1 – The Backdrop

The Church Today

Anyone who works for the Catholic Church is well aware of the problems that we face. They're not only our reality, but they're also fodder for stories in the popular media who seem to want to celebrate our misfortunes. We're seeing declining numbers of parishioners, declining appreciation for and participation in the sacraments, declining vocations, declining donations, an aging infrastructure of Churches and other buildings, scandals in the clergy, and the list goes on.

This situation is not unique to the Catholic faith. Other faiths - Christian and non-Christian alike - are experiencing similar declines in varying degrees. Supporting data is easy to find, and to be candid, I'd rather not start this book by trying to provide any unique or profound insights into the problems that we face. Several people have done so in several other books over the past few years, and I would have little to offer beyond what they've already said.

But while I will readily admit that we have problems, I myself am not one who believes the narrative that the Catholic Church is on a path of continued decline. I believe that we're on the cusp of a revival; that we're poised to make a comeback. The sleeping giant is being awakened, albeit slowly, and we're shaking off some of the confusion that gripped us in the years following Vatican II by returning to an appreciation for our fundamental call to evangelize.

Across the United States and in other parts of the world as well, we're seeing a return to evangelization as a priority. The past three popes have all embraced the idea of a new evangelization, and the global Church is beginning to finally appreciate the wisdom of their direction.

I'm firmly convinced that the Holy Spirit leads and drives the Church, and with him as our leader, it will be impossible for us to fail. We may stumble, we may make terrible mistakes, and we may not always have clarity about what to do next, but we will not fail.

When Jesus gave Peter the keys to the kingdom of heaven, he told him, "You are Peter, and upon this rock I will build my church, and the gates of the netherworld shall not prevail against it" (Mt. 16:18). Often people will hear this and picture the Church defending herself against the netherworld, battling to stay alive but never giving in.

I offer another perspective. I like to think about the Church as being the one on the offensive, charging the netherworld with voracity and pushing on the gates wearing the armor of God. She isn't defending, she's attacking.

But in order for the Church to prevail, she has to be nimble. Our circumstances will change but our mission will not. We simply need to adjust our approach.

The early Church was nimble. When the Hellenists complained against the Hebrews because their widows were being neglected in the daily distribution, the Church immediately identified seven reputable men and laid hands on them to ordain the first deacons (Acts 6:1-6). Were there people in the Church at the time complaining about the restructuring that took place by this action? Perhaps. We don't read about it in the Bible, but it's not out of the realm of possibility. Today I write this book as an ordained deacon some 2,000 years later, following in the tradition that was initiated in that moment of nimble response. And I appreciate the need for us to find again the ability to be nimble.

I've been a deacon in the Archdiocese of Detroit (AOD) for a decade now. After working many years for General Motors, I retired from my job and joined a movement here in our great archdiocese which I support and which I believe is in fact a nimble response to our circumstances here in southeast Michigan, deep in the heart of the automotive industry.

Our response to the declines that we've experienced has evolved over almost a decade, led by our great Archbishop Allen Vigneron but clearly informed and guided by the Holy Spirit. It can be summed up very simply:

We are on the path to becoming a more missionary diocese.

This is our calling; this is our goal. We exist to be missionary, to spread the good news and to go and make disciples.

Does everyone in the AOD support this move? Of course not. Does everyone even understand it? No. If it were as easy as the Church simply setting direction and everyone following it, I'd still be working for GM because there would be no need for my role with the Curia.

Our path to being more missionary has taken us through a series of obstacles and challenges, including some from outside the Church like a global pandemic, social media addiction, and declining morality, and others from inside the Church like resistance to change, boring homilies and bad music at Masses, and perhaps most significantly of late, a very real shortage of priests that's growing more daunting every year.

But do any of these obstacles and challenges give us a free pass to decide not to go on mission? No, they do not.

When Jesus told his followers to go and make disciples of all nations at his Ascension (Mt. 28:16-20), he didn't warn them about all of the problems that they would soon confront. He didn't tell them about the persecutions or the martyrdom or the schisms that were to come. He just gave them a mission to go and make disciples.

And when the Holy Spirit asked our archdiocese to be more missionary, he didn't warn us about the problems that we would face. He didn't warn us that some of the greatest resistance we would experience would come from within. And he most certainly didn't tell us that there would be a global pandemic that would strike just as we were getting started. He just gave us a mission to be a more missionary diocese.

When the reality of the pandemic became clear, there were many who wanted us to stop, to put everything on hold, to forget about the calling of the Holy Spirit and instead batten down the hatches and ride out the storm, hoping that we would survive and make it through. When it was over, we could pick up the pieces and figure out a new direction.

After all, long before the pandemic we were seeing the painful realities of the priest shortage in our archdiocese. It was quite possible that the virus would exacerbate the problem. Many of our older priests were among the most vulnerable due to their age and their declining health. Some of our priests who were contemplating retirement would simply choose to do it now rather than wait for the pandemic to end, which was true for not just the priesthood but for many other walks of life. Perhaps our reality was that we were heading into a series of closings, mergers, and parish clusters in the years ahead that would allow us to ride the attrition curve of our priests.

But Archbishop Vigneron displayed tremendous courage and said no, this was not going to be the plan. If we went that route, we may as well forget about being missionary because all we would do is fight for years to come about which parishes would be the next to be targeted, and we would be doing nothing other than surrendering and accepting a future of continued decline. We were called to be more missionary, and we were going to find a way to do it despite whatever circumstances we may face.

In the years leading up to the pandemic, we had studied a few different ways to handle the priest shortage. While the Archbishop and his Episcopal Council had listened to the alternatives, there was no real desire to make a change until now. After all, the Archbishop had just a few years until his mandatory offer to retire at age 75. Would it not make more sense for his successor to take up this challenge?

I wasn't in on any of those earlier discussions, and I won't try to speak for anyone else, most especially the Archbishop. But what I do know is that prior to the pandemic there was no real appetite for a major restructuring.

When the pandemic came, it seemed like the gates of the netherworld were doing their best to prevail against not just the AOD but the entire world. And that's when the Archbishop decided that he wasn't willing to accept a retreat. It was time for the Church of Detroit to go on the attack. It was time to address the priest shortage and come up with a structure that would allow us to continue to be on mission despite the obstacles that we faced.

The Archbishop decided that it was time for us to move to Families of Parishes.

This is the story of our journey to Families. I tell it from my perspective, that of the one tapped to take the lead in this effort.

Full Disclosure

I've heard it said that the story of the Passover is told very differently from an Egyptian perspective than it is from the perspective of the Jews and Christians. While we see it as a triumph, the Egyptians understandably view it as a calamity. It's always important to know the perspective of the storyteller when listening to a story.

The story which follows here is told from my perspective. It's quite possible – even probable – that the same story would be told differently by others in the AOD who went through our transition to Families of Parishes. It's not that any of the events would be different, but rather that the sentiments surrounding those events would vary from my own.

I've been blessed by this journey in many ways, and my prayer life and my trust in the Lord have greatly benefited from it. But others might not feel the same way, most especially some of our great priests here in the AOD who have had to struggle with some rather significant changes in their ministries.

It's also the case that as I write this book I have scant data by which to say that we have succeeded or have failed. We have about a year under our belt with our 26 Wave 1 Families, and we're just getting started with our 28 Wave 2 Families.

We will ultimately be successful if over time we are a more missionary diocese. This is our goal; this has been our goal for some time now. Families of Parishes have never been our goal. Families are not an end; they are a means to an end. They allow us to structure in such a way that we can hopefully continue on our missionary journey despite the obstacles that we face.

So why tell the story now? Is it premature to do so?

The reason why I feel the need to tell the story now is that there are many, many dioceses around the United States and around the world who are grappling with what to do about the priest shortages that they face, just like us. I've received calls from many dioceses asking us, "What did you do?" I've spoken with people from dioceses in Ireland, Australia, Canada, and all over the United States.

As a person who spent 35 years working in the secular world, I believe with all my heart that we in the Catholic Church need to do a much better job of learning from each other rather than continually creating things from scratch. We need to benchmark, capture best practices, and never be afraid of R&D. By R&D I don't mean Research and Development, I mean Rip off and Duplicate.

I believe that other dioceses can learn from what we did even though we're not done, whether that means using what we did or realizing that what we did will never work for their circumstances. Either way there is benefit to the Church.

That said, let me state my two primary goals in writing this book.

First, I want other dioceses to be able to learn from what we've done. For this reason, I've included clips of presentations, charts, timelines, and other things that others may find beneficial. At times, this content may not be very entertaining, but that's because it's not for entertainment value. In this regard, there is a bit of a project management angle to this book.

Second, I want to tell people about how we have experienced the hand of the Lord in guiding us through this journey. I clearly saw the Holy Spirit leading and driving not only the AOD but also me personally. This is not to put myself on a pedestal. No, far from it. I hope you will see that I frequently struggled to appreciate the Holy Spirit's assistance. Rather, I think it's important that people see how powerfully the Holy Spirit works in our world today. The society we live in has become so secular - so unwilling to see God in the here and now. But he's acting as powerfully today as he did for the early Church if we are but willing to open our eyes to see it. It's my goal to reveal how the Holy Spirit has acted in our journey in order to give others hope that he will act in your life and your circumstances as well if you are willing to trust him.

So with my disclosure complete, buckle up and enjoy the ride. It's going to get bumpy.

Chapter 2 – The Exodus

A Call To Do Something Else

I started formation for the diaconate in 2008. It was a rather tumultuous time in my life when my career with GM was clearly ramping down and my calling to be a deacon was clearly ramping up. God wanted me to obey and apply for the diaconate, but I didn't think he understood how difficult that would be for me. I had three young children who were not far from their very expensive college years, and I had almost 25 years into a career that had paid the bills and then some for my family.

How could I possibly find the time to take classes at the Seminary and be in a formation program for the next four years? Just let me finish my career, God, and when I retire, I'll pursue whatever you want.

But the Lord had a different plan for my life, and he was relentless. I felt a constant tug at my heart telling me that he wanted me to pursue something other than another 15-20 years with GM.

I fought it for as long as I possibly could, but I talked with some priests who I trusted and they convinced me that if this was God's plan, he would clear the path for me. And in ways that I would have never dreamed possible, he did.

In my four years of formation, I felt that the Lord always put my kid's events on days when I didn't have class. He put me into a new job that gave me more time and freedom to pursue the diaconate. And he made it clear to me that there was a bigger plan than I could possibly understand at that point in my life.

Even in the earliest years of formation when I was just getting started on the path toward ordination, I felt a very strong desire to leave the corporate world and to pursue some sort of full-time ministry. I prayed about it quite a bit, asking God that if this is what he wanted for me, he needed to show me how to do it.

I could write another book on how that all worked out, as the story is really rather remarkable. But that's not the point of this book, so I'll simply leave this part of the story with one particular insight.

Shortly after my ordination, I was asked to take on a role at General Motors in Manufacturing Strategy and Planning. This was something that I didn't ask for, and it came at me out of the blue. Initially I resisted it, but I slowly began to realize that this might be a part of God's plan for me.

And so on my way to the interview, I prayed to God a very simple prayer. "If this is what you want for me, make it known to me and I'll accept it on the spot without reservation."

During the interview, he did in fact put it on my heart that this was where he wanted me. I didn't understand why, and I had great reservation about what I was leaving behind, but I immediately said yes. This was the first time in my life when I jumped at what I believed to be God's will for me no matter what the cost. But it would not be the last.

I truly enjoyed the role that I had in Manufacturing Strategy and Planning. I worked with a wonderful group of people, and I picked up a number of skills that ultimately were of great value to me in my role with the AOD. I didn't realize it at the time, but God was guiding me down a path where I could ultimately use what I had learned for his good.

But even though I enjoyed my role, I continued to long for something else. Something in full-time ministry. Something that would allow me to utilize the skills that I had learned as well as the graces of ordination to do something meaningful for the Lord and his Church.

From Call To Action

Through various ministries that I took on after ordination, I was introduced to a few people at the AOD who felt that I might be a good fit for something in the Curia. There weren't any specific plans, but clearly I was tilling the soil for new growth.

In March of 2019, I got the call that I had been wanting for over a decade. Would I be willing to leave my job at GM for a full-time job with the AOD Curia?

My first reaction was one of panic.

This would mean a tremendous pay cut at a time when my wife Anita and I were just starting to enjoy the realities of being empty nesters. The kids were finished with college, which was the biggest pay raise I ever had. The house was too big and we were going to downsize. We were going to travel and enjoy life like we had never done before.

This would mean starting over at a time when I was incredibly comfortable at GM. I knew exactly who to talk to in order to get things done. I had people who I knew I could trust and others who I knew I had to avoid. I could do my job in my sleep, but now I was thinking about leaving it.

For this decision, I didn't jump without considering the costs. In fact, I did more budgets and financial plans than I can count. Every one of them turned up the same: this was going to be a big change for my wife and me. This was going to require us re-thinking our retirement plans.

But no matter what the numbers showed, I believed in my heart that this was what God was asking me to do. If that were the case, wouldn't he take care of us? I began to realize that my faith was pretty strong when things were going well, but perhaps not so strong when I was confronted with complicated decisions that would have a real impact on my way of life.

I was reminded of something that I told my kids when they were in difficult situations: anyone can be the captain of the ship when the waters are calm, but a real captain proves his or her worth in a storm. Maybe I wasn't as much of a real captain as I thought I was.

Thank God for my wife Anita, who has always been a big supporter of me and of my calling. If this is what God wants, she would say, then why are you worried? Just do it.

And so I decided to do it.

Spiritual Warfare, Part 1

But the decision to leave GM came with something that I never expected: a healthy dose of spiritual warfare.

Growing up as a cradle Catholic, I had heard a little bit about spiritual warfare, but I figured that while it might be very real for people like the great St. John Vianney or St. Mother Teresa, there was no way that it would ever be a part of my life.

As I went through formation to become a deacon, I came to a better appreciation for the fact that the devil may well want to thwart my plans to draw closer to the Lord, but I confess that I still held the view that this wouldn't be something that would be common in my life. It's not that I didn't believe in the devil or in his evil plans; I did. But spiritual warfare for a simple deacon? The devil had much bigger targets than me to worry about.

Like so many other things that I have learned and continue to learn in my ministry, I was wrong.

For a few years leading up to my exit from GM, I had experienced some back problems. I had developed stenosis from compression of my spinal cord due to a narrow spinal canal and growing arthritis in some of the lumbar, and it would manifest itself in pain in my left leg.

There was a wonderful Chiropractor at my Church who worked with me to get the pain under control, and I thought that I was done with it. But just about the time that I got the call from the AOD, my leg pain came back.

It got worse and worse, and I began to fear that it might be a big mistake to leave GM at a time when I may well need surgery. Would the surgery even be covered by the AOD? As a new employee, would I be able to have time off to recover? I began to experience doubts about leaving which caused me great concern.

Was it coincidental that this flared up at the same time that I was contemplating a move? No, it was not. It was spiritual warfare. The father of doubts was having his way with me, trying to get me to back out of the move and to stay with GM. Despite my denials, the devil was in fact toying with me, a simple deacon.

I pressed on with my retirement plans and resumed treatment with the Chiropractor, hoping for relief similar to what I had experienced before. But it didn't happen. The pain got worse. I found that I couldn't walk for more than 100 feet without stopping to let the pain subside. And that was my state when I arrived for my first day in my new job, July 1 of 2019.

I remember distinctly being downright panicked about walking around the office and meeting people. I couldn't walk very far, and I couldn't stand up for more than a few minutes without taking a break to sit down or lean against something.

On that first day, every time I was walked to a new area to meet someone, I was surveying the scene and planning how I could sit or lean without being too obvious. I don't know if anyone caught on or not, but my day was rough to say the least.

Why was this happening, I would ask the Lord? I came here at your calling, and you allow this? Can't you just fix me up and let me do the job you called me to do at full strength?

But the answer was no. The Lord was not going to fix this for me. And so I pressed on with starting an entirely new career amidst the pain that I knew I had to address.

By the time I reached the end of 2019, the pain was too much. I also realized that I was living my life with tremendous physical restrictions that were dampening my ability to do the Lord's work, or for that matter to just have fun.

One of the things that was most troubling was that when I would serve as deacon at Mass, I couldn't stand through the entire Eucharistic prayer. Thank God for the fact that, as a deacon, I had to kneel down when the priest held his hands over the gifts and called down the Holy Spirit. That gave me enough of a reprieve to stand up again and finish my duties.

I had to do something, and so I visited with a surgeon to talk about my options. The Lord blessed me with a wonderful friend who works here in the local hospital system, and she referred me to the doctor who she felt was the best at what he did. He was a gifted surgeon who offered me the option of a minimally invasive operation from which I could recover very quickly.

At first, I was thinking that I would have the surgery in the late spring of 2020, since this was a good fit for all of the events that I had planned in my calendar. I had no idea at the time that this would have been a big mistake. By late spring of 2020, all elective surgeries were stopped due to the pandemic. Had I gone with plan A, I might not have had relief for a year or more.

Once again, it was Anita who drove the plan and suggested that I have the surgery sooner rather than later. You're in so much pain, she said, why not just do it now? And so we agreed that I should have the surgery in late January.

To cut to the chase (no pun intended), the surgery went well, the recovery was amazingly quick, and to this day I am without pain in my leg. I don't doubt that someday the pain will come back as the condition creeps its way to another lumbar, but I'll deal with that if and when I need to do so.

When I look back on it now, I realize that, as much as the devil sought to pull me off course, the Lord put wonderful people in my path to get me back on course. For this, I give thanks.

Chapter 3 – Listening to the Holy Spirit

How We Got To Where We Are

To this point, I've covered a little of the history of how I got to the AOD. But in order to appreciate our journey to Families of Parishes, it's critical that any who read this understand the things that transpired in the years prior to our restructuring.

If I were to simply jump into the mechanics of what we did without explaining why we did it, it would be a hollow story that's nothing more than an exercise in project management. So allow me to give some background to help make sense of what we did.

A Most Incredible Man

> *"Some might say that the Archdiocese of Detroit is a most unlikely setting for a large-scale revitalization of the Church. But is it not in the most unlikely settings that the Lord loves to show forth his divine power? Our acknowledgement of our own spiritual poverty is precisely what can lead us to rely wholly on God. Then it becomes clear that success belongs to him alone and not to any human ingenuity. If we have become spiritually dry, we need not fear. Dry wood is perfect for being set on fire!"*

These words are found in the Catechetical Exposition of the profound Pastoral Letter *Unleash the Gospel*. They were written by one of the greatest leaders of the Church I have ever had the pleasure of knowing: Archbishop Allen Vigneron.

I could go on for quite some time about Archbishop Vigneron, but I could never fully describe for you the man he is. He's perhaps the most prayerful person I have ever met. He's a man of great wisdom.

He's a tremendous leader, though his leadership is humble and understated.

When I left GM for this new role, I didn't know him very well. He was the presider at my ordination, and I have a cherished picture of him with his hands extended over my head during that Mass. I knew that people who knew him spoke highly of him, but I didn't have any firsthand experience with him.

In my time with the AOD, I've had the chance to see him in action. He's as genuine as it gets. He humbly seeks the direction of the Holy Spirit and the input of those around him before making decisions, but he's never afraid to make a decision. I couldn't ask for anything more of a leader.

I can say without reservation that he's the best leader I've ever worked for, including my 35 years with GM. And to be clear, I worked with some people at GM who I consider to be tremendous leaders. The Archbishop has the wisdom and clarity to compete with any of the great leaders I've known in my secular career, but he combines it with a humble spirituality that none of them could possibly understand. This is a rather unique and special combination of skills that precious few people possess. Leadership and humility are often considered to be at opposite ends of the spectrum, though our Lord certainly showed us the perfect example of how to master both.

For all of his great leadership qualities, two in particular stand out to me.

The first is his tireless effort to seek input and advice from others. So often people in high level leadership roles don't take the time to do this. I've observed senior leaders who feel that they are too busy to take the time to solicit input, and I've observed those who are too arrogant to solicit input, but I've seldom found people with his level of responsibility who insist upon making informed decisions. He trusts the people around him and he values their input. I've had several personal experiences where he has not only sought out my input but acted upon it, which is rather humbling to me.

The second is his ability to know when to stop the debate and make a decision. In my previous career at GM, we used to say that there comes a time in any vehicle program when you have to silence the engineers and build the car. This concept isn't unique to the automotive industry, and it's most certainly a reality in the Church, where discussions can be extended for what can seem like an eternity by those who prefer philosophy to decisiveness. I've most certainly earned relief from time in purgatory for having endured some of these endless discussions. The Archbishop is always patient, always kind, always listening. But he has a keen ability to realize when enough has been said, at which point he has no reservations with saying that he appreciates all of the discussion but he has made a decision.

Under his leadership – informed by his obedience to the Holy Spirit – we in the Archdiocese of Detroit have been on a rather incredible journey for almost a decade now. When the journey began, I was more of a spectator than a player. But even as a spectator, I could see that something special was happening.

A Most Incredible Journey

A man as wise and prayerful as Archbishop Vigneron was able to see that we in the Archdiocese of Detroit needed to do something to address the growing secularity in our country and to embrace the new evangelization, a favorite topic of Pope St. John Paul II, Pope Benedict XVI, and now Pope Francis. But what should our response be? This is a question which has broad implications, and a misdirected effort could have easily set us off on a path that ended up being less fruitful than what it otherwise could have been.

And so he consulted with his regional bishops, his priests, and other trusted advisors to develop a plan. That plan was rooted in prayer, and it was unquestionably directed toward understanding what the Holy Spirit asked of the AOD rather than telling the Holy Spirit what the AOD wanted of him.

In our Archdiocese, we have four Auxiliary (Regional) Bishops. As we began our journey, they were Bishop Michael Byrnes, who would eventually be named the Archbishop of Agana, Bishop Arturo Cepeda, Bishop Donald Hanchon, and Bishop Francis Reiss, who is now retired. In 2016, with two of these original four Auxiliaries moved on, Bishop Gerard Battersby and Bishop Robert Fisher were ordained as Bishops to complete the Episcopal Council. These fine men are some of the keys to all that we've done in our move to be a more missionary diocese. They are all faithful sons of the Church, and they are unequivocally on board with the vision of Archbishop Vigneron.

We began our journey in 2014 with a year of prayer. This was foundational to everything that we were about to do, and so all of the parishes of the AOD were asked to pray for guidance.

We then followed up in 2015 with a time of listening. In this year, every parish in the Archdiocese was asked to conduct listening sessions with the lay faithful to gather what they had heard in their prayers. What was the Holy Spirit asking of them? What was the Holy Spirit asking of their parish? What was the Holy Spirit asking of the Archdiocese of Detroit? I had the pleasure of conducting one of these listening sessions at my home parish of St. John Vianney in Shelby Township, where I had been serving as deacon since my ordination in 2012.

Two very significant things happened in 2016.

First, there was an act of repentance. A Mass for Pardon was held at the Cathedral of the Most Blessed Sacrament where we as an Archdiocese, led by the Archbishop and his regional bishops, sought to repent for the sins of the Archdiocese leading up to this point. This was very much in the spirit of the humble leadership that our Archbishop embraces. It was a moving event, especially when the Archbishop and his four regional bishops lay prostrate before the altar and sought forgiveness.

Second, we convened a Synod for the entire archdiocese to discern where we go from here given all that had happened in the years of prayer and listening. Synod 16, as it's known, was an historic occasion during which representatives from all corners of the Archdiocese – clergy, religious, and lay people – gathered to pray and reflect together on what will make the Church in southeast Michigan a joyful band of missionary disciples. The Archbishop was a prominent figure in the entire Synod, as one might expect. The results of the discussion which took place at this Synod were captured and given to the Archbishop for him to pray with and use to decide upon next steps.

I'm most certainly not giving sufficient attention here to Synod 16. It was a tremendous event, and it was clear that the Holy Spirit was alive and well in the conversations that took place. While I don't wish to speak for the Archbishop, I think it's a fair assessment to say that for as often as he looks back on the Synod, it was certainly a high point of his episcopate.

2017 proved to be the exclamation point on the sentence that was Synod 16. Again in 2017, there were two very significant things which happened.

First, there was the promulgation of *Unleash the Gospel*, the Archbishop's Pastoral Letter which summarized what we learned, and then provided very clear and concise direction as to what we now need to do to respond to the calling of the Holy Spirit.

In my time in diaconate formation, I've had the pleasure of reading a number of Church documents, from Pastoral Letters to Pastoral Notes to Papal Encyclicals. One of the things that I can say about just about every one that I have read is that, while they are often beautiful documents, they aren't always clear about what to do once the last paragraph has been read. They are intended to give general instruction while still leaving the details open to discussion, debate, and interpretation. While I appreciate the intent, this is a point of frustration to me as one trained in engineering and leadership. If we who are charged with making it happen are unclear about what we are being asked to do, we can sometimes spend more time arguing about what to do than we spend doing it.

But this isn't the case for *Unleash the Gospel*. It's clear, concise, and gives very specific Action Steps which describe what we need to do as an Archdiocese to be more missionary. For this I am very thankful.

If you have not yet read *Unleash the Gospel*, I strongly encourage you to do so. You will no doubt find it a delightful and inspiring read.

The second thing that happened in 2017 was the beatification of Fr. Solanus Casey, now Blessed Solanus Casey. The fact that he is a son of Detroit and that his beatification came in the midst of all of this flurry of activity in our Archdiocese is not a coincidence. Indeed, it was an affirmation that we were on the right track.

By the end of 2017, the table was set for us as an Archdiocese, and it was time to move forward with our plans. But it's never really that simple, is it? Embracing a bold new mission isn't easy, and it doesn't happen quickly.

Chapter 4 – My First Assignment

Parish Missionary Strategic Plans

Despite the buzz about all that had happened up to the release of the Pastoral Letter, the reality was that our progress toward completing the Action Steps from *Unleash the Gospel* was slow. Some felt that the timing for these Action Steps was perhaps overly optimistic. Others felt that the Curia – toward whom most Action Steps were directed – was simply not structured to move fast on implementation.

I won't weigh in as to why I feel that the Action Steps were slow to implement, but I would be lying if I didn't say that I'm in a strange way happy that they were. If it weren't for this, I might never have been given an opportunity to leave GM and work in the Curia.

Because of the slow progress, the Archbishop and his leadership decided that it was time to focus some of our efforts directly on the parishes of the AOD. This was, after all, where the rubber meets the road, to put it in terms that we in Detroit can clearly appreciate. It was time to go directly to the parishes and support them in developing their individual plans toward being more missionary.

In the fall of 2018, a dedicated team of Curia personnel was pulled away from their daily assignments and asked to develop a process by which parishes would be guided through the creation of what was called a Missionary Strategic Plan, or MSP.

The MSP would be a plan that the parish would implement over the next 3-5 years to make themselves more missionary, more evangelizing, more focused on responding to the call of the Holy Spirit from Synod 16.

There was an appreciation for the fact that we would benefit by starting with a few pilot runs of the MSP process with what we called "Partner Parishes," and so nine Partner Parishes were selected to work with this team of Curia personnel on developing their MSPs.

But there was a catch, and that catch proved to be a rather significant one. The decision was made that if these MSPs were to be bold, they would require fundraising. It was felt that bold moves could not be accomplished at no cost. Some today look back on that decision with dismay, but we have to realize that this was new ground that was being tilled and there was no clear way forward, so we did what we felt was best.

These nine Partner Parishes completed their MSPs over the next several months, and they were also given fundraising targets that they were to collect from parishioners. The idea was that half of the money collected would be for the parish to implement their MSP, and the other half would go to the Curia to fund the downtown activities associated with our efforts to be more missionary. (Those downtown activities were to eventually include the funding of the team that I would be called to bring on board.)

It would be an understatement to say that the fundraising part of the MSP process was not popular with the priests of the AOD. In fact, it was incredibly unpopular. They were willing to do what the Archbishop asked of them out of obedience, but they were quite vocal about their frustrations.

That said, we pushed through the Partner Parish MSPs and got the fundraising discussions rolling.

Looking back on what was done, it would be my opinion that much of what was put forth in the Partner Parish MSPs was not particularly bold. In some cases, it came across as though the parishes were looking for ways to spend their half of the fundraising, and that many of the action items were not particularly missionary in nature. Of course, there was some very good work done as well. But in total, we probably didn't meet the rather hopeful expectations of the process.

The effort that went into these first nine Partner Parishes was immense. Beyond the work of the people in the parishes, there was a large team of Curia people working many hours to pull together the process.

There was quickly a realization that to do this work well for the other 200+ parishes in the AOD, we needed a dedicated team and a dedicated project manager to lead the work. And this is what ultimately led to me getting the call in March of 2019, asking me if I would leave GM to take on the project manager role.

The Original Plan

My original job description at the AOD was pretty simple, really. That doesn't mean that it was easy to do, but it was easy to understand. I was asked to learn from what we experienced in the Partner Parish MSP process and use that to refine the process for the remaining 200+ parishes.

The Archbishop and his key advisors wanted to complete all MSPs by the end of 2021, which was a bit aggressive but which I felt could be done.

I would be given a few employees who would work for me directly, and I would be asked to hire some number of contract people (that number would be determined by me as I understood the job more) for getting the work done.

This sounded to me like classic project management, and I was comfortable that I could get it done without being stretched. If I were to be completely honest with myself, I would have to admit that I figured this was going to be a relatively simple execution.

Early on in my role, I settled on two major thrusts to get the process rolling.

First, I wanted to meet with all of the key people in the Curia to get to know them and to capture their thoughts on what worked and didn't work well in the MSPs that had gone on up to this point. These meetings were quite beneficial to my task, and they also allowed me to get to know a little bit about the background, family, and hopes and dreams of many of the people with whom I would be working.

Second, I wanted to have discussions with the people who were a part of the Partner Parish exercise to understand from their perspective what worked, what didn't work, and what they would recommend we do differently to be more successful with the remainder of the parishes. This included people inside the Curia who had been a part of the activity and the Pastors of the nine Partner Parishes.

Within a few weeks of my arrival, we had an All-Priest meeting where we rolled out a timeline for completing the remaining MSPs. The timeline involved four "Waves" of activity, each Wave consisting of a set of parishes who would be brought through a common process, as depicted here.

SENT ON MISSION
The Next Phase of Unleash the Gospel
Projected Timeline to be finalized after Partner Phase

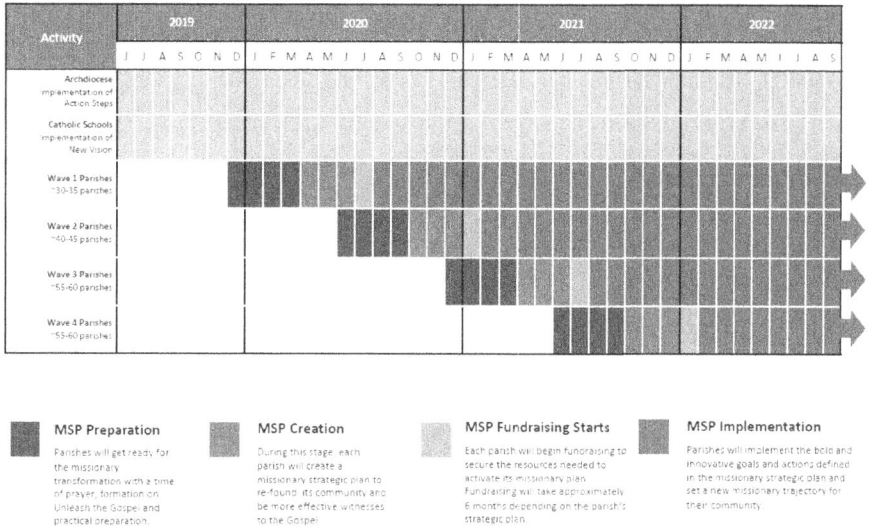

ARCHDIOCESE OF **DETROIT**

Activity	2019						2020												2021												2022							
	J	J	A	S	O	N	D	J	F	M	A	M	J	J	A	S	O	N	D	J	F	M	A	M	J	J	A	S	O	N	D	J	F	M	A	M	J	J	A	S

Archdiocese implementation of Action Steps

Catholic Schools implementation of New Vision

Wave 1 Parishes ~30-35 parishes

Wave 2 Parishes ~40-45 parishes

Wave 3 Parishes ~55-60 parishes

Wave 4 Parishes ~55-60 parishes

MSP Preparation
Parishes will get ready for the missionary transformation with a time of prayer, formation on Unleash the Gospel and practical preparation.

MSP Creation
During this stage, each parish will create a missionary strategic plan to re-found its community and be more effective witnesses to the Gospel

MSP Fundraising Starts
Each parish will begin fundraising to secure the resources needed to activate its missionary plan. Fundraising will take approximately 6 months depending on the parish's strategic plan.

MSP Implementation
Parishes will implement the bold and innovative goals and actions defined in the missionary strategic plan and set a new missionary trajectory for their community.

This All-Priest Meeting was my first exposure to the realities that I was going to face in my role.

The meeting went poorly. Many of the priests were angry and loaded with questions that by their very nature displayed their hostility toward this project. The vast majority of the questions centered around the fundraising portion of the process, with very few if any questions being raised about the need to be more missionary.

This was also my first exposure to a behavior that I've seen in several of the priests over the past few years: a passive-aggressive behavior. The priests are, for the most part, good and holy men who love the Lord and who became priests so that they could serve him and his Church. It wouldn't be right for a priest to be directly or obviously aggressive, so this passive-aggressive approach was a sort of convoluted way of making their point through subtleties, ironic statements, and sometimes even philosophical points used against the premise.

I was much more accustomed to someone just wagging their finger in my face and repeatedly swearing at me, a behavior I had seen quite often in my time working in assembly plants. I suppose that I prefer passive-aggressive to just plain aggressive, but in either circumstance it can be very difficult to make progress.

The Curia staff at this meeting – including me – were for the most part unprepared for the negativity that came at us. We weren't able to sufficiently answer some of the questions, and we didn't come across as being very well organized.

The Archbishop, as he always does, remained prayerful and supportive, and while he was clearly concerned about the negativity that he heard, he also had the wisdom to realize that this was not unexpected and that we needed to keep focused on answering the call of the Holy Spirit from the Synod.

This first meeting with the priests was an eye-opening experience. I was by no means discouraged by how it went, but it left me with a profound appreciation for the fact that I really needed to have my act together before coming before the priests again.

Chapter 5 – Building the Team

Part 1: The Coaches

By early fall of 2019, I was blessed with a team of four people to help lead our activity. Each of these four people was given the title of "MSP Coach." These four are some of the finest disciples I have ever had the pleasure of knowing: Deacon Dave Casnovsky, Christina Hall, Mary Martin, and Kathy Svoboda. Over time, Christina would move on from our team and be replaced by Wade Richards, another disciple, and another gift to our team.

Among other things, these Coaches needed to support the four regional bishops who in turn support the Archbishop in his role. The regional bishops live in their region, so they're spread out across the Archdiocese, which is rather large. I knew that asking someone to support a bishop and region that was far from their home would be problematic, but the Holy Spirit took care of that for me. These four people who came to my team as Coaches were conveniently all living in or very near one of the four regions.

The MSP Coaches are true disciples who love the Lord, who love his Church, who are committed to the mission and to the Archbishop, and who I simply enjoy as people. I really couldn't have asked for anything more than that.

I'm grateful for so many things that they've done, but the one that stands out the most to me is one that may surprise some people: they really taught me how to pray. Or perhaps to put it a little differently, they taught me how to pray better. These fine men and women were prayer warriors, meaning that they let prayer drive most everything they did. I had a good prayer life, but prayer was not as much a part of my everyday decision making as it was for them. They showed me how to integrate prayer into meetings and everyday discussion in ways I had never before done.

One of the first things that we did as a team was to go offsite and use the Amazing Parish principles to talk about who we were and what we were trying to accomplish. This allowed us to develop some guidelines which we have honored to this very day.

Some of the key things that we agreed to were as follows:

- We would always start with prayer and allow the Holy Spirit to speak to us.
- If we couldn't come to an agreement in a meeting, we would hit the pause button, take it to prayer and come back to discuss later.
- We would be prayerful, innovative, and collaborative.

The five of us then went about the work of framing up our plan for getting the remaining MSPs done and of staffing up with the necessary resources to complete them.

Framing up the MSP process was actually an enjoyable task. We realized that what we were doing was directly in line with our archdiocese's efforts to be more missionary, and that was something that gave us all a sense of joy and peace.

With the plan starting to take shape, we did some basic workload analysis and decided that we needed to bring on about 20 contract employees to work with the parishes. I'm a big believer in keeping things simple, and the simplest way to look at this was that we felt that at any given time these people could handle two parishes who were creating their MSPs and two more who were preparing to do so. Both preparing and creating an MSP took a fair amount of training and formation for the leadership of the parish, and this number of roughly four under their facilitation at any given time felt about right. But we also agreed that we wouldn't hire anyone who wasn't right for the job. If we couldn't get 20, we would take whatever we could get so long as they were the right people.

Each of these additional people that we needed would be called a Missionary, and so the Coaches and I began planning the hiring of 20 Missionaries.

There were a few problems that we faced in hiring these Missionaries, and there was one financial concern that seemed to be a minor point at the time but would prove to be a rather significant issue as events unfolded.

One problem we faced was that we needed people who could drive a project and meet deadlines, but who were also spiritual and faithful sons and daughters of the Church. This isn't an easy combination to find, and we knew that finding such people would be complicated.

Another problem was that there wasn't enough money to bring these Missionaries on as full-time Curia employees, so they had to be contract employees. This meant, in turn, that we wouldn't be able to offer them any benefits.

The pay that we were able to offer them wasn't all that attractive either. They were paid on a per diem rate, and the rate – while reasonable - wasn't something that most people would jump to take. This was further complicated by the fact that in late 2019, the job market was hot and there weren't a lot of people looking for work.

And speaking of pay, this is where the financial concern came into play. There was no real budget for my team within the Curia finances. Everything we did was to be paid for by the fundraising that was to go on in the parishes, and that had not yet begun. What if the parishes couldn't raise what we anticipated? What if there were other problems and the money wasn't made available?

We were, in essence, operating in a deficit mode at this point, paying salaries to my team and me based on the expectation of future funds coming in. This didn't sit well with me, but this plan was in the works before I had come on board and so I went along with it.

As it would turn out, this financial concern that I had would prove to be a rather significant issue over time. I never would have anticipated that a global pandemic would be the reason that the plan would start to unravel, but then again, I'm sure no one else would have thought that either.

Part 2: The Missionaries

With the job market as hot as it was, we knew that it was going to be tough to attract and retain good people, and we knew that we had a rather difficult task ahead of us in trying to fill these Missionary roles. But we also knew that we had a very special and powerful weapon on our side: the Holy Spirit.

I spent quite a bit of time praying for the Lord's help. If we didn't get the right people, this would become an exercise of just checking the box at each parish to say that we're done, and that wasn't going to make us a more missionary diocese.

We first tried posting through the conventional route via our own AOD website. Not surprisingly, the results were not all that good. So we upped the ante. We posted on LinkedIn, we spread the message through Facebook and other social media, the Coaches and I directly contacted people we thought might be good candidates, and we sent a message to all of the recent graduates (laity) of Sacred Heart Major Seminary, which is located right here in Detroit.

When we advertised the Missionary jobs, we spoke of the ministry, of the mission, of the need to do what the Holy Spirit asked of us from Synod 16. We didn't mince words and we didn't dance around the fact that these were going to be very important but also very difficult jobs.

Our efforts paid off to the tune of 26 applicants. This was rather astounding to me, but at the same time I was fully aware that the Holy Spirit was most likely the reason for most of them applying rather than our efforts.

On January 13 and 14 of 2020, we conducted our interviews. We took three rooms at Sacred Heart Major Seminary and had three teams of people interview each candidate. The questions for each room were grouped so that we could identify different facets of their fit for the job.

The interview questions were as follows:

Group 1 – Motivation and Skills

- Why do you believe that you are a good candidate for this position?
- What motivates you? What challenges you?
- Have you read the Pastoral Letter *Unleash the Gospel*? What did you like or dislike about it?
- Have you ever facilitated or chaired meetings of a group of people? Been a part of developing a strategic plan?

Group 2 – Prayer and Faith

- Please describe how and when you pray.
- Please describe your feelings about the Catholic Church and the Catholic Faith.

- Do you believe that the Holy Spirit is acting in the world today? If so, how?
- What does "Evangelization" mean to you? Do you evangelize others?

Group 3 – Self Assessment

- What are your greatest strengths? What are your greatest weaknesses?
- Can you provide an example of when you have been innovative? Collaborative?
- How comfortable are you with using Microsoft tools (Excel, Word, PowerPoint)?
- Describe how you would deal with a cynical or disinterested pastor or Leadership Team member.

Some of the candidates were taken aback by the questions about Prayer and Faith. Needless to say, they had never been asked about that in an interview before. But this is what gave us great insight into their heart, which is a big part of what would ultimately determine their success or failure as a Missionary.

So allow me to mention again the drawbacks of the job of a Missionary: low pay, no benefits, and a very difficult job where you will often be rejected. What an appealing job description, eh? But when the Holy Spirit does the recruiting, you simply can't fail.

Among the 26 applicants, we had 22 bachelor's degrees, 18 master's degrees, four doctorates and one who was just about to complete her doctorate. We had seven people who attended classes at Sacred Heart Major Seminary. We had three who spoke Spanish, and one who spoke Aramaic and Arabic.

But what was even more impressive was the backgrounds of the people who interviewed. We had an executive vice president of a large automotive supplier, a psychiatrist, three people who owned and operated their own companies, and even one who served under President George W. Bush as Army General Counsel, the civilian equivalent of a five-star general. We had one ordained deacon, another in formation, and another who would soon be in formation for the diaconate.

There were a few folks who decided through the interview process that this job wasn't right for them. I appreciated their honesty. There were a few who we felt wouldn't be able to do the job. And when the dust settled, we brought on a total of 16 incredibly talented Missionaries.

The names of these fine disciples we hired are as follows: Kate Baumer, Connie Borg, Don Buchalski, Mary Ann Hannigan, Brenda Hascall, Adora Kassab Ibrahim, Sue Lang, Deacon Steve Morello, Michael Nanna, Wade Richards (who eventually became a Coach), Erin Shankie, Paul Spankie, Joe Schmidt, Karina Stevens, George Strimpel, and Ben Weir.

We were also blessed to have Gabby Rodriguez, yet another disciple of the Lord, working as part time administrative support for our team.

The talent in this fine group of people is beyond what I would have ever imagined. Not only are they bright and hardworking, but they are committed disciples of the Lord from the first to the last. I'm forever grateful that they agreed to be a part of our journey, and for the fact that they have so positively impacted my prayer life and my love of the Lord.

Needless to say, after this experience I spent a lot more time in prayer giving thanks to the Lord for leading all of these wonderful people to us.

The "Chapel"

So the team was complete: four Coaches, 16 Missionaries, part time administrative help, and me. But there was another player on the team that no one really knew about except me, and perhaps Anita. That was my chapel. Since the start of this journey, it's been here in the chapel that I've found solace, peace, and deep prayer. My chapel is kind of like the 12th man on the football team, providing me strength and courage.

In the second half of 2018, Anita and I had come to the conclusion that we needed to downsize our home. Our kids were all in college or graduated from it, and we no longer needed a four-bedroom colonial in the heart of Rochester Hills.

Anita had lots of great ideas about what she wanted in our next home, but I only asked for a few things. I wanted a natural gas outdoor fire pit that I could turn on and off as needed without having to smell like smoke. I wanted a large entertaining space directly connected to the kitchen so that we could have big parties and not cram everyone around the kitchen island, which is pretty much where everyone ends up at a party. And I really wanted to have a place where I could go to pray.

As a deacon, I'm asked to say morning and evening prayers every day. When I was first ordained, it felt like somewhat of an obligation. As I got more comfortable with it, it felt like a relief in my day. Today it feels like a privilege. The beauty of praying the Liturgy of the Hours is something that takes time to appreciate, but once it becomes a part of the rhythm of life, it blossoms into a necessary way of dealing with life's anxieties and troubles.

But what I've found over the years is that I struggle to focus on my prayers when I'm in the house. There's always something distracting me, taking away my focus. It might be something as disruptive as a phone call or something as subtle as a nagging feeling that there's laundry in the dryer that needs to be folded, but there's always something.

Some people are able to set up a prayer space in their house, perhaps a spare room or even just a comfy chair in the corner of the living room. But that just doesn't work for me. I pray best when I can separate myself from the everyday and pray in isolation.

One of the best places I found for this kind of isolated prayer was the Chapel at Sacred Heart Seminary where I took classes for the diaconate. I just love praying there, and I can really immerse myself in it.

Sometimes I can find good prayer at my home parish of St. John Vianney, but that can be distracting because when someone comes in, there's a certain obligation to be the deacon and greet them.

The best option that I could come up with for good prayer was to have a separate structure on my property which was devoted to prayer. A chapel of sorts.

And so when we moved, we bought a home further north of the city in a rural community called Bruce Township. We found a beautiful home on 2.5 acres where we can sit on our back deck and watch the deer stroll through most every day. We even have a groundhog that lives under our shed who has become somewhat of a pet to us.

In the back of the lot we have quite a few trees, and we purchased a pre-made shed and had it delivered into a small clearing. We next had to get electricity to it, which was no small task. I rented a trencher and my son Nick and I spend quite a bit of time trenching back to the shed. That's a job that I'll never do again. I'm quite grateful that Nick had both the physical strength and the caring heart to do most of the work for me.

With the shed powered up, I went about finishing off the inside with a small heating unit for the winter, an overhead fan for the summer, and nice but understated wood paneling and trim work to make it comfortable.

Anita and I had some debate about how to furnish the inside. She wanted something like a church pew with a kneeler, but that was not for me. I wanted a La-Z-Boy recliner. I can't get deep into prayer on a hard bench. I joked with Anita that if we had it her way, perhaps we could purchase a hair shirt to add to the fun, but I don't think she appreciated my humor. She joked with me that the chapel would eventually become my place for a nap if I got too comfortable in a recliner.

In the end, because I spend far more time down there than her, I got my recliner.

We call this wonderful place of respite our chapel, but I'm well aware that it doesn't meet the Church's requirements of a Chapel. Thus, I speak of it as our chapel (lower case "c") rather than our Chapel (upper case "C"). I'm probably not correct in doing this, but I would offer to any who might find fault that my intentions are good even if my nomenclature is flawed.

The chapel is very likely the best thing I have ever done for my own personal prayer life. When I'm in there, it's all about prayer. I can focus on my prayer. I'm not distracted. I can get carried into deep and meaningful prayer that I struggle to find elsewhere.

As I look back on things, I realize that the Holy Spirit was a big part of why I have that precious space. It was there that I had the opportunity to spend much time in prayer, seeking the Lord's guidance through the troubled times that were soon to come in the world and in my role with the AOD.

This is why I consider the chapel to be a part of the team that has helped the AOD through our transition to Families.

Chapter 6 – Failure to Launch

Spring Training

While our new crop of Missionaries was bright, educated, and committed to the Lord and his Church, they were also being asked to lead an effort which none of them had ever experienced. And so we knew that it was incumbent upon us to train them and get them ready.

We developed a rather extensive training plan which would take place over six weeks starting on March 2, 2020. The training was to take place in an open area at St. Scholastica, a parish just across the border of Detroit and as centrally located as we could find. Fr. Jim Lowe, the pastor at St. Scholastica, is a wonderful and very prayerful man who was fully supportive of our efforts and was quite willing to assist us in any way.

There were six primary focus areas that were to be covered in the training.

- **Understanding of the departments of the Curia.** This involved meeting with the heads of each major department and having them explain to my team how their area functioned. This would be important for our Missionaries as they got questions from parishes about who to contact on specific issues.
- **Appreciation for the Mission.** Our team needed to be fully immersed in the journey that the AOD had been on, including an understanding of the timeline getting us to this point, deep dive discussions on *Unleash the Gospel*, and training in Evangelization.
- **Spiritual Development.** This was an absolute necessity for not only the Missionaries, but for the Coaches and me as well. If we were going to be faithful to our task, we needed to be grounded in a sound spirituality. This aspect of the training

involved daily Mass, prayers to start morning and afternoon sessions, and the use of a wonderfully gifted young priest, Fr. Patrick Gonyeau, to give our team spiritual direction.

- **Meeting of key players outside the Curia.** We brought in key people from outside of the Curia, especially some of the top advisors to the Archbishop, to tell us what they felt about our task, and then join us at Mass and for lunch.
- **Deep dive training on the MSP process.** Quite a bit of time was given to learning how MSPs would be created, learning about the tools that supported their creation, and doing a mock MSP as a team so that everyone understood how to carry out their role.
- **Off-sites/Field Trips.** We knew that it would be incredibly boring to sit in a classroom for several weeks, so we arranged off-sites – aka field trips – to see sites in the Archdiocese of Detroit that make us special. This included visits to the Cathedral of the Blessed Sacrament, The Shrine of the Little Flower, the Solanus Casey Center, and others.

A matrix summary of the training plan is provided below for reference.

	9:00 AM	9:30 AM	10:00 AM	10:30 AM	11:00 AM	11:30 AM	12:00 PM	12:30 PM	1:00 PM	1:30 PM	2:00 PM	2:30 PM
Monday, March 2, 2020	Welcome - Moderator	HR, IT discussion					Lunch		Introduction to Families of Parishes			
Tuesday, March 3, 2020	UTG Formation					Mass	Lunch		UTG Formation			
Wednesday, March 4, 2020	Prayer before Meetings			Spiritual Formation		Mass	Lunch		SHMS Offerings		Certification	
Thursday, March 5, 2020	Evangelization 101					Mass	Lunch		Off-Site - Shrine of Little Flower			
Friday, March 6, 2020	Chancery Tour			Drive back to Scholastica		Mass	Lunch		Missionary Opportunity Assessments		Team Time	
Monday, March 9, 2020	Healthy Leadership Teams					Mass	Lunch		Heathy Leadership Teams			
Tuesday, March 10, 2020	Coach Break Out Sessions					Mass	Lunch		Communications Tools and Vision			
Wednesday, March 11, 2020	Catholic Cemeteries	Spiritual Warfare		Spiritual Formation		Mass	Lunch		Youth Ministry			
Thursday, March 12, 2020	Diveristy and Inclusion				Bishop Battersby	Mass	Lunch		Off-Site Blessed Sacrament Cathedral			
Friday, March 13, 2020	Schools Vision		Schools Break Out			Mass	Lunch		Team Time		Mission of the Laity	
Monday, March 16, 2020	IT Tools and Vision					Mass	Lunch		Off-Site - Our Lady Star of the Sea			
Tuesday, March 17, 2020	Effective Meeting Facilitation				Guest Speaker	Mass	Lunch		CLI DMI Survey			
Wednesday, March 18, 2020	Dynamic Parish		Spiritual Formation				Lunch		Benchmarking and Big Book of Bold Ideas			
Thursday, March 19, 2020	Visioning Day Defined		Visioning Day Wave 1 Results			Mass	Lunch		Off-Site - Solanus Casey Center			
Friday, March 20, 2020	What is Bold?		Goals and Metrics			Mass	Lunch		AOD Fundraising Use		Catholic Foundation	
Monday, March 23, 2020	Guest Speaker on Prayer	Costing out MSP Items, Parish Audit Services		Team Time		Mass	Lunch		CCS Role and Process			
Tuesday, March 24, 2020	Encounter, Grow, Witness Toolkit					Mass	Lunch with +AHV		Path to Missionary Discipleship		Practice Sessions Overview	
Wednesday, March 25, 2020	MSP Smartsheet				Guest Speaker	Mass	Lunch		Off-Site - Sacred Heart Major Seminary			
Thursday, March 26, 2020	MSP Creation - Introduction					Mass	Lunch		MSP Creation - Introduction			
Friday, March 27, 2020	MSP Creation - Family Evangelization					Mass	Lunch		MSP Creation - Family Evangelization			
Monday, March 30, 2020	MSP Creation - Parish Culture					Mass	Lunch		MSP Creation - Parish Culture			
Tuesday, March 31, 2020	MSP Creation - Parish Function					Mass	Lunch		MSP Creation - Parish Function			
Wednesday, April 1, 2020	Team Time		Spiritual Formation				Lunch		Off-Site - St. Anne			
Thursday, April 2, 2020	MSP Creation - Sunday Experience					Mass	Lunch		MSP Creation - Sunday Experience			
Friday, April 3, 2020	MSP Creation - Catholic Schools					Mass	Lunch		MSP Creation - Catholic Schools			
Monday, April 6, 2020	No Training - Holy Week											
Tuesday, April 7, 2020	No Training - Holy Week											
Wednesday, April 8, 2020	No Training - Holy Week											
Thursday, April 9, 2020	No Training - Holy Week											
Friday, April 10, 2020	No Training - Holy Week											
Monday, April 13, 2020	MSP Creation - Technology and Communications					Mass	Lunch		MSP Creation - Technology and Communications			
Tuesday, April 14, 2020	MSP Creation - What not to do					Mass	Lunch		MSP Creation - What not to do			
Wednesday, April 15, 2020	MSP Creation - Refining, Timing, Metrics					Mass	Lunch		MSP Creation - Refining, Timing, Metrics			
Thursday, April 16, 2020	Catch up time for anything leftover					Mass	Lunch		Catch up time for anything leftover			
Friday, April 17, 2020	Retreat					Mass	Lunch		Retreat			

And so on March 2, 2022, we welcomed our brand new 16 Missionaries to St. Scholastica and we started the training.

Along with the excitement that I was feeling as I drove in for our first day, I was also feeling angst about what was going on in our country and how it was going to affect our efforts. The Coronavirus was dominating the headlines and a lot of people were dying from it. I had a very uncomfortable feeling that all of our efforts were about to be overshadowed by a train that was coming down the tracks and headed our way.

What Happened?

Just two weeks into our training, the bottom fell out. The AOD closed the Chancery, parishes were grappling with whether or not they should stay open, and the world began to panic.

I'm quite certain that anyone reading this book could easily describe how you felt at this point. I myself was scared, but I was also in a bit of a state of denial. This couldn't be happening, could it? We're far too advanced of a society to have something as small as a virus take us down like this one did, aren't we? Perhaps if we just shut down for a few weeks, this will all go away.

When the buildings were shuttered, our team immediately reverted to online training using Microsoft Teams. We had never planned for this, and it was a rather significant pivot for us. But as it turns out, this was by no means our last pivot, nor was it our most significant pivot.

The online training wasn't nearly as effective, but it did work. We continued on with the hope that things would clear up and we would soon be back together to finish our training at St. Scholastica.

Down in my chapel, the Lord heard quite a bit from me in these dark days. Why did you call me here for this? Can you just make it end soon so that we can get on with the task you gave me? Where are you, Lord?

It's not that I ever lost faith or lost trust in the Lord, but this was quite a curveball. Had I just stayed with GM, I could have no doubt continued doing what I was doing from home. In fact, I would have probably seen a rather significant increase in my workload as there would have no doubt been a need for more strategic analyses on what-if scenarios. But instead I was wondering if we would even be able to keep our jobs. If the parishes were closed, there would be no good way to complete MSPs and no need for my team to exist.

After completing another two weeks of training, the pandemic impact around the country was much worse. It was clear to me that nothing was going to be opening up soon, and it was equally clear to me that my team didn't really have a role that was going to be needed any time soon.

My direct supervisor is Fr. Jeff Day, the Moderator of the Curia. As Moderator, he's also the leader of the Cabinet, which is essentially made up of the six Directors of the major departments in the Curia. He's a wonderfully pastoral man and a joy to work for. During the pandemic, he stepped into the crisis and led us in admirable ways. He called for twice a day Cabinet meetings, where we would make sure that we were on top of all things Covid, and he established regular communications – at least weekly – with everyone in the Curia to be sure that there was a visible presence of leadership at all times.

The importance of leadership presence in a crisis can't be overemphasized. Even if people grow tired of the communications, there's an inherent sense of comfort that comes from knowing that those in charge are doing their best to control what they can control and to plan for what's ahead. A void of leadership in a crisis can result in chaos. Fr. Day did a wonderful job of making sure that such a void would not happen in the AOD by making himself visible and available to the people in the Curia.

He and I had a few conversations about where to go from here with my team, and I essentially proposed one of two options. Option 1 was that we keep moving forward, finish the training, and find something to do as a team while we waited for the parishes to reopen. Option 2 was to shut down operations and let everyone go.

After some discussion with the Archbishop, the agreement was to use Option 1. The Archbishop realized all that we had gone through to bring my team on board, and he also realized that they were a valuable part of his plan to engage the parishes. Thus, it made sense to keep us intact – at least for now.

At the same time, it was clear that this was a decision that would need to be revisited over time. If things continued to decline, we may need to go to Option 2. I understood this and agreed to it. Although I didn't want to see this effort end, I also couldn't justify keeping it going if there was no hope of us adding value any time soon.

Pivot Again

The Coaches and I had a lot of discussion about what we should do with our team after the training was complete. Although there were lots of options on the table, we all agreed that we needed to do something to continue to advance the goal of being a more missionary diocese. Even a global pandemic was not going to stop us from doing whatever we could to follow the direction of the Holy Spirit here in the AOD.

We settled on three activities that we would pursue.

The first activity had to do with parish intercessory prayer teams. We all knew that prayer was going to be critical for keeping us close to the Lord amidst the pandemic, and our parish intercessory prayer teams were the best vehicle we had for supporting the parishes of the AOD behind the scenes. We formed the existing teams, brought on new teams and trained them, and established a number of online prayer venues to drive our efforts.

The second activity was a somewhat complex outreach to the community that we called "Calming the Storm." Our goal was to be a support group for people in need due to the pandemic. People had lost their jobs, their homes, and even access to their places of worship, and they needed support. We established a team of people who would call or email anyone who contacted us through our websites, ads on social media, and other outreach efforts. We kept on top of the homeless shelters, food banks, and other support services in the area which were still open for business so that we could refer people in need. We spent quite a bit of time listening to and praying with people. In some cases we got in our cars and delivered whatever was needed to help people out.

The third activity was one that ended up being quite beneficial to us in our efforts to form Families of Parishes, though we had no idea at the time that we were going to Families of Parishes. We established something called "Pastor Connect." Every member of my team was given a list of 15-20 priests in the diocese that they were asked to call frequently – daily if needed – to listen to them, pray with them, clarify AOD Covid policies for them, or whatever was needed. Some of the priests greatly appreciated our contacts and developed wonderful and long-lasting relationships with members of my team. Others, quite candidly, wanted nothing to do with us. This particular activity may sound a bit odd to some people. Why would priests need this? It's important to realize that our priests were scared at the start of the pandemic just like everyone else. But additionally, they were isolated in ways that many of us were not. I was frustrated being stuck inside for months on end, but I had my wife and kids there with me. Many of the priests returned to their rectories with no one else living there. They couldn't say Mass. Their offices were closed. They were much more isolated than most of us, and they needed to talk.

We asked everyone on the team to be a part of two of these activities, and then they were charged with organizing their efforts to get it done and reviewing the plan with the Coaches and me.

Each of these activities yielded results that were quite awesome. We drove a lot of prayer, we helped a lot of people get assistance in a time of need, and we helped a lot of priests cope with the isolation that they experienced. This was great.

But at the same time, this was not what we were hired to do. It was becoming evident that there was very little hope of a quick return to MSPs, and even though it sounds harsh, the reality was that we were a financial burden to the AOD that could quickly be eliminated. I pretty much assumed that this was going to be the case.

This was the focus of much of my prayer time in the chapel. What do you want of me now, Lord? What do you want me to do?

Chapter 7 – And Now For Something Completely Different

My Marching Orders

I tend to keep pretty good notes on things. This is largely because I know that my memory sometimes fails me on the details, and I need my notes to remind me of specifics. Remembering concepts, direction, and the big picture is easy. But details? I'm not so good.

This struggle with detail was clear to me in my undergraduate studies at Wayne State, where I had to take a lot of math classes. My major was Electrical and Computer Engineering, and much of the work was math-based. I could never remember the formulas, although I could remember the concepts behind why they mattered. I often found myself deriving the formulas on my own during an exam because I simply couldn't remember what they were. A big part of the problem was that I was also a fullback on the Wayne State football team, and that took an awful lot of time and energy. By the time practice was over, I was too tired and too beat up to try to memorize anything.

But for all of my detailed notes, the specifics around April and May of 2020 are a little bit foggy. I think that a big part of the reason for this is that I really didn't want to remember anything.

This was a very dark time for me. I had made the jump from GM, but it turns out that the jump might have been a big mistake. I thought I was flying high and following God's will in my life, but everything was crashing to the ground.

Then something happened that was totally unexpected. The Archbishop told the Cabinet that he had made the decision that we were moving to Families of Parishes. We needed to get ready for him to make a formal announcement at Pentecost, which was on May 31, 2020.

What are Families of Parishes, I wondered? I had never heard of them.

At first I simply thought that this was something that the Curia would do after my team and I were gone. It didn't really matter all that much to me.

As we began to learn more about Families, I started to realize what a big change this was going to be. This wasn't just a restructuring; this was a significant change to the way that priests would function. They would need to cooperate, collaborate, and work together in ways that they don't today to support multiple parishes. And if one of them retired or moved on, there might not be a backfill because, to put it bluntly, there's no one on the bench to replace them.

I knew that we were experiencing a decline in the number of priests, but I had no idea how significant it really was. This chart became the subject of much discussion and a key reason for why we needed to move to Families:

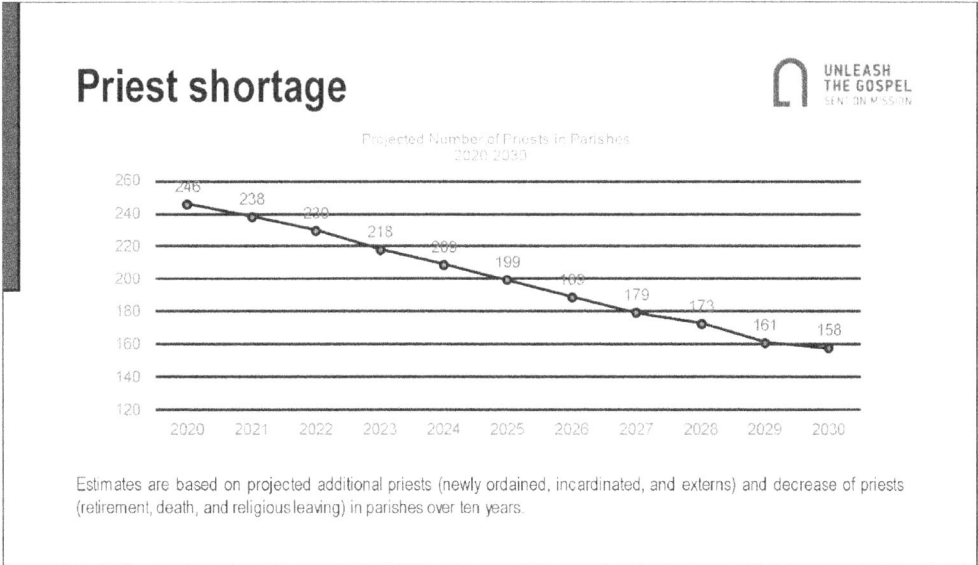

Priest shortage

UNLEASH THE GOSPEL
SENT ON MISSION

Projected Number of Priests in Parishes
2020-2030

246, 238, 230, 218, 209, 199, 189, 179, 173, 161, 158
2020, 2021, 2022, 2023, 2024, 2025, 2026, 2027, 2028, 2029, 2030

Estimates are based on projected additional priests (newly ordained, incardinated, and externs) and decrease of priests (retirement, death, and religious leaving) in parishes over ten years.

With 217 parishes, we were only a few years away from having less than one priest per parish. If we didn't do something, we were headed for a very painful future of mergers, clusters, and parish closings.

I found all of this very interesting, but again, it wasn't my issue to deal with. It was clear that this would eventually affect my role as deacon at St. John Vianney, but that would take time and I would eventually adjust.

I went down to the chapel and prayed as I always did, and I was spent. There was no future for my team, and I needed direction.

I was comfortable that I could find something else to do. Most likely GM would take me back, at least in a contract role. But my team? Some of them had left jobs, even left companies that they started or owned, to do this role. This seemed so unfair to them.

I prayed to the Lord and, as I sometimes do despite knowing that it's not the right way to pray, I gave God two options. I could shut us down completely and let everyone go, or I could fight to keep our team doing what we were doing with the hope that we would be able to come back to MSPs in the near future. So which one was it going to be, God? You just tell me and I'll do it.

But God, as he often does, threw me a curveball. I'll summarize the message as though it were a conversation, but as you well know, prayer doesn't work quite like this.

> God: I want you to lead the effort for Families of Parishes.

> Me: With all due respect, I think you misunderstood my question, God. That wasn't one of the options.

God: I want you to lead the effort for Families of Parishes.

Me: I don't even know what that means.

God: Trust me.

Me: I don't want to lead that. It's going to be painful. And that's not what I wanted for my ministry. I left GM to be more missionary, not to run another big project.

God: Is it your ministry, or mine? I want you to lead the effort for Families of Parishes.

Me: Are you sure about this?

God: I have trained you for years for this. I gave you experiences in project management, strategic planning, and leading large organizations. Use it now for this purpose.

Me: This is going to require a lot of help from other people.

God: I gave you a team.

Me: Yes, but we didn't hire them for this. We didn't train them for this. They may not even want to do this.

God: I gave you a team. Use them.

Now, clearly I'm laying this out as though it were a tennis match between God and me, and that's taking advantage of the poetic license that I have available to me as I write about it two years later. But this is the essence of the first part of that prayerful exchange.

The First Step

At this point, my mind was racing. How could this make sense?

In my mind's eye, deep in prayer, I saw a raging river in front of me. The water was swirling and pushing forward almost as though it were angry. I knew in my heart that the river was deep, and even though I could just barely make out the bank on the other side, the river was wide enough that I knew that crossing it was going to be dangerous.

But I knew that the Lord was asking me to cross it.

I didn't understand how this would be possible. I had no bridge, no ropes, nothing to cling to, no path to make it across. I felt a sense of anxiety and fear. Was the Lord giving me a task that I simply couldn't do? Lord, I do believe, help my unbelief (Mk. 9:24)! But I knew that he wanted me to do it, and so I said yes, of course I'll do it.

And then one rock appeared in front of me, just past the sand and into the river. It was as if it was calling me to step onto it. And so I did. But that only got me a few feet from the shore. Where would I go from here? I told the Lord that I was grateful for the rock, but where was the next one?

You don't need the next one yet, he told me. You need to learn patience. You need to trust me. You need to let me drive. You'll get the next rock when I decide that the time is right.

And so I stood there on that rock, fighting my own natural instinct to try to take the reins and do it myself. Maybe I should just continue forward on my own? I knew that this was foolish; I would never make it across. Maybe I should jump back to the shore and give up?

I knew that I needed to trust the Lord. If he asked me to trust him and let him lead, then that's what I needed to do. Little did I know how often that lesson would come back to me in the years ahead.

Now, I don't claim that I had a vision. I'm not a prophet. I'm not even always very good at prayer. Of all of the nine men in my ordination class, I'm quite confident that I was the least likely to get a prophetic word from God. They were all much more spiritually mature than me, and I knew it.

So it may be that this wasn't a vision but was rather just my way of trying to make sense of what was happening. I suppose I'll never know for sure, at least not on this side of the veil.

But I do believe with all my heart that God doesn't call the qualified, he qualifies the called. If this was what he wanted from me, then I was going to do it, and I trusted that he would give me whatever I needed to get it done.

And so I immediately walked back from the chapel and called Fr. Day. I told him that I heard in prayer that God was asking me to lead this project. I told him that this was a very big change for our archdiocese, and if we didn't have someone driving the plan, there was a big risk of failure. I told him that if this was something that was agreeable, I would take my team and do another major pivot: we would lead the effort to move to Families of Parishes.

Quite frankly, I didn't even know what that meant. And I didn't know if my team had the desire to do it. Maybe they would just quit?

Fr. Day listened carefully and agreed to talk it over with the Archbishop.

The Green Light

Fr. Day called me the next day and told me that the Archbishop supported my plan: my team and I were to lead the effort to form Families of Parishes.

Another rock appeared in front of me in the raging river, and I stepped on it.

He also asked that I come to the next Cabinet meeting and tell them about what was happening.

Our Cabinet at the time was made up of a number of fine people for whom I have much respect. Besides Fr. Day and me, we had Fr. Steve Pullis, Edmundo Reyes, Jeff Wagoner, Kevin Kijewski, and Krista Bajoka. Fr. Pullis, who headed up our office for Evangelization and Missionary Discipleship, is a great priest with a gift for preaching and a wonderfully extroverted personality that makes him very popular in the AOD. Edmundo Reyes ran our Communications Department. Edmundo is a communications expert and a true disciple. Jeff Wagoner was our CFO. Jeff came to the AOD after many years with the Ford Motor Company. He brings with him quite a bit of valuable experience in the world of finance and accounting. Kevin Kijewski was our Superintendent of Catholic Schools. Kevin is a lawyer who had seen Catholic Schools experience in a few other dioceses prior to coming to the AOD. Krista Bajoka has a long history with the AOD, having worked for several years in the Curia. She was the right-hand support person for Fr. Day.

Speaking to this group about my plan was something that I knew had to be done, but it was also something that I dreaded. We were having lots of discussions about budget cuts to address the reduced revenue coming in from the parishes, and I'm sure that some (maybe even all) of the members of Cabinet assumed that one big cut was to eliminate my team. If I came forward and explained that we were not going to be eliminated but were instead going to refocus our efforts toward Families, they might view it as me trying to save my job and the jobs of my people.

I knew that this was not the case. I was trying to be faithful. But I could certainly understand why they might feel that way.

Besides, if the Archbishop wanted to do this right, he would probably need to hire a consulting firm to lead up our move to Families, and my team was no doubt a less expensive alternative than going down that path.

But despite the sound reasons that I had for moving forward as I did, I had a bad feeling in my gut when I had to speak to them about the plan.

When I did discuss it with them, it was met with apprehension, though everyone was polite. However, anyone who has worked in the Church knows that polite doesn't necessarily equate to approval.

There clearly wasn't resounding support, and even I must admit that I felt a certain sense of guilt about what I was proposing. We were most certainly looking at budget cuts, and if my team stayed, that would mean that others would have to cut more.

I started to doubt myself. Maybe I misunderstood what God wanted of me? Could this really make sense? I have no idea what I signed up for and its coming at a very bad time when we simply can't afford it. What if I mess this up and waste a lot of money along the way?

I wish I could say that it all turned out well. To be fair, much of it did turn out well, but I think that to this very day there is frustration amongst some members of the Cabinet about the fact that others had to take bigger cuts so that my team could stay. In fact, I don't just think this, I know that it's true. At least one person on the Cabinet has been quite clear with me that this is how he feels.

Looking back a few years later, I can see evidence that I was in the right. First, my team did in fact rise to the challenge and did a remarkable job that I don't think any consultant could have done for us for reasons that will be explained later in this book. Second, the Lord has affirmed to me time and again that this is what he wanted me to do. And third, the journey has been brutal at times. I most certainly didn't set myself up for a picnic. I set my team and me up for a very difficult ride.

But one way or another, I got the green light and it was now time to figure out how to manage this major project for which I was now the project manager. While I had a certain sense of relief that my team was able to move forward, I also had great concern that we needed to do this right, and we had no playbook to follow. It was time to get busy.

The Biggest Pivot Of All

So now that we had the green light, it was time for yet another pivot on my team. Only this one wasn't a small pivot; this was a complete change in direction. I trusted that the Lord had given me this wonderful team of talented Coaches and Missionaries for a reason, but now I had to ask them if they wanted to be a part of a rather dramatic shift in what we were asking of them. Would they want to make yet another major pivot away from what they hired on to do just a few months earlier?

I didn't take their willingness for granted. Indeed, I expected that some might have viewed this as the last straw. They had been hired to do MSPs, then came the global pandemic and a major switch to carrying out three activities which we had never suspected were coming our way, and now another dramatic pivot to driving Families of Parishes.

Since our training ended and we had switched to the three activities, we had established that we would meet virtually every morning for prayer and report outs. Each morning meeting started with Scripture and prayers of intercession which lasted about 15 minutes. A few years earlier, I would have probably laughed if someone told me that I would be starting a 60-minute meeting with 15 minutes of prayer, but the Coaches convinced me that if we were serious about seeking the guidance of the Holy Spirit, then we needed to listen to his direction each and every day in prayer. Now that we've been praying together for a few years, I can't imagine not doing it, and I can say without doubt that it's been something that's made us a much stronger team.

The day after we got the green light, I used our morning meeting to explain to them what was happening and how they could – if they wished to do so – be a part of this next change in direction. I tried to be as honest as possible in telling them that I had some idea of what we were going to do, but that there was no way I could give a lot of details because I simply didn't know them at this point.

I made it very clear that if they wanted to leave, if this was not something that they wanted to sign up for, I fully understood. There would be no hard feelings if they decided to walk away from this.

I told them that this wouldn't be easy. There was going to be resistance, pushback, and maybe even some hostility toward them personally for what we were going to do.

They asked some questions, but I didn't have a lot of answers. I could only speculate about what we might be doing.

They were asked to pray about this for a few days and then decide if they were on board or if they wanted out.

Much to my surprise - but also much to my liking - they were all on board and they all stayed. This was remarkable to me. This was proof to me that this was a team of people who was committed to the Lord, to his Church, to our Archbishop, to *Unleash the Gospel*, and to making our archdiocese more missionary.

I found another rock in the river and took another step forward.

In the trials and tribulations that were soon to come, I would see further proof of their commitment. This team is a rather remarkable group of people, and I am to this day quite thankful for them.

Prayer, Relationship, and Responsiveness

At this point in my still somewhat new career with the AOD, I confess that I was feeling a little bit distressed. Yes, we were moving forward on a new path, but what had I gotten myself into? I knew that we were at a significant point in our journey, and I knew that it was a good time to stop and reflect on what worked and what didn't work for our team up to this point before just moving into the next phase.

This became a significant focus for me in my chapel time. What do you want me to see from this, God?

In my reflections, I began to see that there were three key things that made anything we had done successful. By the same token, any time these three things didn't get done, we saw failure. These three things were prayer, relationship, and responsiveness.

Our team had grown together in ways that I would have never dreamed possible over the past few months because of our common time in prayer. We opened our hearts to the Lord and to each other every morning. We rotated the prayer lead to different members of the team, and each person brought their own personal spirituality into the mix.

Candidly, I would have never believed how much prayer can draw a team together if I had not experienced it myself. I'm forever grateful to this wonderful team for helping me see this, and I'm forever committed to the idea that prayer is a critical element of the success of any team.

Relationship was the second learning. When my team called our priests as part of the Pastor Connect program, we built some very solid relationships with some of the men. To be clear, this was not true across the board. Some of the men wanted nothing to do with my team. But when there was openness, a relationship developed which blossomed into trust and mutual respect. We never planned to lean on those relationships as we moved into Families. In fact, we didn't know about Families when we started Pastor Connect. But having those relationships made our move to Families much easier.

I knew a VP of Labor Relations at GM who used to say, "You can't build a relationship in a crisis." His point was that so often in the automotive world, Union and company leadership ignore one another for three years and then gather around the table to negotiate another contract. There's no relationship, there's no trust, there's no basis for compromise. If we could work on getting to know one another better in the off years, the negotiations would go much better.

The same is true for working with our priests. Let's be honest: most priests dislike the Curia. In the AOD, we often hear it said that they dislike "Downtown," because our Chancery is in downtown Detroit. When my team was able to develop a relationship, it was interesting to see that the priests with whom we worked well didn't consider us part of the Curia. They considered us to be separate from it. And to be truthful, we had no problem being so labeled because it was a sign of respect.

As for responsiveness, this one may very well be motivated more by my personal pet peeves than by our actual experience, but it is indeed critical and it's something that I made a priority for my team.

I've heard so many people talk about how they called someone in the Curia or emailed them and got an answer three weeks later, or perhaps never got an answer at all. I myself experienced this with people in the Curia both before I worked there and after I came on board.

I understand that people are busy; I am too. But it's downright disrespectful to not reply to someone in a timely manner. My rule of thumb is 24 hours or less. My people are well aware of my sense of urgency. I ask it of them and I demonstrate it myself with them and with others who contact me.

If you find that you're too busy to respond to people in a timely fashion, then perhaps it's time to re-think how you approach your day. When I was a young manager, I used to be frustrated that my people were constantly bothering me with questions. After a while, I realized that the only reason my job existed was to be there to answer those questions. If they all knew what to do, I wasn't needed. Thus, from a very early point in my career, I've always found ways to leave open chunks of time on my calendar to respond, to discuss, to show people that I care about them. In some jobs I had to book time in my calendar every day for this purpose, but it was always worth it.

Prayer, relationship, and responsiveness are three things that drive success in any project, and they did for us in Families of Parishes. Granted, each one of these has a reward of its own that goes beyond the project, so we don't necessarily use them to hit milestones and deliverables. But they most certainly help drive the successful achievement of milestones and deliverables, whether that was the focus or not.

Chapter 8 – A Nimble Response

What are Families of Parishes?

Over the past several years, we in the AOD – much like other dioceses around the world – have used different strategies in our parishes to deal with the various challenges that we've faced, whether those challenges be priest shortages, shifting populations, or other factors. Those strategies primarily have been closings, mergers, and clusters. It's important to understand the difference between these options and Families of Parishes before moving forward.

Closing a parish is never popular, even if there are very few parishioners remaining. People are understandably attached to the Church where Mom and Dad got married, or where their children were baptized, and so on. I remember that when GM built the Detroit/Hamtramck Assembly Plant in the early 1980's, there was a Church that was to be demolished to make room. People were literally chaining themselves to the doors when the bulldozers showed up. It was not a pretty site. Closures are an option of last resort.

In a merger, two or more parishes are combined into one new parish. Consider a hypothetical example of the merger of St. Mary and St. Joseph. The two parishes both lose their names and they become one new parish, call it St. John Paul II. The new parish now has two campuses, but there is now one staff, one parish council, one finance council, and so on. In theory this makes everything easier for the pastor to lead, but in reality he's left with a number of problems that end up consuming much of his time and energy. People continually lament the loss of St. Mary or St. Joseph, and they complain ad nauseam about trying to get used to the new name of St. John Paul II. As he tries to build a new culture of the combined parishes, he finds instead that there are camps of people from each of the old parishes who refuse to cooperate with one another.

Clustering two or more parishes offers a different model which keeps the parishioners content but burns the pastor out very quickly. Consider St. Mary and St. Joseph again. They're clustered and they remain as St. Mary and St. Joseph, and they both keep their staffs, parish councils, finance councils, and so on. The parishioners have kept their sense of identity, but now the poor pastor has doubled his meetings. The administrative burden of his office begins to overtake his ability to be with the people.

Here in the AOD, we've had our fair share of closings, mergers, and clusters, and we've experienced difficulties with all of them.

A Family of Parishes is a bit of a hybrid of the good that we find in clusters and mergers. A Family is a grouping of parishes, usually three to six, in which each parish retains its name and its identity, much like in a cluster. But there is potential to reduce the number of support organizations, thus reducing the overall administrative burden, much like in a merger. The priests who are a part of the Family are responsible for all of the parishes in the Family. There are different ways to organize the priests in the Family, and as you will see later, we in the AOD are using two models.

In the AOD's approach to Families, the Moderator or One Pastor takes on a large portion of the administrative burden for all of the parishes in the Family, thus freeing up the other priests to be more missionary with the time they now have available to them. This is key to our move to Families because if we do this well we will add clerical firepower to our efforts to be more missionary even though there are fewer priests.

One of the great benefits of Families is found when a priest retires or moves on to another assignment. In a conventional one pastor over one parish situation, the new pastor comes in and everything changes. Probably everyone reading this book has either been directly involved in a difficult pastor transition or knows someone who has. When the people don't like what they see in the new pastor, they Church shop to find a parish they like better, or they start attending services at a non-Catholic community, or in the worst case, they just give up on their faith altogether.

In a Family of Parishes, this is not the case. Take a hypothetical example where we have four priests *In Solidum* who collectively pastor four parishes. Each parish continues on with its own unique identity, but they begin to combine resources and ministries across the Family where it makes sense. Now one of the priests retires, and he's not replaced. The four parishes continue on with their unique identity just as before, only now the three remaining priests cover the four parishes. There may be a reduction in Masses offered due to the fewer number of priests. There may be a senior priest who is brought on for weekend help. But to the parishioners, not much has changed except for those who may have dearly loved the priest who retired. But the Family Pastoral Council continues as before, the Family Leadership Team continues as before, the directors continue as before, and so on.

Later in this book, there will be a more detailed explanation of how we have chosen to deploy Families here in the AOD. At this point it's important to simply understand at a high level what a Family is and why we are moving toward this structure.

There's one very important point of clarification that I need to make which I would ask that you keep in mind as you read this book. A Family of Parishes isn't a thing, it's a collection of parishes. A Family isn't a juridic person from a canon law perspective, and it isn't a legal entity from a civil law perspective. We often use phrases that speak to the Family doing something or the Family being responsible for something, but in reality it's the parishes within the

Family who do the something or who are responsible for the something, not the Family. This may sound like a trivial point, but quite a bit of time dealing with Families has taught me that it's not trivial at all, especially when it comes to canon and civil law issues.

The Givens

Here in the AOD, there were a handful of things that were givens in our move to Families. These givens became the parameters around which my team and I designed the process and timeline for completing our journey.

The first given was that the Archbishop wanted the move to be completed in about two years. There were a number of reasons why this was the case.

One reason was that he was at that time 71 years old, and he wanted to be sure that this effort was complete and somewhat settled prior to him submitting for retirement, which all bishops are required to do at age 75. This was a very prudent thing to do. If the archdiocese were to experience a leadership change part way through this process, there would be potential that the new bishop might decide to put a hold on the move to Families or even cancel it. We didn't want to expend all of this time and energy on a move only to have it stopped mid-stream. Of course, the next bishop will have the ability to take us out of Families if he so chooses, but it will be much less likely if the transition is complete.

Another reason was the need for expediency to reduce the pain of making the transition. This is something that most people in the secular world clearly understand, but that many of our priests struggle to grasp.

Anyone who has been involved in a significant restructuring knows that dragging it out can be frustrating and distracting. It's very much like the analogy of removing a band aid: it's painful to pull it off slowly, so the better approach is to rip it off completely in one quick yank. If a restructuring is slow, people will use that time to spread rumors, to stand around the water cooler with other employees and wring their hands worrying about their jobs, and to look for other jobs on the outside so that they can feel a sense of control over their future.

The second given was that there had to be significant involvement of the presbyterate in designing what our Families would look like. There was no way that we could select the parishes in the Families or create the Family structure in a dark room with a small team of Curia employees and hope that everyone would accept it.

The third given was that there needed to be great transparency in everything that was done. We were well aware that there would be doubts among the priests about what was happening, so we needed to communicate and over communicate what was decided at each step of the journey to be sure that everyone understood where we were headed and why.

The fourth given was that we needed to continually remind ourselves and others that the reason for this move to Families is that we need to structure ourselves to be on mission despite the obstacles that we face. As we often say, the move to Families isn't an end, it's a means to an end. In a very practical sense, this meant that we needed to root our work in the calling of the Holy Spirit and in prayer, and that we needed to sense check what we did by putting it up against *Unleash the Gospel*. This may sound odd, since *Unleash the Gospel* doesn't mention Families of Parishes at all. But if it was truly an inspired document that came from all of that prayer and preparation work, then it should provide insight to our next steps.

FOP Leadership Teams

One of the first tasks that we as Cabinet took on was to determine how to assign the teams of priests who would decide many of the details for how our Families would be structured. This may sound simple, but in fact it was something which required significant discussion and debate. After all, this was the vehicle by which much of the foundational work for our Families would be determined. If we made mistakes here, they would propagate through everything else we did afterward.

In order to decide how many teams to establish, we needed to first decide at a high level how we wanted Families to be structured. We settled on the fact that there were to be three basic groups within a Family, and that each group needed to be studied.

The first group was the governance and leadership of the Family, including most importantly the priest themselves. How would the Family be led by its priests, deacons, and supporting councils? There were options to be considered, and we needed a team of priests to decide which were the best options for the AOD.

The second group was the people who work directly with the faithful; those who have ministries which work closely with parishioners.

And the third group was the people who support those who do direct ministry.

With this understood, we agreed to form three FOP (Families of Parishes) Leadership Teams: Governance/Leadership, Mission Direct, and Mission Support. As to the number of people on each team, we felt that 8-10 was a manageable number of people who would be able to collectively drive to agreements.

That said, picking the people to be on these three teams was also a critically important thing. We needed to have team leaders who were wise and had some years of experience in problem solving, and we needed to have others on the team who could contribute to the discussions without dominating or being afraid to speak up. The teams were made up of primarily priests, but there were some lay people who were selected as well.

I don't recall exactly how many iterations we took at deciding on the leaders of these teams and the others who would fill them out, but it was certainly more than just one or two.

The three leaders selected were Fr. Tim Birney for Governance/Leadership, Msgr. Chuck Kosanke for Mission Direct, and Fr. Ed Zaorski for Mission Support. These three are all fine men, excellent priests, and great leaders to boot. I have much respect for all three of them.

Once the full contingent of people on the teams were selected, we felt it was important that each team have a clear description of what was being asked of them and when it was due. Hence, I created Charters for each team. This would prove to be a common approach to kicking off teams associated with our move to Families: everyone got a Charter.

With the players selected and Charters approved, we asked these teams to get started. For consistency, the leads of each FOP Leadership Team were invited to all meetings of the other two teams.

It's All About The Priests

Without question, the most significant decisions to be made regarding a restructuring to Families (or something like Families) revolve around the way that the priests will work together. We believed this to be the case from the start, and now that we have the wisdom of several Families launched, we know that it is indeed the case.

If you step back and consider a move like this from 10,000 feet, you can see why this is so important.

To the average parishioner, a move to Families might go completely unnoticed. They may occasionally see a different priest presiding at Mass, and they may hear about events going on that are bigger than just their own parish, but this may not even register to them as a change.

To the Staff, a move to Families is fairly significant because it will most likely change the way they go about their everyday work. Not so much for the person who greets people at the front desk, but for pretty much everyone else, a change will be required. Business Managers will be asked to work together and think about the finances of the entire Family rather than just one parish. Religious Education Directors will need to come together to talk about how to best handle their function across the entire Family and not just their parish. Parish Pastoral Councils – at least in our case – are no longer needed once the Family Pastoral Council is up and running. And so on.

But in the end, these Staff members still have pretty much the same life that they always did outside of their nine to five (or nine to nine) working hours at the parish. And they do have the option of looking for another job if they don't like the Family structure.

Deacons like myself are significantly impacted, as we now serve all of the parishes of the Family rather than just our home parish. This can be a rather profound change to our ministry, but again, we still go home to the same wife and children, and we have many things that we do outside of the Church which remain constant.

But the priests? This is a big change for them. They're accustomed to being king of their own castle, so to speak, and the Church functions in such a way that they can for the most part run their castle as they wish. Of course, there are boundaries to what they can and cannot do. But they enjoy a surprising degree of freedom which you won't find in many other occupations. I can say without hesitation that a priest has far more freedom in his parish than any assembly plant manager has in his or her plant.

In my early days as a deacon, I was shocked to find out that even the Bishop has very limited ability to address a problem that he sees in a priest under his episcopate. He can suggest, he can consult, he can counsel. But he really can't force. In an extreme case he can employ canon law to remove a priest from his pastorate, but this is rare and not something that anyone really wants to do.

Families force the priests to work together in ways that they may not enjoy. Especially in the *In Solidum* Model (which will be discussed in more detail), they are asked to make decisions in a collegial manner rather than just having the ability to decide on their own. This is a significant change and one that does not come easy to men who have for the most part lived on their own and done things as they wished for many years. This was, to be candid, not the way that many of them wanted to finish their priesthood.

And so it was that we kicked off the Governance/Leadership Team first in our timeline. What they decided would be the foundation for everything else that would follow.

For those who are not involved with the Church, you may wonder how it can be that anyone can attend a Catholic Mass anywhere in the world and it will be the same despite the freedoms that our priests enjoy. How do we keep such a rigid structure amidst such loose rules for discipline and control?

There are three basic things at play here. One is, of course, the Holy Spirit. He has been our Paraclete since Christ ascended into heaven to be at the right hand of his Father, and he will continue to be with us until Christ comes again in glory to judge the living and the dead. He keeps us on the straight and narrow, even if some of us sometimes stray from the fold.

The second is canon law, the code of laws for the Catholic Church. Canon law drives the universal Church, and particular law can be written for a specific diocese if needed to drive the local Church.

The third is obedience, which is something that simply doesn't exist in secular organizations. When a member of the clergy is ordained (both priests and deacons), we vow to obey the bishop and his successors. This is something that would be impossible to take lightly. My vow of obedience is an absolute for me, and I'm quite certain that it is for most in the clergy. Thus, even though a bishop can't force a priest to do something, the vow of obedience that the priest took holds significant sway over how he will ultimately respond.

Chapter 9 – The Plan Begins To Take Shape

Governance/Leadership FOP Leadership Team

In June of 2020, the Governance/Leadership FOP Leadership Team began to meet. The plan was that they would get some of their work behind them before the other two FOP Leadership Teams would begin, as the others needed to know at least directionally where Governance was headed in order to do their work.

The Charter for this team was as follows:

Governance/Leadership Team

Team Charter

This team is charged with developing one model (or multiple models if required) of governance for Families of Parishes for the following functions:
- Priests
- Parish Pastoral Councils
- Parish Finance Councils
- Parish Leadership Teams
- Parish Finance Officer

For each area, this includes developing new titles (if a change in title is needed) and primary roles and responsibilities.

This team is also charged with providing suggestions for necessary revisions to the priest assignment process in support of revised roles and responsibilities for priests in Families of Parishes.

Considerations

- While one model of governance is preferred because it would be the easiest to implement, it is possible that more than one option may be needed to support the variety of needs of the Archdiocese.
- Canon law must be comprehended in any proposed solution.
- This team need not consider deacons at this time.

Timing: This team will meet from 6/1/20 through 9/1/20

This team was the most important and the most complex of the three FOP Leadership Teams. We had benchmarked some other dioceses to learn what they had done - most especially the Diocese of London, Ontario, our neighbors to the south who had already gone to Families. And for any who may be wondering, that's not a typo. The first country directly south of Detroit is Canada. The folks at London were most gracious with their time in support of our efforts, and for this we are quite grateful. In fact, I learned a lesson from their generosity and I've tried to be equally gracious to other dioceses who have contacted me about our efforts.

London had gone to something called the One Pastor Model of governance in all of their Families. In a One Pastor Model, there's one priest who is in charge (the Pastor), and he has one or more Parochial Vicars who report to him and help him pastor all of the parishes in the Family. This is a very clear and simple model of governance, but it drives a rather significant downside for us here in the AOD.

In order to get to a One Pastor Model, it's necessary for the priests who are not the Pastor to agree to being Parochial Vicars, or Associate Pastors, who report to the Pastor. In our case, that would have meant asking many of our current Pastors to resign their role as Pastor and accept a role as a Parochial Vicar. This was in fact what London had done, and they were able to make it work.

Here in Detroit, this simply would not have worked. There was no way that many of our priests would willingly resign their pastorates. I can't blame them for this, as I would struggle to do so myself if I were in their shoes.

It's my believe that at least some of the reason this wouldn't work in Detroit is that we live in the heart of the automotive industry, a business which is influenced by the successes and failures of the United Auto Workers (UAW). In this town, the idea of giving up something that was gained through bargaining, toil, or seniority isn't popular.

I'm quite familiar with the culture of the UAW, as I was in leadership positions at four different assembly plants, all of which had hourly workforces that were UAW-represented.

To be fair to the UAW, I'm quite certain that I benefited from their efforts as far as my pay, my vacation days, my benefits, and so on. Even though I was salaried and not in the union, there's a carry-over effect that made our jobs as salaried employees better. But in the end, working with the UAW was quite difficult, and it often led to decisions and activities that defied common sense.

Our priests, of course, are not unionized. But the union mentality is something that has oozed its way into our culture here in southeast Michigan, and I have no doubt that it has in some way impacted our presbyterate as well.

The One Pastor Model was one option that the Governance/Leadership Team made available to our Families, but only three of our first 26 Wave 1 Families used it.

The other option that this team chose was called the *In Solidum* Model. This is, without question, a complicated model of governance that's difficult to understand and operate in our American way of thinking.

By way of a simple explanation, *In Solidum* essentially means that a group of priests together work to pastor a group of parishes. All of the priests are equals in this effort, meaning that there's no one priest who is the leader. Right off the bat, this will probably make anyone who has been in a leadership position a little bit nervous, and justifiably so. If no one is in charge, it's tough to make any significant progress. As they say, a camel is a horse by committee, so isn't that what we're going to get?

The *In Solidum* Model is specifically allowed in Canon Law. In fact, a document released in June of 2020 by the Vatican Congregation for Clergy called it out as an option to be considered. That document is called *The pastoral conversion of the Parish community in the service of the evangelising mission of the Church.* It's a very thoughtful document that's worth the read. In our case here in the AOD, it was a tremendous boost to our efforts because it focused on two areas that were near and dear to our journey: the need to evangelize, and the potential for groupings (Families) of parishes.

I don't think that the timing of the publication of this document at the very start of our efforts to restructure - and far along into our efforts to be more missionary - was a coincidence. I think that it was yet another indication from the Holy Spirit that what we were attempting to do was good.

There's a position called for in the *In Solidum* Model which is a leadership position of sorts. That position is called the Moderator. In an *In Solidum* Model, one of the Priests *In Solidum* is selected by the Archbishop to be in this Moderator role. The Moderator is considered to be the "first among equals," which means that he represents the parishes of the Family in juridic matters and he is the tiebreaker if there's something about which the Priests *In Solidum* cannot agree.

It doesn't take a lot of effort to see that the Moderator position comes with quite a bit of grey, both in terms of the vagueness of the role and in terms of its impact on the color of the hair of the one who is given the title. The desired state is that the Priests *In Solidum* all get along and that they make decisions fraternally, so when is it time to be the tiebreaker? And how does one step in and do so without abusing the intent of fraternal decision making?

The beauty of the *In Solidum* model is that none of the priests are asked to give up their pastorates because they collectively pastor all of the parishes in the Family. The difficulty is that such a relationship does not lend itself to clear roles and responsibilities, and so making decisions can be very difficult.

One of the ways that our Archbishop eventually helped us navigate this complexity is by the use of something he called the Covenant, which will be detailed later.

As far a supporting organizations go, this team decided that there was a need for a Family Pastoral Council (FPC), a Family Leadership Team (FLT), and a Family Finance Team (FFT) which would support the Moderator in his role. But at the same time, they were fully aware that this couldn't just be another set of meetings with another set of groups which would be piled on to the existing meeting structure. And so their recommendation was that once the FPC was up and running, all Parish Pastoral Councils be thanked for their efforts and concluded. The same was true for Parish Leadership Teams once the FLT was up and running.

However, by canon law every parish must have a Parish Finance Council. These teams needed to remain in place. This does not mean, however, that there needs to be separate meetings for all Parish Finance Councils and the FFT. It's possible that all could meet on one night, though if they do it would be important that matters unique to one parish be dealt with only by the Parish Finance Council members from that particular parish.

Mission Direct and Mission Support FOP Leadership Teams

Once the Governance Team was starting to firm up their recommendations, it was time for the Mission Direct and Mission Support Leadership Teams to begin their deliberations about how to structure the rest of the Family.

The Charters for these teams made it clear that whatever they came up with needed to support our efforts to be more missionary. Those Charters are as follows:

Mission Direct Team

Team Charter

This team is charged with developing one model (or multiple models if required) of governance for Families of Parishes for the functions that directly minister to the faithful, including but not limited to:

- Directors of Religious Education
- Youth Ministers
- Music Ministers

This team is also charged to reflect upon *Unleash the Gospel* and our call to be more intentionally missionary, with consideration for self-funding new mission-focused positions through the economies of scale gained by families of parishes coming together. These new positions may include but are not limited to:

- Director of Evangelization
- Director of Community Engagement

For each area, this includes developing titles and primary roles and responsibilities.

Considerations

- While the primary function of this team is to address organizational issues, it will also be important to consider common tools to be used in support of efficiency and common business practices

Timing: This team will meet from 8/1/20 through 11/29/20

Mission Support Team

Team Charter

This team is charged with developing one model (or multiple models if required) of governance for Families of Parishes for the functions that support parish ministry to the faithful, including but not limited to:

- Human Resources
- Information Technology
- Parish Finance Officer (high level description to come from Governance Team)
- Maintenance

For each area, this includes developing titles and primary roles and responsibilities.

Considerations

- While the primary function of this team is to address organizational issues, it will also be important to recommend common tools to be used in support of efficiency and common business practices

Timing: This team will meet from 8/1/20 through 11/29/20

These two teams ultimately settled on the idea that there were to be six areas or functions to be covered if a Family was to be on mission. Those areas were as follows:

- **Mission Support** – covering finance/accounting, HR, IT, and facility maintenance.
- **Discipleship Formation** – covering formation and catechetics.
- **Engagement** – covering outreach and the path of discipleship for parishioners.
- **Evangelical Charity** – covering the implementation of Catholic Social Teaching within the Family.
- **Family Ministries** – covering all aspects of ministering to the nuclear family.
- **Worship** – covering worship services, prayer, and other liturgical experiences.

Engagement was an area that was for the most part new to us in the AOD. We knew that our brothers and sisters in the Protestant Churches did a pretty good job here, and we realized that it made sense for us to try to do some of this ourselves if we were to be more missionary.

In the ideal, a Family would have six Directors named to handle these six areas, and those Directors, along with the Priests, would constitute the leadership of the Family. Our reality has been that in some cases, most especially the inner city and rural Families, it wasn't possible to have six Directors, and so they ended up having less than six people cover the six functions. In addition, in situations where money was particularly tight, some areas were covered by volunteers rather than using paid positions.

One of the great things that these teams did was to define not just the director roles, but also the vision for which ministries would fall under each of the directors. This would be very important as we moved into forming the directors in their roles. If they were inconsistent in their responsibilities from one Family to the next, training them would be difficult.

The Playbook

As these three FOP Leadership Teams were completing their work and reporting out on what they had decided, it was clear to me that we needed to document what they concluded in something that we could reference as we moved forward. I initially believed that this would be a relatively simple task. This proved to be a somewhat naïve belief.

I knew that we needed to call this document something catchy, something that would carry meaning just by its title. To me, the answer was clear: The FOP Playbook. I've played on and coached many sports teams over the years, and it was always the Playbook that showed the team what was supposed to happen and guided their efforts.

The other thing that I liked about the title "Playbook" is that what actually happens on the playing field is never quite what the Playbook calls for. As a fullback, I was well aware of how the X's and O's were supposed to move on any given play, but I was also well aware that when the ball was snapped, there was no telling what actually might happen. The play didn't change, and the goal line was the same, but the realities of football were such that the actual execution would have to vary somewhat if we were going to score. This was true for our move to Families as well. What worked for a Family in the city of Detroit was not the same as what worked for a Family in the rural areas to the North, but we still needed something to give us parameters, direction, and a common vision.

And so I began documenting the results of the three FOP Leadership Teams in the FOP Playbook.

I think it's fair to say that the Playbook has taken on a significance that I didn't anticipate. I was looking for a reference manual and not an encyclopedia, but as we moved forward with our efforts it tended more toward the latter than the former.

The Playbook today has major sections for Governance, Mission Direct, Mission Support, Schools, and Missionary Strategic Plans, as well as Appendices for particular law in support of Families, detailed norms for consultative bodies, and select quotes from the 2020 Instruction from the Congregation for Clergy.

Picking the Families

One of the more important things that needed to be determined was which parishes would be in which Families. We had 217 parishes, and we developed some very simple guidelines for how Families should come together:

- There should be 3-6 parishes in a Family. Less than three will not sufficiently enable the benefits of Families, and more than six could become cumbersome. Exceptions to this are possible when it makes sense to do so.
- All of the parishes in the Family must share a border with at least one other parish in the Family. Having parishes spread too far apart will diminish some of the benefits of sharing resources within the Family.

The agreement was that the defining of parishes in Families would be done by the priests themselves. In each of our four regions, the regional bishop and vicars forane from the region would lead the charge, facilitating the priests of the region through the process of selecting the Families. The Coach from my team who was assigned to the region would work with the group to help co-facilitate the discussions and drive toward a conclusion that fit the timeline.

The Curia had come up with a suggested set of groupings which we assumed could be used as a starting point for the priests' discussions. We thought that if they were provided with this list, it would prime the pump and they would vary as they saw fit. That proved to be a mistake. Many of the priests felt that we were dictating the answer to them - that the Curia was making decisions that should be left to the priests. We very quickly abandoned this idea and pulled back all of the copies of the proposed groupings.

Discussions around establishing the Families weren't easy, and they weren't quick. Some of the men had very strong feelings about who they wished to be partnered up with in a Family. This proved to be problematic. We were trying to set up Families based on criteria that was best for the Family and not based upon who got along with whom. After all, the priests would eventually change assignments but the Family would go on. It's understandable that relationships came into play; this is human nature. But it required quite a few meetings after the meeting to work through these issues.

When the dust settled, we ended up with 52 Families. If you consider that we started with 217 parishes, it comes to roughly 4.2 parishes per Family on average. I viewed this as a success, and I think most in the Curia did as well.

These 52 proposed Families were eventually given to the Archbishop for his approval, and he approved them all.

It's worth note that today we have 54 Families rather than 52. The reason for the additional two is that two of the proposed Families were broken into four Families, primarily due to them being too large.

Chapter 10 – Project Management

A Clear Focus

We on the Cabinet decided that this Families initiative was so significant that we needed to have discussions on FOPs at least once per week. We agreed to meet every Wednesday morning – virtually, of course, as we were all working from home.

Looking back on this time, it's interesting to note that the Cabinet was working pretty well together. I think that this is primarily because we really had only two major priorities: survive the pandemic and implement Families. There was no discussion or debate about the need for either one of these, and there weren't very many distractions like those we experience in more normal times. In addition, there was a need to meet much more frequently than usual, and this caused us to develop stronger relationships with one another.

This clear focus was not unique to the AOD Curia, of course. It was true of most every organization at that time. Whatever you had been working on needed to be reconsidered in light of the realities of the pandemic.

Organizations tend to rally around a common cause, and even more so around a common enemy. I recall very clearly how my leadership at GM reacted when the horrific events of 9/11 were taking place. After the second plane hit, the assembly plants around the country started calling in and asking for direction. Should they shut down and send everyone home?

Guy Briggs, our Manufacturing VP at the time, was a man who I truly admired for his leadership. He was always able to step back and see things in the bigger picture, and in so doing he was able to provide direction that was more profound than what might have arisen from just the heat of the moment. He set up a video call for all of the assembly plant managers and a few of us back at headquarters to talk things over. By the time the call took place, it was clear that what was happening was a terrorist attack.

After listening to the discussion, he made a statement that really stuck with me. He said, "We need to keep running. If we shut down, that's exactly what those bastards want." And so we kept running.

In the weeks that followed, our company had a very clear focus: helping our country get on its feet. Even though much of the country was virtually shut down for fear of what might be next, we kept producing vehicles. We even started a campaign called "Get America Running Again." We offered huge discounts to get people to buy our vehicles and keep the country moving forward.

GM didn't save the country, of course. But we did what we could and we had a very clear vision of where we were headed. We all understood it and we all lined up behind it.

In a similar way, the Curia was now very focused and driven to get through the pandemic and to get Families up and running.

The downside to this, of course, is that neither staying afloat financially nor restructuring was a particularly fun or fulfilling initiative. Surviving the pandemic meant agreeing to budget cuts which none of us wanted to do, and implementing Families meant helping our priests align in ways which very few of them wanted to do.

The result was that even though our time together was focused, it wasn't necessarily enjoyable. But in fairness, I don't think that there were very many businesses or churches anywhere in the world who were kicking back and enjoying life in mid-2020.

Why do I bring this up? Because the focus that we had was something special that drove us to work together in a way that was needed but that's often missing in curias and parishes around the country. Far too often we don't say no to anything, and this can result in stretching the organization so thin that few things get done well.

Where there is focus, there are good results. Where there is confusion, there are poor results.

It's my belief that the confusion that we sometimes see in curias and parishes is not only due to over commitment, but it's a form of spiritual warfare as well. The devil knows that if he can get us moving in too many directions at once, we'll fail at most of them. Hence he plays on our desire to be kind and tricks us into taking on more than we can handle.

Perhaps I'm overthinking this, but whether I am or not, I would strongly advise that before any diocese sets down the path of a major restructuring like Families of Parishes, they must first seriously consider what kind of resources and effort it will take to do it well, and in turn what other activities they will pause or drop to allow time to do things right.

The Project Timeline

To help drive our efforts, it was clear that we needed a simple project timeline. A well-done timeline is a thing of beauty because it gives a visual of where we are and of what comes next, which in turn keeps everyone focused. I had detailed timelines and high-level summaries that I lived by, and I used those timelines at Cabinet meetings, meetings of my team, and every All Priest Meeting we held to be sure that we all knew where we were in the process.

The high-level timeline from those very early days is shown here.

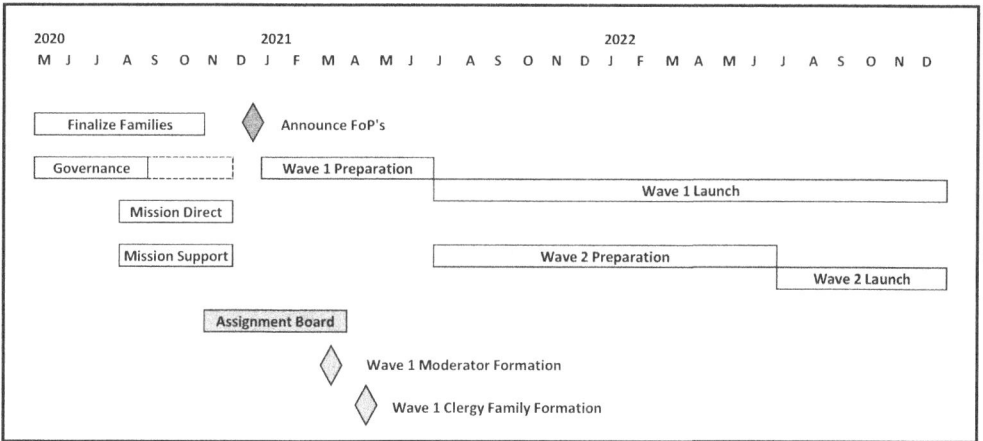

As I look over this timeline from some of our earliest planning, it's remarkable how closely we held to it. We pretty much hit all of the major milestones despite all of the problems, headaches, and pushback.

But hitting a timeline doesn't necessarily mean success. Success will ultimately be determined by how effective we are at being more missionary, and this is something that will take quite a while to understand.

When the timeline was rolled out to the priests, we got the reaction that we fully expected: this is far too aggressive. The Church doesn't work this way. We take decades and centuries to make significant change. There were several comments made about the belief that I was mistakenly driving this thing as if it were a GM project, and that I didn't understand the Church culture.

In fairness, I didn't (and still don't) fully understand the Church culture. I had been a deacon for seven or so years, but that's relatively short in Church years and it didn't provide me with anything close to the experiences that many of the priests had.

But at the same time, I had been through many reorganizations at GM, and in comparison this FOP timeline was ridiculously slow. Two years to restructure? At GM we would announce a change on Friday and we would be in the new organization on Monday morning.

This was one of many situations that I've had to navigate in my role where a fine balancing act was needed. It was important to respect where the priests were coming from because their experiences are real and must be honored, but it was also important to drive them to deadlines and milestones because without them they would simply not change.

I truly do admire our priests. They are men who have given their lives to the Lord. They've given up the chance to have many of the things that I have: a wife, children, the ability to secure my future financially, and so on. They have my respect and my admiration.

And so driving them to do something that they collectively didn't want to do was very hard. It took a toll on me when priests would come after me with negativity, whether it was to my face, by email, or in anonymous comments in surveys following some of our meetings. Not only was I the poster child for something that many of them didn't want, but I was also a rung beneath them on the hierarchical ladder, if you will, since I was just a deacon. And I can say that this point was made clear to me on multiple occasions.

I've often feared that someday I may be assigned to a parish where the pastor hated what I did in this role. It would certainly make my diaconal ministry more difficult. To be honest, I still have that fear to this very day.

Transparency

There's an interesting dilemma when it comes to being transparent. If you don't share progress along the way, people will feel that you're holding back information. But if you do share progress along the way, people will be frustrated with seeing partial plans that by their nature require a little bit of trust in knowing that more is to follow.

This was our struggle, but we landed clearly on the side of sharing whatever we knew along the way despite what criticisms may come with doing so. With this in mind, we set up monthly All Priest Meetings to share our progress and welcome feedback.

But agreeing to be transparent isn't the same as making it happen. The way things are said, the order in which they're rolled out, and the professionalism by which this is done all matter. In this regard, we've been blessed with a rock star of a Communications Director in Edmundo Reyes. He led us in all Communications matters and did a superb job. Edmundo is outstanding at what he does and he is a truly committed disciple of the Lord.

But even with Edmundo's skill, transparency proved to be difficult due to the pandemic. Throughout our journey, we faced two significant obstacles.

First, we couldn't meet in person, so everything had to be done by Zoom. Zoom is a wonderful tool for many things, but sharing complex and controversial topics over Zoom feels a bit cold and uncaring.

I remember when one of the executives I worked with at GM was fired over the phone. It was awful, and it showed no respect for the years of dedicated service that she had given to the company. All of us were shocked that something so significant could be done in so callous a way. I couldn't help but feel that – although the circumstances were certainly very different – perhaps we were doing something along the same lines.

Second, it was simply not possible to leave all of the mics open for discussion at these meetings. Having roughly 200 people on a Zoom meeting who all have the ability to ask questions freely would be disastrous. We would never get through our material. In addition, many of the priests didn't have a firm grasp of technology, and they had no idea how to use the mute button.

In order to take questions, we asked the priests to type them into the chat box. Then Edmundo played the role of facilitator and read the questions for one of us to answer. This was by no means ideal. We rarely got through all of the questions, so many needed to be answered after the meeting. Besides that, a few of the priests felt that perhaps we were simply not answering the tough questions because we had the ability to pick and choose which to answer. This was never the case, but in any sort of a restructuring, trust is critical and so the fact that some had doubts cast a shadow over our efforts to be transparent.

Every meeting would start with the Archbishop offering prayers and his reflections on our journey. His prayers were based off of a Scripture passage that he read, and his prayers were always deep and rather lengthy. This was wonderful, and it allowed the men to really appreciate his spirituality, his concern for them, and his continued reminders that what we were doing was in response to what the Holy Spirit called us to do.

At most every meeting, we invited someone or perhaps more than one person to report out on how their activity was progressing. That could be the leader of the Governance/Leadership FOP Team, or the leader of the Mission Direct or Mission Support Team. It could be one of the Bishops talking about his region's efforts to align the Families.

Toward the end of every meeting, I would show the timeline and talk about where we were and what came next.

We had done some homework with another diocese that had gone to something like Families, and they offered us some valuable insight into something they did which we adopted for use at all of our meetings. At the end of every meeting, just before the Archbishop's final comments and blessing, we would put up three polling questions which the men would vote on through the Zoom app. The reason this was so important was that it gave us a sense for the pulse of the total group's feelings rather than just a select few who managed to get their questions answered during the meeting.

These polls were, in my opinion, incredibly helpful to us in understanding what the majority of the priests thought, which in turn would help us to figure out what to do next. For example, through polling we found that most of the men agreed that we needed to do something to address the priest shortage. They may or may not like Families as the solution, but they agreed that something needed to be done. This not only gave us insight as to where to go from there, but it also helped to silence the rather vocal minority who were convinced that we didn't need to do anything and that this plan was a waste of time.

The polling was live and the results were immediately shared at the meeting so that everyone could see them. I became a bit like a game show host as I filled time talking while the poll was taken, and then commenting on the results as they were shared.

The polling questions that we asked were of a very specific nature. We didn't try to steer them into giving answers that were obvious, but we also never asked questions that would invite a mutiny. This wasn't easy to do. It was my job to write the questions, and it was always difficult to walk that line.

By way of example, this was a question from our September 2020 All Priest Meeting:

> The following best describes my emotions about moving into Families of Parishes over the next two years:
>
> - I am fearful/concerned
> - I am neutral at this point
> - I am looking forward to it

The results were that 44% of the men were fearful/concerned, 37% were neutral, and 19% were looking forward to it.

It was important to know that almost half of the men were fearful or concerned. We knew that the number was high, but this helped us understand just how high. At the same time, it surprised us that one in five were looking forward to the move.

But we didn't offer a response like, "I hate it," or "I refuse to do this." It was true that some of the men felt this way, but trying to address a response like that would not be beneficial to anyone.

Within a day of the meeting itself, we sent out surveys asking the priests to rate every presentation and to offer comments. I was the one who gathered the results to the surveys, and I confess that I was at times pleased and at times shocked by the anonymous verbatims.

What was pleasing was that many who responded had a sincere desire to do what the Archbishop was asking of them, even if they didn't fully understand it.

What was shocking was just how rude some of the comments were. To be clear, the rude comments were not common, but at times things were said that I felt were quite unbecoming of a priest.

These All-Priest Meetings were well attended. I think that the Zoom format probably increased participation because some of the men live quite far from the Chancery and would skip in person meetings just because of the drive. But I also think that the topic of Families was rather significant to them and they were more inclined to attend for that reason alone.

If I were to give advice to any diocese looking to move to Families or something like it, I would offer that you should meet and communicate information with your priests as frequently as possible. There were some who told us that we bombarded them with too much information, but there were many more who said that they appreciated us doing so even if they struggled to keep up with it.

Chapter 11 – In The Trenches

The Unsung Heroes

Up to this point, I've described a lot of work that was going on with the Cabinet, the FOP Leadership Teams, and the priests. But what, you may be wondering, was my team of 20 people doing?

To start this discussion, I must confess that I wish I would have done things a little bit differently with respect to my team's work in those early days. I chose to let us silently work behind the scenes, and I didn't give us a lot of spotlight. While this is a humble and typically Catholic approach, it came with a downside: most people didn't know or appreciate all of the incredible work that we were doing in the trenches.

I can say without hesitation that the work my team quietly did was absolutely critical to any success we've had with Families of Parishes. But I'm not sure that very many people in the Curia would echo that thought, primarily because I didn't talk about it much. As time progressed and budget cuts became a reality, this would come back to haunt me because people simply didn't appreciate what we were doing.

I think it's important to make this clear up front for two reasons. First, I want to acknowledge how critical a role they played in helping the AOD move to Families. I owe this to them because I didn't do a good enough job of crediting them up to this point. And second, I want to make it clear to other dioceses that it's my opinion that simply setting up a few teams of priests and Curia personnel to drive a restructuring as significant as a move to Families will not work. Someone needs to be thinking about and actively addressing a number of things in the background like those that we addressed or the restructuring will fail. In some dioceses they've hired consultants for this work, and that's always a possibility. But I say – admittedly with bias – that having our own internal team of people who really got to know and care for our priests was a tremendous advantage. I think that we were, quite frankly, a bargain compared to what the AOD would have paid for outside consultants who would have struggled to get the same results as we did.

So allow me to brag a bit about the silent heroes of this FOP effort, my Coaches and Missionaries.

With the support of the Archbishop to keep the team together, we had a very clear sense that we had to deliver results that both justified our existence and moved the needle forward not just on Families but more importantly on the changes needed to be a missionary diocese.

We began with a series of discussions about what were the major streams of work that needed to be done to support the effort. These discussions were informed by whatever information we had from other dioceses who had move to Families or groupings. After much debate, we agreed on nine areas. Each of these areas was turned into what we called an FOP Work Team which was charged to carry out the Charter that would guide their efforts. These Work Teams were as follows:

1. Benchmarking
2. Priest Support
3. Clergy Survey
4. Parish Survey
5. Deacon Mission and Formation
6. Laity Education and Formation
7. Prayer Support
8. Clergy Formation
9. MSP Revision

I'll give a little bit of detail on each of these in the chapters which follow, but before I do that I'll describe how we staffed these teams and how I had yet another moment where it became clear to me that the Holy Spirit was guiding our efforts from the very start.

Once these teams were defined, I spent some time with the group walking through the Charters for each of them. I then asked that they all take a few days to pray over which teams they felt called to be a part of, after which I would assign them as best I could to balance the workload.

When they turned their work team preferences over to me, it was yet again remarkable how well it turned out. The teams almost built themselves.

Their preferences were very well distributed across the various work teams, which was good. But what was even more amazing was how well the skills which they had learned on the outside played into their role.

Our Benchmarking Team ended up with a Missionary who ran his own strategic consulting firm, another who worked for many years in strategic planning for a large power company, and a lawyer.

Our Clergy Support Team had a Missionary who was finishing up doctoral studies in Organizational Leadership.

Our Diaconate Education and Formation Team included two Deacons who loved their ministry as deacons and who were full of ideas about how to apply *Unleash the Gospel* within the ranks of the diaconate.

Our Clergy Survey and Parish Survey Teams ended up with a Missionary who had done parish and priest survey work for the Archdiocese of Omaha, a Missionary with a doctorate in Evaluation of Research and Statistics, and another Missionary who had spent many years collecting and analyzing data for the State of Michigan.

Our Laity Education and Formation Team had a Missionary who spent an entire career in marketing.

Our Prayer Support Team consisted of Missionaries, Coaches, and others in the Curia who were prayer warriors.

I could go on, but I think this gets the point across. These people were not placed on my team by happenstance. The Holy Spirit knew way back when we were interviewing what the plan was, and that plan was far beyond anything that I could have ever reasoned or even imagined at the time.

As I looked over the teams and reflected upon how we got to this point, another rock popped up in the river.

Benchmarking Work Team

One of the first teams that we got rolling was the Benchmarking team. That team had a brief and focused mission to collect data that the three Leadership Teams could use for their work.

Their Charter was as follows:

AOD Families of Parishes
Benchmarking Work Team

<u>Charter</u>
This team is charged with gathering benchmark data which has already been captured and seeking out new data as appropriate to provide clear and concise information

regarding what to do and what not to do from other dioceses. The target audiences for this information are the three leadership teams and the Cabinet.

Considerations

- Much data has already been collected but it needs to be filtered and organized.
- While the Parish Care and Sustainability Department has the lead for this activity, there are a few Missionaries with significant industry experience in benchmarking who could contribute to this effort.

Timing

This work would need to be timed to meet the needs of the three leadership teams, and may continue into the Preparation Phase if required.

We broke up our work into three areas which you might expect – Governance, Mission Direct, and Mission Support. Our job was to contact other dioceses who had gone to Families or something like Families to learn from them what they did that worked and didn't work. We had some data that had already been collected by the Curia Parish Care and Sustainability Department, but we wanted to round it out.

The fine Missionaries who did this work were outstanding. They had business and strategic skills that would match up with any strategic planning department in any organization.

The work that this team did was shared with the FOP Leadership Team, and it was much appreciated.

There was a sidebar activity that came from this team's work which we had not anticipated. As we got together to talk about what each member had learned, it became clear to me that there were other things we were learning which didn't fit into the three categories but which still needed to be comprehended in our move to Families.

I captured these other things and put them into a presentation which I gave to our Episcopal Council in September of 2020. I called that presentation, "Strategic Lessons Learned from Benchmarking." I brought to their attention five points which we had gleaned from these benchmarking conversations. Those points were as follows:

1. **Each Family must have a clearly defined leader with clearly defined roles and responsibilities.**
   - This is not unique to the Church; it's true in business, military, and even volunteer organizations.
   - While the idea of communal leadership sounds intriguing and even Biblical in some regard, it is ineffective, and it has been shown to fail.

2. **Clergy must be trained in what is expected of them in Families.**
   - We are undertaking a significant and dramatic change in the way we preach and teach the Good News of Jesus Christ.
   - We cannot effectively make this change if the Clergy does not clearly understand the new ground rules.
   - Training for Clergy should be mandatory, and it must be good.

3. **Organizational Structure within a Family must be defined to a great extent.**
   - There is a tendency to take a hands-off approach; to let each Family decide what is best for them.
   - This is a mistake for two primary reasons:

- o Many clergy prefer to be told what is expected; they don't know what to do.
- o If we don't specify, we will have inconsistencies.
  - We will not be able to deploy common training and take advantage of best practices.
  - Clergy who move from one Family to another will lose valuable time trying to figure out how the new organization operates vs. the one they just left.

4. **Common Tools within a Family must be defined to a great extent.**
   - Common tools lead to reduced costs, sharing of best practices, simplified data collection when needed, and other benefits.
   - We have a tremendous opportunity to do this right with the move to Families
   - However, this requires that the common tools be developed, tested, and ready to be deployed from the first Family launch.

5. **Curia Support for Families must be clear and concise, and it needs to be spelled out prior to the launch of the First Families.**
   - Without clearly defined support from the Curia, Families will develop their own plans, and they will reject help from the Curia in the future.
   - Curia needs to take the lead and have clear direction from the very start.
     - o This may include reorganizations, new Charters, and clear alignment of Curia personnel to specific Families or to specific positions within Families.
     - o Curia cannot afford to evolve after Families are in place; it needs to be proactive.

The degree to which we ultimately implemented each of these five points varies. In some cases I think we nailed it – specifically two, three, and five. As you will see, the *In Solidum* Model of governance that we settled upon is not a good application of the first point, and we just didn't do a very good job with point four.

Our Benchmarking Team finished up their work and disbanded rather quickly. I've always believed in my time in leadership that when a team's work is done, it's imperative to disband them and not just continue to meet for the sake of having meetings.

Priest Support Work Team

We were well aware that the move to Families would be difficult for our priests, and from the start we wanted to do whatever we could to help them through it. With this in mind, my team partnered with Msgr. Patrick Halfpenny from the Office for Clergy to form the Priest Support Work Team.

Msgr. Halfpenny is a delightful priest with a deep spirituality that is as natural to him as breathing. He loves the Lord and the priesthood, and he was the right man to try to help the priests of the AOD through this move.

Although it was formed with noble intentions, our Priest Support team was one that I have to say was never fully utilized despite the good work that they did. We put things in place to support our priests, but very few of them took advantage of the good things that were offered.

The Charter for this team was as follows:

AOD Families of Parishes
Priest Support Work Team

Charter

This team is charged with developing and implementing specific actions to support the priests of the Archdiocese as we transition to Families of Parishes. Areas of support will be determined by the team, but should consider all aspects of ministry - human, spiritual, intellectual, and pastoral.

Considerations

- The specific needs for priest support will vary over time as we move toward FOP's.
  - During the discernment, some of the presbyterate may experience fear, anxiety, and stress.
  - Once a governance model is decided, some of the presbyterate may experience loss and grieving if they are asked to assume new roles in FOP's.
  - Once FOP's are implemented, some of the presbyterate may experience sorrow or perhaps even anger over the changes.

Timing

This work will continue throughout the FOP process, potentially even after the final families are in place in July of 2022.

This team first set up an advisory group of priests who were asked about what help they felt the priests of the archdiocese needed. Based on feedback from those discussions, they brought in a priest from the Diocese of London to speak about his experiences with Families at one of our All-Priest Meetings. After this, they set up a series of talks that were made available to all priest of the archdiocese on Boundaries and Thresholds, Embracing Transition: Spiritual Growth in Times of Change, Isolation, and Managing Anxiety in Time of Stress. All of these talks were given by respected people from the Church and from the secular world, and all of them were excellent.

Sadly, only a few dozen people attended each of them, and that includes some of my team who were there for support. We recorded them and sent the link out to all priests, from which we got a few more views. But the response to this effort was weak at best.

It wasn't a mistake to have this team do what they did. Indeed, it's clearly a need. But the truth is that it's very difficult to get men who help others with their problems to come forward for help themselves, even when they may benefit from it.

To ignore this need would have been a mistake, so I'm glad that we did what we did. I would advise that any diocese who moves to Families be sure to address how they will support their priests through the transition. But I do look back and wish that our response rate would have been better. Perhaps this is something that other dioceses can think through and put plans in place for a better response rate than we got.

Clergy and Parish Survey Work Teams

It probably goes without saying that as an engineer, I love data. To some people, data is boring and flat. To me, it tells a story. And so I took particular interest in the Clergy Survey and Parish Survey Work Teams.

Their Charters were as follows:

AOD Families of Parishes
Clergy Survey Work Team

Charter

This team is charged with developing or perhaps selecting a survey to be sent to all priests and deacons in the AOD. This survey will capture the gifts and desires of the clergy, as well as the challenges.

Considerations

- There are several purposes for this survey:
  - Allows the clergy to express their desires as changes are made for FOP's
  - Allows the Assignment Board to consider results when making assignments
  - Allows for alignment of clergy interests and backgrounds with parish culture
- While this team is to be led by the Clergy Department, the MSP Department is quite willing to assist.

Timing

This work should be complete by Dec 1, 2020.

AOD Families of Parishes
Parish Survey Work Team

Charter

This team is charged with developing or perhaps selecting a survey to be sent to all parishes, perhaps to parish councils or leadership teams, in the AOD. This survey will capture the strengths, gifts, and opportunities for the parish.

Considerations

- There are several purposes for this survey:
    - Allows the parishes to express their needs as changes are made for FOP's
    - Allows the Assignment Board to consider results when making assignments
    - Allows for alignment of clergy interests and backgrounds with parish culture

Timing

This work should be complete by Dec 1, 2020.

These teams did some really great work, and there was an offshoot to what they did that I didn't anticipate going in, much like what happened with benchmarking.

The Clergy Survey team decided to develop a robust set of questions to ask all of our priests and deacons about their interests, hopes, and fears for their ministry in light of where we have been and where we are headed.

But how would we best go about developing the questions? Should we just brainstorm what the questions should be? We probably could have come up with some good ideas, but this wasn't something that we had a lot of skill in doing. Should we defer to existing clergy surveys that some companies who do this type of work already have available? There are many out there, but they aren't necessarily tailored to our needs.

The same discussion was raised with respect to the parish surveys. There are lots of parish surveys on the market; should we create our own or use an existing survey?

The solution we came to was the result of something that we did many times in our journey: we went back to *Unleash the Gospel.* We pulled statements out of the Pastoral Letter and broke them down into questions for both the clergy and the parishes.

One simple example is shown here:

> ### *Unleash The Gospel* Reference:
> o "Parishes are to be founded upon prayer and a culture of encounter with Jesus" – from Vision for Parishes

> ### Priest Survey questions:
> o How much time do you spend in prayer each day? (<30 min, 30-60 min, >60 min)
> o How strong is your desire to teach others how to pray? (Scale 1-10)

> ### Parish Survey questions:
> o Do you have a parish intercessory prayer team?
> o Do you have one or more Rosary groups?
> o Do you have other prayer groups that meet regularly?

The Clergy Survey Team surveyed all of the priests and deacons via a link to a Smartsheet (database), while the Parish Survey Team developed a process for gathering data that was a bit more involved.

For parish surveys, we set up a three-part process. The pastor of each parish was asked to select ˜10 people to participate in all three parts of the process. First, these people were given an anonymous survey to rate their responses to the questions we had developed. Next, the entire group was gathered for a live discussion about the culture and history of their parish. Finally, there was another live meeting held where we walked the group through a structured SWOT analysis of their parish (Strengths, Weaknesses, Opportunities, and Threats).

If a parish completed all three parts of the process, we produced something we called a Parish Culture Report which summarized all of the data. These Culture Reports were a rather helpful summary of what key people in the parish felt about the things that they were good at and the things that challenged them.

The clergy survey data was used by the Priest Assignment Board, and the Parish Culture Reports for each parish in the Family were ultimately given to the priests, deacons, and directors of the Family so that they could get an appreciation for each and every parish in the Family. The goal was to help them to better understand and appreciate those parishes which they didn't know very well.

Survey Insight

I mentioned previously that I believe that data tells a story, and this was certainly the case for our clergy and parish survey data. The story is one that I believe is quite important not only to our efforts to be more missionary here in the AOD, but to any diocese who wishes to do the same. And since we're all called by the Great Commission of our Lord to go and make disciples, that includes pretty much every diocese.

The priest survey data was confidential, and I wasn't able to review the information that was submitted. In truth, I didn't want to see it. I would never want to run into a priest in the diocese and know any intimate detail about him. It's none of my business, and I wouldn't want my private thoughts being reviewed by random people in the Curia either.

But I did ask to see the aggregate results because I thought they might give some clues about where we are strong and where we may have shortcomings. And that data most certainly did provide us some insight, especially when paired up with the parish data that we collected.

Because we had commonly designed the clergy and parish surveys to be aligned to *Unleash The Gospel*, both surveys covered seven key areas. Those areas were:

- Sacraments, Liturgy, and Prayer
- Inward Evangelization (evangelizing those in the pews)
- Outward Evangelization (evangelizing those who do not come to Church)
- Administration and Operations
- Staff and Lay Leadership
- Pastoral Care and Christian Service
- Sent on Mission (familiarity with *Unleash The Gospel*, proclamation of the Kerygma, etc.)

By looking at the data from both the priests and parishes in these seven key areas and comparing it to our mission as an archdiocese, we found some helpful insights. In February of 2021, I presented an analysis of this data to our Episcopal Council, and since that time I've shared that same analysis with many others. Here's a summary of what we found.

- **The Mass and the Sacraments** - The vast majority of our priests enjoy preaching, teaching, and confession. The parishes rated themselves highly in these areas as well.

Analysis: we are very good at and we enjoy the liturgical and sacramental fundamentals of the faith. This is very good.

- **Becoming a more missionary diocese** – Only 34% of our priests enjoy praise and worship, and only 11% have done any street evangelization. Our priests rate their own strength in outward evangelization as relatively low, and our parishes gave the lowest overall scores to outward evangelization. Analysis: we need to think about how we will actually become a missionary diocese given these results.
- **Youth Ministry** – Only 34% of our priests enjoy young adult ministry, only 23% enjoy youth ministry, and only 15% enjoy singles ministry. Analysis: we need to think about how we will attract the youth and young adults to the faith given these results.
- **Christian Service** – Our priests rated their skills very low here, and our parishes rated this as the second lowest area of strength. Analysis: we need to think about how we will support our priests in this area.

This may look a bit bleak, but there's good news here.

We must first realize that we can't change where a man's enjoyment lies. You can't force someone to like something. But our move to Families of Parishes comes with new Director positions which have tremendous potential to shore up areas where our priests are not as interested. This will, of course, require that these Directors be empowered to do their jobs as they are defined. Families come with the potential to free up our priests to do more of what they enjoy and to let the directors take on more of what the priests don't enjoy. This is a tremendous opportunity for us.

But in order for us to realize the potential from this opportunity, we need to be willing to look at how we function as Church. Far too often we see that virtually everything is run by or supported directly by the priest, which in turn means that we cap the number of ministries that we offer as a Church based on Father's schedule, or his age, or even his interest. This is a problem today, and it will get significantly worse as we see a continued decrease in the number of priests if we don't do something different.

When I began working for the AOD, long before my team was up and running, Anita and I called a local Protestant mega church that was really doing great work. We wanted to ask them about what they did that made them so successful, that helped them to grow so much in the past several years. They had dozens and dozens of ministries being offered, from Scripture study to rock climbing to community support.

So we called them and explained our desire to the receptionist who answered the phone. She understood and said that they were quite willing to tell us whatever we wanted to know. After all, we're in this together as disciples of Jesus Christ. But, she said, who did we wish to speak with? I told her: the Pastor. After all, wouldn't he be the lynch pin for everything, the CEO and CFO and COO of the entire organization?

When I said this, she chuckled. "Our Pastor," she told me, "has no idea what ministries are going on. He gives his Directors his blessing and then his Directors lead the charge for their areas."

What a difference from our Catholic way of doing business! But here today, with our Director structure for Families of Parishes, we have the ability to emulate some of that. Maybe not all of it, because we have our requirements to meet, and their structure is probably too extreme for what we are ready to accept just yet. But if, for example, we were to empower a Director of Evangelical Charity to do his or her job, and if we get the right person who is passionate about it and who can bring on great volunteers who are equally passionate, we can move mountains without needing Father to work outside his preferences, to be at every meeting, and to approve every decision.

The data did indeed tell a story. There is a way to continue to be more missionary even as our priests decline: we need to involve, trust, and empower the laity to a much greater extent than we do today. And in the end, our goal is to be a more missionary diocese. There was wisdom in the structure that our FOP Leadership Teams had defined.

Chapter 12 – Preparing The Deacons And The Laity

Deacon Mission and Formation Work Team

There's much to be said about the diaconate, both here in the AOD and elsewhere. In Church years, the permanent diaconate (henceforth referred to here as the diaconate) is something that's still quite new and not even close to fully understood or appreciated. The diaconate was only reestablished just over 50 years ago.

As a deacon myself, I have some fairly strong opinions about what a deacon is and what a deacon can and should do in his ministry. I believe that we deacons are an untapped font of help which the Church here in the United States has not yet figured out how to use to her benefit.

We deacons have experiences that our priests largely don't have. We have experiences in the workplace, in the marketplace, and in our neighborhoods. We have experiences as husbands and fathers. We know the realities of having difficult in-laws, of trying to be a disciple of the Lord while still trying to climb the corporate ladder, and of balancing the realities of our ministry with the very real demands of our marriages and our responsibilities to our children. But for the most part, these experiences are not utilized well in our ministries.

The complexity here is that the diaconate is a ministry of service, and that service has typically been defined as service to the poor, the homeless, and the sick. And to be clear, these are services that a true deacon enjoys. Some of my most fulfilling ministries in my time as a deacon have come from serving the homeless, from jail ministry, and from bringing communion to the homes of those who are too sick to come to Mass. This is where we truly see the face of Jesus: in those who are most in need.

But we can do more, and at least from where I sit, we should be asked to do more. Anyone who has worked in the Church understands the need for organization, for structure, for follow through, and the like. These are things that many of us deacons live and breathe in our secular careers, and we can help the Church if she were to ask. In my humble opinion, the Lord gave the diaconate back to the Church as a resource to help her through some of the difficult times ahead as we see growing secularity and a reduction in the number of priests.

But with all of that said, my role in the AOD was not to get involved in this facet of the business. My role was to implement Families of Parishes, and so we established a FOP work team to study and recommend the best way for the deacons of our archdiocese to adjust for Families. The Charter of that team was as follows:

AOD Families of Parishes
Deacon Mission and Formation Work Team

Charter
The team is charged with establishing and implementing the best possible means to involve the diaconate community in the FOP model.

Considerations
1. Clearly Deacon Breen, Diaconate Program Associate Director, must be involved in this effort
2. There are three deacons and one man in diaconate formation in the MSP Department

Timing

Timing for this work team will depend upon what they determine to be the best approach.

This team took on a role that none of the others did, but for a very sad reason. Our Associate Director of the Diaconate, Deacon Kevin Breen, was experiencing declining health and he needed support to get his work done. Our team became that support.

Deacon Breen passed away in January of 2021. He was a wonderful husband, father, and deacon, and in my formation he was my mentor. His loss was a tough one, and it came amidst the craziness of the pandemic when it was very difficult to pay respects and say goodbye. He was a very large man, a gentle giant with a heart for the Lord and for service.

Rest in peace, Kevin.

Eternal rest grant unto him, O Lord, and let perpetual light shine upon him.

One of the key decisions that this team had to make was how deacons would support Families. Would they continue to be assigned to one parish, or would they be assigned to all of the parishes in their Family? To me this was a pretty simple discussion. I felt that deacons should follow the lead of our priests and be assigned to all of the parishes of the Family. But not everyone felt that way, and there was a fair amount of discussion and debate about this.

In the end, the conclusion was that all deacons in a Family would support all of the parishes in the Family, and further that they would take direction and counsel from the Moderator or One Pastor of the Family. This latter decision was so that we didn't get into a situation where a deacon was taking direction from multiple priests, which would have been very tricky if not impossible to navigate.

As of the writing of this book, this team is still up and running as they support the transition of Deacon Breen's successor, Deacon Chris Beltowski. Deacon Chris is another fine, prayerful man for whom I have much respect.

Laity Education and Formation Work Team

As is obvious from all that I've discussed thus far, quite a bit of our time and effort around Families was focused on the clergy. But we couldn't ignore the laity, and so we formed a team to deal with this group as well. (The laity here is considered to be the people in the pews and not the lay people who work on parish staffs.)

Addressing the laity with respect to Families was a complicated matter. First, there's the issue that many in the laity will simply not notice that anything has changed, so if we spent too much time talking to them about Families it might have a negative effect of building up expectations with not much to follow from their perspective. Second, we would ideally approach the laity of the Family through the priests of the Family, but this was not really possible in Wave 1 because our priests were not yet even fully aware of what to expect for themselves much less their parishioners.

With this as a backdrop, the Charter for this team was as follows:

AOD Families of Parishes
Laity Education and Formation Work Team

Charter
This team is charged with developing and/or selecting training materials to educate the laity in AOD about what FOP's are and why they are needed. They are also charged with doing the educating and training across the diocese in whatever means they deem appropriate.

Considerations
- Recommended areas of education and training (the Team may propose to alter this list)
  - What is a Family of Parishes?
  - The value of best practices, including the **SPARK** database of best practices from around the country
  - The value of common tools
  - Inter parish community building
  - Transition and change management for laity

Charter
This training will be required for both the Discernment Phase of FOP's (June 1 – December 1, 2020), and the Preparation Phase of FOP's (December 1, 2020 – July 1, 2021).

This team, like so many other FOP Work Teams, did an excellent job. And as was true for benchmarking and for surveys, there were a couple of interesting offshoots of their labor that we didn't expect going in.

We had envisioned three so called "Family Gatherings," which were to be events where all of the priests, deacons, staff, and laity of a

Family would gather to get to know one another and to get them used to meeting as a Family. These Family Gatherings were not intended to be Q&A sessions about what Families are and why we are moving to them. We were happy to support such discussions in whatever way we were requested to do so, but these meetings were for the spiritual and social growth of the Family members, most especially the laity.

The team decided to focus the three Family Gatherings around the path to discipleship that's described in *Unleash the Gospel*, which is the Encounter-Grow-Witness (EGW) model. The concept behind EGW is quite simple: we as Church need to help people encounter the Lord in some fashion to get them to know who he is, then we need to give them opportunities to grow their faith, with the plan that once they have grown they will be willing to witness to the Lord and draw others to the faith. This is a very basic and yet very effective model of evangelization, and we've employed it in many aspects of our efforts here in the AOD, including our Family MSP process.

The first Family Gathering was thus focused on the idea of encountering the Lord and one another in our Family, the second around growing in those relationships, and the third around converting that growth into witnessing ourselves to those we get to know through our Families and ultimately to those who live within the boundaries of our Families but who do not join us at Church.

Once a Moderator or One Pastor was named, the Missionaries would work with him to set up dates for these three meetings. We met with mixed results. Some of the Moderators and One Pastors were happy to make this happen, while others were apprehensive to say the least.

This team developed a standard slide deck for each meeting, but each Missionary was encouraged to alter the deck as they saw fit to meet the needs of their Families.

Early on, our priests were content to just let us run through our standard process, but as they progressed many of them asked to vary from it and instead set up the third and sometimes even the second and third Family Gatherings to their liking. This was fine with us; if the priests were leading the charge, we were probably better off.

With 26 Wave 1 Families, our team ran just shy of 80 of these Family Gatherings. Each one took a fair amount of planning in advance and follow up when done. Every Family Gathering had at least two people from my team in attendance. This was so that the leader could facilitate while someone else did all of the background work. All of the Gatherings were on weekends or weeknights, but I didn't hear a single complaint from anyone on my team about this. They were content to do whatever was necessary to help us achieve the mission. I never took for granted their commitment back then, and I look back on it now with great respect. I've never worked with a team of people who were as committed to their work as this team, and I suspect that I never will have the pleasure of doing so again.

Overall, the Family Gatherings were a success. Early on, we struggled through some technical issues trying to do mixed meetings of both in person and online, but they largely accomplished what we had hoped for which was getting the laity to get to know one another and whetting their appetite for what was coming with Families.

Laity Education and Formation Observations

In the course of these Family Gatherings, we made two very important observations. While these observations have been helpful to our efforts here in the AOD, my primary reason for mentioning them here is that they will likely benefit other dioceses who make similar moves.

First and foremost, there was a palpable excitement amongst many of the laity that quite frankly caught us off guard. We had quite a few people come forward to offer their thoughts, some of which are summarized in the following statements.

- "It's about time that the Church is doing something to address the priest shortage. We hear about it all the time but we didn't think that the Church had a plan. This is great to see."
- "I have no idea if this concept of Families of Parishes will work or not, but I do know that we've been declining as a Church for some time now and I'm happy to see that we're finally doing something to invite people back."
- "What can I do to help? I'm happy to offer my time and talent in whatever way is needed."

If these are fairly common sentiments amongst the laity, then it raises some interesting questions that we do well to ponder.

- Why is it that every time we run an event in our parishes, the same people come forward to lead it when there are other people out there who want to help but aren't engaged? There are many good people out there waiting to be asked, but we haven't found a good way of asking them.
- Why have so many Catholic dioceses around the country waited to do something to address the priest shortages that we face? We are a Church of tradition, and we have some things that are timeless. But structure is not one of them. The early Church was quick to react and adjust, always with the mindset that we would do whatever was necessary to go and make disciples. Too often today we are so mired in what once was that we struggle to see what must be.

In this regard, I'm once again compelled to speak about the wisdom and foresight of Archbishop Vigneron. He started this journey late in his episcopate. He could have easily sat back and comfortably rode into the sunset. But he had the courage to put the needs of the Archdiocese of Detroit ahead of his own, and he took on this most difficult task of restructuring so that we could be ready to handle the priest shortage that we know is coming at us. In fact, it's a priest shortage that's already here.

The second observation that we made from these Family Gatherings was something that we ourselves were too late to properly address, but that others would do well to think about if you are planning a restructuring. While we had put a significant amount of effort into getting the clergy ready, and we were now putting a fair amount of effort into getting the laity ready, we had not done enough for the parish staffs. And they were understandably upset about this.

Why, they would ask us, have I not heard anything about Families until this Family Gathering? I know you've been meeting with the priests, but they haven't shared anything with me. Am I going to lose my job? Is my job going to change?

In fairness, we had done a few things to work with the parish staffs leading up to our Wave 1 launch, but we were in a bit of a predicament. We didn't want to go around the priests and share info with their staffs, but we also realized that the priests probably didn't know enough about the change themselves to share it with others.

That said, looking back on our efforts now with the benefit of experience, we simply should have done more to inform, involve, and support parish staffs in our initial move to Families. By the time we got around to launching Wave 2, there really wasn't a need for this because most everyone in a Wave 2 parish had already talked to people in a Wave 1 parish and they knew what to expect.

Perhaps we should have had a FOP Work Team devoted to Parish Staff Formation? Perhaps we should have done more to encourage the priests to share info with their Staffs? Perhaps there was some other approach we could have used? I don't know that I have a good solution, but I offer this for others to consider as you plan your journey.

Chapter 13 – Preparing For Launch

Prayer Support Work Team

> *"Intercession has always been the hidden engine of the Church's mission. It is not by accident that the co-patrons of the missions are St. Francis Xavier, who traveled as far as Japan to preach the Gospel, and St. Thérèse the Little Flower, who spent her entire adult life in a cloistered convent, offering all her prayers and sufferings for missionaries around the world. Intercessory prayer cultivates the soil for the sowing of the Word. It can stir up spiritual hunger in a whole city or region, so that the hearts of even those who are far from God are prepared to hear the Gospel when it is preached to them."*

This is a quote from Marker 10.2 of *Unleash the Gospel,* and as I've said, I didn't fully appreciate what this meant when I came to the AOD. But through the patient mentoring and the steady example of my Coaches and Missionaries, through my many hours of prayer in the chapel, and through the witness of so many great people at the AOD, I've come to a new appreciation for the value of intercessory prayer.

It was in this spirit of appreciation for the great need for intercessory prayer that we formed our Prayer Support Work Team. Their Charter was as follows:

AOD Families of Parishes
Prayer Support Work Team

Charter
This FOP effort cannot be successful if it is not covered in prayer. This team is charged with creatively directing prayer in support of all phases of the FOP process.

Considerations
1. This will include intercessory prayer teams at parishes, the prayer activities teams, and perhaps other groups.
2. This group should make a special effort to enroll people to pray for our priests by name as they work through changes in their roles as a result of FOP's.

Timing
This team will need to be engaged throughout the FOP process.

This team was made up of prayer warriors – those who not only love to pray for others but who actually feel compelled to do so as their calling because they have the charism of intercession. They were rather remarkable in that they never sought or appreciated the spotlight. They simply wanted to intercede for our efforts and to bring on other people who would do the same.

There were a number of parishes in the AOD who already had Intercessory Prayer Teams, but this FOP Work Team was on a mission to add more of them and get them properly trained in what it means to function as an intercessor. They contacted priests and explained the value of forming such a team, and they offered online training for new and existing teams to grow their numbers. They brought in guest speakers to offer their thoughts on why intercessory prayer is necessary. In fact, I had the great pleasure of speaking to this group.

They came up with proposed wording for a prayer for Families of Parishes which the Archbishop accepted with one minor modification, and we now use that prayer to kick off many of our meetings.

They offered what we called "Regional Prayer Surges" for each of the four regions, which were online meetings to heighten awareness of the need for and value of intercessory prayer.

They worked with a group of cloistered nuns who agreed to pray for every priest and deacon in the archdiocese by name.

They invited Archbishop Michael Byrnes, a former auxiliary bishop of the AOD, to speak to the intercessors. Archbishop Byrnes is a tremendous believer in and supporter of intercessory prayer.

And they used their own time and talent to create videos for both educational and promotional purposes to attract people to intercessory prayer.

The interesting thing about intercessory prayer is that we'll never have proof that what they did made a difference. But I look at it this way: when I drive my car, I don't think much about the engine doing its job. But if the engine were to fail, I would be stopped dead in my tracks. This is how intercessory prayer works. When we have it, we don't think enough about how valuable it is. But if we didn't have it, we too would be stopped dead in our tracks.

This team kept the engine healthy, and they continue to do so to this day.

Clergy Formation Work Team

One of the more daunting tasks that we needed to tackle was the formation of our clergy in terms of helping them understand what Families are and how their roles would change within the Family structure. This was something that we had to get right, since the clergy would make or break our success in the transition to Families.

The Charter for the Clergy Formation Team was as follows:

AOD Families of Parishes
Clergy Formation Work Team

Charter
Once the Governance Team has determined the model for governance, formation will be needed for the leadership. It is assumed here that this will likely mean a lead pastor for the FOP.

Considerations
- This is a very significant element of successful implementation of FOP's.
- This formation should comprehend a combination of typical "classroom" training, immersion visits to missionary parishes, immersion visits to families of parishes in other dioceses, and other creative means of showing pastors how to be as successful as possible when leading a FOP.

Timing

Formation will not occur until after the Governance Team has done their work and the new pastors are selected.

This team agreed first and foremost that any formation we did needed to have both a spiritual and a formational aspect to it. We also agreed that we needed two versions of formation for each wave, the first being formation for Moderators/One Pastors by themselves, and the second being formation for all clergy (priests and deacons) of the Family as a team. This meant that the Moderators/One Pastors had to attend two formation sessions.

We eventually settled on a plan for two days for each session. Both the Moderator/One Pastor Sessions and the Family Clergy Sessions would have day one focused on the spiritual, and day two focused on the tactical aspects of Families.

Planning for the logistics of these sessions was not an easy thing. We had approximately 300 priests and deacons who needed to participate, and some of them needed to participate more than once. Just getting the men to sign up and commit to being there took quite a bit of effort from my team.

We had severe restrictions on the number of people who we could gather together at the local retreat centers due to Covid, so some of the Wave 1 sessions needed to be offered at local parishes. This meant that we also had to plan for the meals, refreshments, etc. on our own.

As was true of so many other aspects of our journey, the Lord took care of us. He gave our team a wonderful Missionary in Kate Baumer, who not only had planned several retreats as a youth minister but who also was a talented musician who took on the music for all of our Masses and Holy Hours. She took the ball and ran with it, and this was a tremendous blessing to me.

For Wave 1 Families, our Moderator Formation was on April 14-15, 2021. Day one was all about discernment, with talks from the Archbishop himself and two priests, plus a holy hour of adoration with a homily on discernment from another priest. Day one concluded with a social hour.

Day two involved a series of talks on what Families are about, how a Moderator can serve as a first among equals, and what challenges the Moderators/One Pastors could expect as they moved into their new role. Day two also had Mass at noon, which was presided by the Archbishop.

For the Wave 1 Family Clergy Formation Sessions, we decided to host them by region. These four sessions took place in May and June of 2021.

Day one for the Family Clergy Formation Sessions was similar to how day one for the Moderators was run, but there were different priests doing the talking. Once again, the Archbishop spoke at every session.

Day two was more of a how-to discussion with detail about the governance structure of Families of Parishes, Mission Direct, Mission Support, and an introduction to the Covenant. As was true for the Moderator/One Pastor session, day two had Mass at noon, which was presided by the appropriate regional bishop.

Based on my observation, verbal feedback from people who attended, and the formal surveys afterward, I would have to say that the Wave 1 Formation Sessions were moderately successful.

The men generally liked day one, as it was somewhat like a retreat for them and it concluded with time for them to socialize with one another. Day two was not quite as popular, as the reality of the changes that were coming their way became clear.

There was an undercurrent of apprehension at all five of these sessions. Was this move to Families actually going to happen? There were many examples of programs that the AOD had taken on in the past which were eventually abandoned; perhaps this was just another.

The dialogue at times teetered on the edge of being confrontational. It was clear that there were some priests who simply didn't want to make this change, and they were quite intent on making their feelings known to everyone in the room.

Based on what we learned from Wave 1, we adjusted the Wave 2 Formation Sessions quite a bit. We had a similar format for day one, but for day two in both the Moderator/One Pastor Session and the Family Clergy Session, we brought in Wave 1 priests to speak to their real experiences for each and every talk. This was very well received by the Wave 2 priests.

Both the feedback and the surveys for the Wave 2 Sessions was quite a bit more positive than what we saw in Wave 1.

MSP Revision Work Team

One of the great joys that I had during the chaos of the pandemic and the move to Families was planning for the next generation of MSPs which were to come once the Families were launched. I found solace there because it brought me back to why I came to the AOD in the first place – to help this diocese be more missionary in response to the call of the Holy Spirit.

In truth, the work around Families was taking a toll on me. I had made the decision to shift my focus and do something with my ministry for the rest of my working life, and I had taken a big financial hit to do it. But leading the move to Families was not what

I had in mind when I came here. Even though I believed in my heart that I was doing what God asked of me, what I was doing now felt a lot like the project management work that I did when I was with GM, and while I was fully aware that there was a missionary element to it, for the short term it was back to project management timelines, excel files, status updates, and the like. Thinking about MSPs was a relief and a joy.

On the flip side, there were very few people outside of my own team who had any interest whatsoever in MSPs. Everyone was focused on survival and launching Families; MSPs were simply not something that rose to the top of the list. For me, this was mission critical (pun intended). I very clearly saw two great benefits of doing a Family MSP.

First, doing one would be something around which all of the Family leaders could rally. It would cause them to start thinking as a Family, planning as a Family. It would cause them to think about things in terms of their new role rather than the one they previously held, which I was quite certain most people would still be hanging on to for dear life.

Second, this was both a symbolic and a very real sign that we were moving past the frustrations of restructuring and getting back into what we had intended to do pre-pandemic: be strategic about how we will go about being more missionary.

I've always noted that the greatest leaders I've known in life were those who were able to plan for tomorrow while still dealing with the realities of today. It's not that they ignore today's problems, but rather that they have the skill of being able to simultaneously handle today's problems while at the same time strategizing for where we will be once today's problems are behind us. Strategy and leadership are a lot like playing chess: you can be checkmated if you don't deal with the immediate, but you can lose a long and slow battle if you don't think several moves ahead. I like to think that I've learned enough from the great leaders with whom I've worked that I can channel some of their wisdom into what I do.

The Charter for this team was as follows:

AOD Families of Parishes
MSP Revision Work Team

Charter
This team is charged with revising the MSP process to work with Families of Parishes such that it more successfully achieves the goal of making the AOD into a missionary diocese.

Considerations
- The MSP process for parishes as designed was likely too abrupt. Spending just one day on a proposition and looking for a plan is insufficient for a true strategic look.
- This team has the ability to completely rethink the MSP process.

Timing
- The execution of a family MSP cannot begin until the family is formed and the leadership is in place (clergy, leadership team, and at least the majority of the staff).
- This may start as early as spring of 2021 assuming one or more families moves quickly to adopt the new model, but may not start until fall of 2021.

There were a few things that we learned from our pilot parishes that we carried into the Family MSPs. For starters, we needed to keep it simple, hold short meetings rather than the marathons we experienced with the partner parishes, and we needed to use tools that are readily available rather than creating new ones.

The other thing we learned was something that I knew was right but that was very controversial: we couldn't mandate any sort of fundraising. The reality was that the fundraising activity in the partner parish phase garnered a lot more attention than did the need to be missionary. This wasn't by design, but it was our actual experience. Not only that, but asking parishes to move into fund raising right after a pandemic seemed rather insensitive to what the parishioners were going through.

While the idea of eliminating the fund raising was appropriate and well received by the priests, it was also a difficult decision that I needed to sell to many different groups in the AOD. The problem was that many departments in the Curia had already spent money for the MSP effort in anticipation of the fund raising money coming in, and the biggest culprit of all was me and my team. Our entire effort was to be covered by the fund raising, and now there was none. This was one of the key issues in our budget discussions which would follow, most of which were not pretty.

We ultimately decided that the Family MSP would be a series of six modules, with the idea that each Module would be no more than 90 minutes in length. It's my belief that when it comes to meeting length, the mind can only absorb what the butt can withstand. However, to complete a module in 90 minutes required that some homework be done by each person on the team in advance of the meetings. The alternative was to do the homework during team meetings, which meant that they would go over 90 minutes or we would need more than six meetings.

The Family MSP was to be completed by the Family Leadership Team, which was generally the priests and directors of the Family. Deacons were welcome, but many deacons work full time and can't make meetings during the day which everyone else on the team would clearly prefer. My team would facilitate the completion of the Family MSP, which we couldn't wait to do. After all, that was what we originally hired on to do, and we were excited about the idea of finally doing it.

The flow we decided upon was as follows:

- **Module 1** – Describe the process and review the tools. This included a review of a rather helpful database that we had developed internally called **SPARK**, which captured best practices from around the country in different areas of ministry. SPARK was actually developed by my wife Anita, and I must say that it's quite a wonderful tool.
- **Module 2** – Utilize the "Detroit Model of Evangelization" for two demographics. The Detroit Model is an online course that provides training on how to structure parish programing according to an Attract-Encounter-Grow-Witness paradigm. Each Family would be asked to work through the details for one demographic that was currently coming to Mass (for example, families with young children who attend Mass) and for one demographic that was currently not coming to Mass (for example, families of children who attend Catholic School but do not come to Mass).
- **Module 3** – Discuss the Sunday experience in terms of hymns, hospitality, and homilies.
  Module 4 – Discuss other Sacraments and liturgical experiences such as baptisms, weddings, confirmations, etc. as to how we can make them a more evangelizing experience and follow up with people afterward.
- **Module 5** – Develop the initial Family MSP from the ideas brainstormed in Modules 1-4.

- **Module 6** – Discuss what things the Family will stop doing to free up resources, then finalize the **MSP** and review next steps.

The Family **MSP** that was ultimately developed would be nothing more than a starting point. The **MSP** is a living document that should be maintained and updated as the Family grows and learns.

If utilized properly, the Family **MSP** has the potential of being a wonderful strategic tool for the leaders of the Family. If not, it runs the risk of being just another exercise that never got traction.

Chapter 14 – Thank God Ahead Of Time

A Most Selfless Response

As 2020 progressed, the realities of the financial crisis that we faced in the Curia were becoming painfully obvious. Parishes had closed their doors and gone to on-line Masses, and with that the donations to the Churches declined as well.

I must say that throughout the pandemic, donations here in the AOD were remarkably strong. We did in fact see a reduction, but the reduction was not as bad as we might have feared. Even at my home parish of St. John Vianney, I was somewhat shocked to see so many wonderful people mailing in donations every week because they couldn't be there in person. This was remarkable and a credit to the fine men and women of the AOD.

But despite the tremendous generosity of the people, there was a still reduction in collections, and that reduction translated directly back to less money coming into the Chancery. It was clear that we had to make some pretty serious cuts if we were going to survive.

The decision was made that all departments needed to take a 25% budget reduction. This could be achieved through cutting projects, reducing hours worked, or by reductions in personnel. In my case, virtually all of my costs were people, so getting to 25% meant aggressively reducing our people costs.

For my team, it was pretty easy to see our way to a 20% reduction by cutting everyone back to four-day work weeks. This was, at least in my mind, a must. But that didn't get us to a 25% reduction.

Around this time, one of the Missionaries made a personal decision to leave the team. I never like losing people, but in this particular case, it helped us toward our reduction target, and so I was quite relieved that this had happened. But when I did the math, I still needed to cut two more Missionaries to get to my numbers, even with everyone on four days.

In my time with GM, I'd been involved in many headcount reduction initiatives. I'd sat in the room with other leaders for hours on end where we decided who we would keep and who would be let go. I hated these discussions, but I knew the game and how it was played, and I understood my task here with the AOD.

But in my heart, this was different. I had hired people away from jobs that they could have kept doing, only to release them a few months later. This didn't seem fair. And besides that, who would I cut? They all had the same seniority, and they were all wonderful disciples who did whatever was asked of them. There were no easy answers.

My wife will tell you that I had some sleepless nights over this, and I mean that quite literally. There were some nights when I literally got out of bed after several hours of trying unsuccessfully to fall asleep and just started working again at two or three in the morning.

Eventually I decided on the two that I would ask to leave, and I prepared to call each and every member of my team to personally speak with them about what was happening. But the Lord was tugging at me with a thought that I couldn't really make sense of. He was asking me to call the two to be cut last - that the conversation might be different than what I had planned if I would trust in him. Of course, it wasn't quite this clear and concise, but there was an inkling there that I felt was coming from the Holy Spirit's direction.

And so I did as he asked. And as was true so many times on this project, something happened which I would have never anticipated.

As I called the first people on the list to tell them that they were going to be cut back to four days, a handful of them gave a response that was so selfless that it literally choked me up.

"Do you need to fire anyone?" they asked in one form or another.

"Yes, I do. I can't get the reduction I need without doing so," I replied.

"Then cut me back to three day's pay. Or two. I really don't care. I'll work five days because I believe in what we're doing, but I'm happy with whatever I'm paid. But don't fire anyone. They're all such good people!"

One of them actually told me that she believed so much in what we were doing that she was going to work for free. I told her that this was a bit too much – I wanted to pay her something, even if it was just to pay her for one day a week.

Before I ever got to the final two on the list, I had enough reductions to let everyone stay on at four days, with some being paid for less than four.

Another rock in the river, to be sure.

I once again found myself in the chapel telling God that I was sorry that I didn't trust him more from the start. If I could have just a fraction of the great confidence in the Lord that Blessed Solanus Casey showed throughout his life, I would be a much better disciple and a much happier person. Blessed Solanus was known to often say, "Thank God ahead of time."

When I thought that my team was going to be disbanded, God took the lead and saved us. When we formed teams to lead an activity that we never planned for, God gave us the skills that we needed.

When I thought I had to cut people, God had a better plan. I was slowly starting to understand that this effort really was something that God wanted, and that I was very lucky to be chosen to lead such a graced project.

Chapter 15 – Guide Rails

The Covenant

Over the past several years across the country and likewise here in the AOD, most of our parishes have been led by a single priest. In years past, a parish would have two or more priests. But as their numbers have dwindled, we've evolved into a situation where most priests today work solo.

One of the consequences of this is that many of our priests experience a sense of isolation. They come home to an empty rectory and have no one with whom to have dinner, to share a story, or to simply watch TV. Many of us take these everyday things for granted, but if we lost them we too would eventually feel isolated.

How priests handle this isolation is very personal. Some deal with it well and enjoy their time alone, using it for spiritual and personal growth. But there are some who struggle to handle it and turn to alcohol or other substances to numb the loneliness that they feel. At times this gets out of control, and habits develop. And if there is no one else in the house to keep them in check, these habits can turn into crippling addictions which can ruin their ministries and their lives.

Archbishop Vigneron is well aware of this issue, and from the start of our move to Families he was confident that the relationships that the priests would develop with brother priests in their Family would help to alleviate some of the isolation that they feel. In fact, now that we're far along into Families, this has proven to be the case.

But for those who are accustomed to living alone, the thought of being asked to develop relationships with other priests who they may or may not like isn't easy. There's a need to talk about how those relationships will be supported and grow, and how they as a team will handle conflict. There's also a need to talk about some very practical issues that they will have to work out to make sure that their integration into the Family is as smooth as it can be.

With this in mind, the Archbishop asked that a document be created which would assist the priests in having some of these types of issues agreed to and submitted for his approval. He called this document a Family Priests' Covenant.

There were a few priests who objected to using the term "Covenant" for this purpose, arguing that this is a Biblical term with ramifications that go beyond any agreement that a group of priests in a Family could enter into. But the Archbishop was clear that he felt that Covenant is the right term, and so we stuck with it.

The Covenant is a somewhat lengthy set of questions which the priests of a Family are asked to complete together. Some might argue that perhaps such a document is necessary for in *In Solidum* Family but not for a One Pastor Family, but we chose to ask all Families to complete one.

The Covenant is made up of three parts. Part One deals with interpersonal relationships, with 12 questions around things like how they will pray together, whether or not they will live together, how they will individually strive to be better shepherds to the parishioners of the parishes of the Family, and so on.

Part Two deals with inter-parish relationships, with a handful of questions – each having sub-questions to call out more detail - around things like how they will handle days off, coverage for vacations and retreats, and so on.

Part Three deals with canon and civil law matters. While there are only six questions in this section, they are rather involved questions which we've had to reword on more than one occasion to get them right. These questions deal with significant matters like how they will align themselves to support the parishes in the Family, how they will balance the ministry load across the parishes, who will take primary responsibility for any schools in the Family, etc.

Once the priests of the Family have completed their Covenant, they send it to their regional bishop. The bishop looks it over and provides feedback if he sees reason to do so, and they re-write it based on the feedback for submission to the Archbishop. The Archbishop has the final say in whether the Covenant is sufficient or not. If he supports it, he gives his approval and it's complete.

The Covenant is to be completed within 90 days of the Family being formed, and it must be revisited within 90 days of any change in priests in the Family. This point was promulgated in particular law by the Archbishop.

One lesson learned for us was that there needs to be a defined process for tracking and eventually storing the Covenants. Someone needs to be responsible for knowing which have been submitted, return by the regional, resubmitted, and bought off by the Archbishop. It sounds a bit trivial, but part way through Wave 1 we realized that we had a tracking nightmare on our hands, and we struggled to figure out where each Covenant was in the process. This made for some hard feelings with some of the priests, which is certainly understandable.

I confess that when we first talked about these Covenants, I didn't appreciate their value. It seemed to me that we were making too big of a deal out of things. Wouldn't the men just naturally have these conversations as they formed a Family? But I was wrong. Covenants have proven to be a tremendous way of not only jump starting the discussions, but also of forcing some of the difficult discussions that need to be had which might otherwise have been ignored.

Canon, Particular, and Civil Law

I'm not a canon lawyer. I've never had a desire to be one. But as a result of my position, I've been pulled into more canon law discussions than I would have ever dreamed. And I've even had some brief introduction to areas of civil law that come into play with Families.

What I've learned from all of this is something that I would strongly advise other dioceses to consider: be sure to have a good canon lawyer as a part of your team as you move into Families. If you don't, you run the risk of doing something that may seem innocent but could wind up getting you into quite a bit of trouble. We have a couple of aces here in the AOD in Michael Trueman and Msgr. Ron Browne, and we are blessed to have them.

I won't even attempt to give a good discussion of the details of this part of the business. To try to do so would only show my ignorance of the topic. Instead, I'll offer some high-level thoughts for anyone considering a move to Families.

As far as canon law goes, it's important to know that there are canons which directly or indirectly relate to the *In Solidum* Model. Our very wise canon lawyers here in the AOD have come up with a list of such canons, and they are as follows:

- Canons primarily associated with *In Solidum*:
  - 517§1 – the ability to use the model for care of parishes
  - 542 – constitution of the team and possession
  - 543 – basic references to the way in which the team will function
  - 544 – vacancies within the team
- Canons related with *In Solidum* made by reference of the primary canons:
  - 521 – qualifications of priests *In Solidum*

- 522 – stability in office the same as parochus
- 524 – assigning priests to parish(es); and consultation to that end
- 527 – taking possession
- 528-530 – obligations toward the parish
- 533 – obligation of residence
- 534 – Mass intention for the people of the parish(es)

As far as particular law goes, Archbishop Vigneron promulgated direction in six areas. The details are in Appendix 1 of our FOP Playbook. The six areas are as follows:

   I.   As concerns the Family of Parishes Priests' Covenant
  II.   As concerns the Family of Parishes Pastoral Council
 III.   As concerns the Parish Finance Council (PFC)
 IV.   As concerns the Family Finance Team
  V.   As concerns the Mission Support Director
 VI.   As concerns the Vicariate Pastoral Councils

As far as civil law goes, we had the attorneys who represent us in civil law matters look over our key documents for their thoughts. Those key documents were primarily the Playbook and the Covenant. They made some minor changes, most of which had to do with the legal ramifications of hiring and firing individuals given the Family structure. There is a certain complexity here in that the Family itself is neither a juridic person in canon law nor a legal entity in civil law, and as such the Family does not and cannot employ anyone. People are employed by the parishes of the Family, and in many cases we have directors who are employed in Parish A but who are supervised by a Moderator from Parish B. These situations needed to be addressed in such a way that the Moderator is given certain authority throughout all of the parishes in the Family.

Our civil lawyers also concluded that Families drove no substantive change in direction with respect to liability insurance, the Americans with Disabilities Act, and the Affordable Care Act. Families do drive a possible change with respect to the Family and Medical Leave Act because it was assumed that all of the employees of all of the parishes and schools within a Family would need to be aggregated and counted with respect to the 50+ employee threshold.

Some may read all of this and think it a bit silly. Why, you may wonder, does all of this legalistic thinking matter? Are we not a Church?

But the reality is that, while these legalistic issues may not come up often, when they do come up it's very important that we are clear and concise, and that we have our ducks in a row.

Shots in the Dark

There's no way to avoid the fact that our move to Families was difficult, and that some people very much objected to it. Those who openly expressed their frustration were primarily from the presbyterate, but a small number of laity objected as well.

The vast majority of complaints about Families were in one of two categories. The first was that people didn't want to change what they knew to be the Church and the priesthood as it is today. This is understandable. Change is hard on just about everyone. The second was that people simply misunderstood what was happening, and in their misunderstanding they offered concerns that were easily addressed with facts.

Sadly, some of those who objected resorted to rather shameful tactics of deceit and fear mongering in the darkness of anonymity. Someone – or perhaps some group – sent out a series of anonymous emails and snail mails with false statements about Families, asking priests to resist and parishioners to write to Rome and complain.

These anonymous attacks claimed that we were violating or abusing in some way not just canon law but civil law as well. They tried to drive fear into the hearts of our priests, telling them that if they agreed to be in a Family, there would be legal implications for them personally.

The fact that these attacks were anonymous spoke volumes about the integrity of whoever was behind them. We were happy to address any and all concerns that were raised, and in some cases people brought forward legitimate concerns that we did in fact need to consider and react to. But this was a rather childish way of raising possible concerns.

That said, these pathetic attacks did have an effect on our efforts to form Families. Some of the priests expressed great concern. If this was true, they were putting themselves at risk. And so we had to decide how to react to the accusations, or for that matter if it made sense to react to them at all.

After some debate, we decided that we needed to host a meeting with our priests to address most of the issues that were raised in the anonymous attacks. But this would be our only response. We wanted to reassure our good priests who had concerns, but we were not going to pander to someone or some group who lacked the courage to come into the light and share their concerns with integrity.

At this meeting, we brought in canon and civil lawyers to address the lies that were put forth, and I had the great pleasure of telling the group that we were not going to address any more anonymous attacks. I chose my words very carefully because I didn't want to come off the rails and resort to saying things that violated my calling as a disciple of the Lord, but I was clear enough that it earned me my first appearance in a Church Militant story.

I'm aware of four anonymous messages that went out to our priests and several parish staff members. There may have been more, but candidly I really don't care. As far as I know, there were no more anonymous attacks that came after we launched Wave 1, but I could be wrong about that.

As is true in all walks of life, one can never successfully advance any cause without being honest, candid, and up front with those who are impacted. Did we make some mistakes in our approach to Families? Yes, we did. And we had to make some course corrections. But we always did our best to be transparent with the presbyterate about these things. Those who throw stones from the shadows will always cause trouble, but in the end, we need to have the courage to move forward in the light when a cause is worth pursuing.

Chapter 16 – We Have Ignition

Milestones

As we approached the launch of Wave 1 on July 1st of 2021, we had quite a bit of discussion about how to assure that Families were making progress. We knew that if we simply asked the priests of the Family to get organized per the Playbook but gave them no timing requirements, very little would change. This is by no means a criticism of the priests; this would be true for anyone in any function. Reorganizations aren't popular, and people will resist the change for as long as they can, so timed milestones are necessary to keep things moving forward.

With this in mind, we developed a Milestone Timing Chart which we then shared with the Moderators and One Pastors at their Formation Session, and then with the Family Clergy at theirs. That chart was as follows:

Event	Description	Who Leads	Timing
Family Gatherings 1, 2, and 3	Opportunities for people in the parishes of a Family to get to know one another and pray together	Missionary will contact priests of Family and will lead these sessions	March – July 2021
Moderator Retreat/Formation Session	Moderators will pray, reflect, and learn together about their role	Clergy Office and MSP Department	April 14/15, 2021
Family Clergy Retreat/Formation Sessions	Clergy of Family will pray, reflect, and learn together about their role.	Clergy Office an MSP Department	Four Regional Sessions in May and June

	Covenant will be started.		
Clergy Support Sessions	Sessions to share best practices and offer formation and support	Curia	Monthly starting in May
Commissioning Mass for Family	If possible, with Regional Bishop presiding	Moderator	Between 7/1/21 and 10/1/21
Complete Family Priests' Covenant	Template comes from Office for Clergy	Moderator	Draft by 8/15/21
Select Mission Support Director	As described in FOP Playbook	Family Clergy	Complete by 9/1/21
Select people for Mission Direct Director positions	As described in FOP Playbook	Family Clergy	Complete by 10/1/21
Family Missionary Strategic Plan	Creation of specific plans to help Family be more missionary	MSP Department	Begins as early as October depending on Family
Establish Family Leadership Team	As described in FOP Playbook	Moderator	No later than 12/31/21
Formation of Family Leadership Team	Formation using Amazing Parish tools	MSP Department	Q1 2022
Establish Family Pastoral Council	As described in FOP Playbook	Moderator	No later than 12/31/21
Establish Family Finance Team	As described in FOP Playbook	Moderator	No later than 12/31/21

The priests' reaction to this chart was pretty much what we had expected: it's too aggressive. Many of the priests expressed concern that they couldn't hit many of the dates. However, we moved forward with the understanding that the Families would do their best to hit the dates, and if they for some reason struggled we would handle that on a case-by-case basis.

For my own team's benefit, I went back to my many years of manufacturing experience with GM and set up a means for visually tracking all of the Families to see how they were progressing at hitting these milestones. I'm a big believer in making things visual. As much as I believe in the goodness of people, I've come to understand that you get what you inspect, not what you expect.

The tracking tool we developed was called our dashboard, and we had a dashboard review every Tuesday morning after prayer. We rotated through the four regions at these meetings so that we hit all of the Families in each region every four weeks. As every Family had a Missionary assigned to it, we had the Missionaries speak to the dashboard to not only talk about how their Families were progressing to the milestones, but also to talk about any successes, problems, or areas where they could use help.

It was a bit rough getting this process up and running, since most of the people on my team had not been used to this kind of tracking in anything they had done prior. But once we got in the groove, I think it's fair to say that everyone bought into the process and saw value in using it.

We still review the dashboard every Tuesday morning, and we'll continue to do so until our project is complete.

Director Training

As the Family directors were being put in place, it was time for my team to begin our ramp down from Wave 1 and to start to move on to Wave 2. As we slowly ramped down our work with Wave 1 Families, the baseline Curia departments would need to ramp up theirs. We chose to jump start that handoff with a mid-October Kick-Off training session for all of the directors from all of the Families. That training was held at the Seminary.

Our Curia Mission Direct organization, called Evangelization and Missionary Discipleship (EMD), had reorganized to support the Mission Direct structure in advance of the Wave 1 launch. They broke up into groups that supported each of the five mission direct areas, namely Discipleship Formation, Evangelical Charity, Engagement, Family Ministries, and Worship. My wife Anita was actually the lead for Engagement and Family Ministries, once again making for many hours of dinner time conversation.

Support for the Family Mission Support Directors didn't require any restructuring at the Curia; we were already aligned in this area.

EMD developed a series of six online courses to facilitate the training process. These included an introductory course for all directors and one course for each Mission Direct area. The introductory course provided a general overview of all the areas of Mission Direct and Mission Support as outlined in the Playbook, leadership and management strategies for moving forward, and inspiration for leaders to see the missionary potential of the Families of Parishes model.

These online courses served as a way to get everyone on the same page as it relates to the vision for Families of Parishes, and they can be used again for future training of Wave 2 directors and people who are named to director positions down the road. All directors were asked to review these online courses prior to the October Kick-Off.

At the Kick-Off, the EMD leads for each of the five areas and the Mission Support lead from the Curia all gave presentations to the Family directors on their role. We also ran through some examples of real circumstances that they might face in their Family and asked them to talk as a Family about how they would handle them.

The Kick-Off Training was well attended and it was well executed. But there were a few problems that we ran into.

First, some of the Families had not yet named any directors because they had missed the milestone dates for doing so. Some of these Families sent substitutes to come to the training, but not all.

Second, we were experiencing an interesting dynamic that I didn't anticipate. Many of the directors who were named were in fact priests in the Family. This was clearly not what was envisioned by the Mission Direct FOP Leadership Team. They had envisioned laity taking these roles. After all, one of the key points to having a Family of Parishes was that we wanted to free up the priests who were not the Moderator from being burdened by administration and thereby allow them to do more work that only priests can do. But in many cases, the priests of the Family jumped right back into more administrative roles by becoming directors.

And third, where lay people were named to director roles, some of them felt that they were not able to effectively carry out their role as a director, either because they had so many other tasks on their plate that they simply didn't have the time to devote to their new role, or because their Moderator had not given them the green light to do what they needed to do to be successful.

Despite these problems, the training was generally well received, and the people who came appreciated the fact that we were trying to work with them.

Following this training, each of the five mission direct leads from EMD and the finance lead from mission support began hosting regular meetings with all of the respective Family directors in their areas. These meetings are still happening. They're generally held monthly, though sometimes more frequently.

A key benefit of this focus on the Family directors is that we as Curia can now get to all of the parishes in the Archdiocese by holding meetings with just over 50 directors rather than needing to work with each of the 200+ parishes. If there's something new to discuss around catechetics, for example, we meet with the directors of discipleship and share it with them. They have the responsibility for rolling it out in their Family as they see fit. This greatly simplifies the process.

Of course, if the directors aren't empowered to do their jobs, or if there's poor communication between them and the Moderator or One Pastor, they're given information which they aren't free to distribute or act upon.

I believe that our director structure is a key to us being more missionary as the number of priests decline, and I believe that in the long run we will benefit greatly from this. But time will tell if this will come to pass.

Expanded Report Outs

As we got further into the launch of Wave 1, probably sometime around November of 2021, I realized that there could be great value in expanding our Tuesday report out sessions to other groups in the Curia, but I had a strong suspicion that getting there wouldn't be easy, and I was right about that.

I had a vision that someday we would talk about a region and report progress, issues, and concerns from not only my team's perspective but also from that of other areas of the Curia. If we all reported what we were seeing and hearing about a Family, we stood a much better chance at having a coordinated plan to support them.

But in the Curia, we have a tendency to work in silos. The consequence of working in silos is that people tend to hold information close to the vest and thus don't readily share with others. This isn't because they're hiding things to be deceitful. No, these are very good people who have every desire to see us be a more missionary diocese. Rather, it's because when you work in silos you have no real experience with sharing info with other departments, and so you don't see any value in it.

And so I twisted some arms to garner support for these more broad Tuesday report outs. Some supported the idea, but some saw it as a nuisance and a waste of time for their people. None the less, we got the meeting populated with people from each of the six support functions for the six director roles.

For the first few weeks, the other folks just listened to my team report out on what we knew about the Wave 1 Families. At the end, we asked for any questions or comments, but got very few.

Eventually I allotted time on the agenda for the other groups to speak up about what they were seeing, and that drew some looks of confusion. What would they speak about? I told them that this was their choice, and if they wanted some space on the dashboard to track key things, we would be happy to make that happen.

I had confidence that they would eventually figure out what to do, and eventually they did. Our conversations became more robust as the weeks progressed.

It's my belief that this type of broad discussion offers great potential for us in the Curia – and for anyone in any Curia – to start thinking about the Family as something that we serve as a coordinated unit rather than something that we serve from multiple vantage points. Think of the difference between a restaurant and a hospital. When you arrive at a restaurant, they coordinate all of their activities in order to maximize your enjoyment as a customer. When you arrive at a hospital, on the other hand, they coordinate everything around the convenience and availability of the doctors, nurses, and technicians in order to maximize their internal efficiency. The enjoyment of the customer, i.e., the patient, is simply not considered. I much prefer the approach of the restaurant to that of the hospital, and I'm quite certain that others would agree with me on this point. If we're going to serve our Families well, we need to rethink our efforts to be more like a restaurant. These cross-functional report outs are an attempt at getting us to think this way.

Chapter 17 – How Did We Do?

Wave 1 Experience

As of the writing of this book, we're about a year past our Wave 1 launch and just about to launch Wave 2. I've been contacted by 20+ dioceses around the world who all ask pretty much the same question: is it working?

The most honest answer I can give to this question is that I don't know yet. I can provide data and observations, but in order for us to be successful, we have to truly find our way to being a more missionary diocese.

So let's begin with some data for our 26 Wave 1 Families:

- We've run 73 Wave 1 Family Gatherings and we're now scheduling them for Wave 2.
- We've completed 23 Family Commissioning Masses.
- 92% of the Families have Covenants that are approved or on the way to being approved.
- 70% of our Families have named five or more of their six directors, and 12% of our Families have named none of their directors.
- 14 Family MSPs are complete or nearing completion.
- 21 Support Teams are up and running (FPC, FLT, or FFT).

When we started on our journey to Families, we were fully aware that some were going to take off well and some would struggle. This data suggests that this is indeed the case.

As you might expect, there are stories behind the numbers, and every Family has its own uniqueness. Some of the Families who have named all of the directors have really just named them but done little else, while some who have named no directors yet are actually up and running but just hesitant to formally name the people.

Of the MSPs we've seen so far, they are generally pointed where we had hoped. Families are coming up with plans to work as a Family on things that will make us more missionary. But I would hesitate to say that they are particularly bold. Perhaps this is a good thing; perhaps slow and steady is a better approach given that we are in the midst of a complex restructuring.

Moving away from data and into observations, we've seen some very good things and some concerning things.

Starting with the positive, we're most definitely seeing the impact on isolation that the Archbishop had envisioned. Priests within a Family are meeting, talking, and praying together. Sometimes a portion of their time together is spent complaining about Families, but the bottom line is that they are together. Some of our priests have openly shared that this is a big benefit of Families.

The Covenants have proven to be a very good way of driving the necessary conversations about how the men will work together. The process of completing their Covenant is slow and tedious, but the benefits that come from having done so are obvious.

The Commissioning Masses that have been done to formally kick off the Families have been quite beneficial. We are a people of liturgy, and a liturgical launch is something that has a very positive impact.

The Family Gatherings have proven to be a big hit. The laity like being invited to be a part of forming the Family and getting it moving in the right direction.

Our regional bishops are doing a great job of supporting their Moderators and One Pastors in their roles, meeting with them and praying with them. This should not be interpreted to mean that the Moderators and One Pastors have it easy. Their jobs are very difficult. But it's far better to have your bishop trying to help than not.

And the Curia is in fact united around the idea of Families. I don't think you could find a person in the Curia today who doesn't realize how big of a change this really is. Almost every one of our jobs has been impacted in some way – better for some and worse for others. Having a common goal is a wonderful thing for any organization.

But we've got problems as well.

The Achilles' heel of the *In Solidum* Model is priestly fraternity. If just one of the priests in a Family is obstinate, uncooperative, or has an ax to grind with Families of Parishes, it can severely hamper the ability of the Family to move forward. This is by far the biggest problem that we face, and there are no easy solutions to dealing with such problem cases. We're struggling to come up with strategies to work on this issue.

In many ways, I sympathize with the priests who are resisting our move to Families. We're asking them to make a very significant change to their priesthood. Not only were they formed in the Seminary for a different approach to ministry, but many of them have lived that different approach for dozens of years. To pull that away from them and tell them to think and act differently is quite challenging.

On the other hand, many of us find it very disheartening that what drives some of our resistant priests to fight the move to Families is primarily their unwillingness to give up their kingdom. Some are very comfortable as king of their own castle. They make the rules, they call the shots, and they have a loyal following of staff and parishioners who would do anything for them. In most cases, these men have earned this respect through their ministry, which is a credit to their priesthood. But when they're asked to give that up and work as a part of a team, they feel threatened.

Some are threatened because they want to remain as king. Some are threatened because their weaknesses are going to be exposed for their brother priests to see. Some are threatened because they grew up in cultures where the priest was treated like royalty and they always pictured themselves in that role someday.

I don't want to dwell on this point because the majority of our priests are either on board with Families or willing to give it their best shot. And further, some of those who are most resistant are in fact excellent priests who have given their life to the Lord and who serve their parishioners with a pastor's heart. But for any dioceses who wish to restructure to Families or something like it, I offer that a subset of your priests will be by far your greatest obstacle.

Perhaps the most significant frustration that my team and I experience is when we speak to parishioners who understand and appreciate the need to move to Families and who are excited about the possibilities, but they tell us that their priest is not on board and is telling them not to cooperate. We've had parishioners leave one parish with a priest who is fighting Families and register at another who supports simply for this reason. This isn't something that we want to happen, but it does speak to a very serious problem within a small portion of the presbyterate.

Another problem is that some of our Moderators have surprisingly limited leadership skills. This was not completely unexpected, but the degree to which we're seeing it is surprising. We've seen some of the men avoiding conflict and seemingly paralyzed by the thought of making decisions that many in secular leadership positions would consider to be minor. In this regard, we've engaged the Catholic Leadership Institute to provide fundamental leadership training to any priests who are interested. That will start later this year.

As mentioned earlier, we're seeing quite a few priests taking on director positions, which is problematic. One of our key objectives in Families was to free up priests to do more missionary and evangelical work, but if they jump into director positions, they limit their ability to do so. In addition, this cuts out the laity from taking on a share of the challenges that we face. We are working hard to get out of this situation for Wave 1 Families, and we are being very clear with Wave 2 Families that this is something they should avoid.

We're also seeing some of the Families name their directors but not follow the structure called for in the Playbook. For example, the Family may have a Mission Support Director named, but the business managers in the parishes aren't reporting to this person. This may sound trivial, but it's not. If they don't report to the MSD, they often have allegiance to their parish only and they may resist working with the MSD on common issues that affect all parishes in the Family. We are trying to get Families to align to the Playbook, but this is not an easy task.

So are we succeeding with our move to Families? The jury is still out. We may not fully understand for years.

But are we directionally correct? I think the answer is yes. Both data and observations give us reason to believe that we're on a path to making the AOD a more missionary diocese.

Appeals to Rome

It probably comes as no surprise that there were appeals made to the Congregation for Clergy in Rome by some of our priests regarding our move to Families. This is, after all, a fair and legitimate option available to a priest if he feels that he has been wronged in some way.

The details of the appeals and the details of the response from Rome are private, but it's fair to offer a summary of what we were told by Rome.

In general, the Congregation for Clergy offered support for our move to Families of Parishes. They were complimentary of many of the steps that we took, and for this we were grateful.

They also offered us feedback which we took to heart and thus made appropriate adjustments. Their feedback is summarized in four points.

- There is a preeminent mutuality among the Priests *In Solidum* that must be safeguarded and pervade the care of the parishes for which they are responsible. The priests assigned *In Solidum* care for all parishes to which they are assigned and fulfill the obligations of pastors in those parishes (cf., cann. 528-530). This is clarified in the arrangement they make with each other in the Covenant. The Moderator is not a superior to the others. The Priests *In Solidum* necessarily participate in the tri-munera of their office in care of the parishes, including the munus regimini that is not solely possessed by the Moderator.
- The Priests *In Solidum* form a college that is responsible for all the parishes in the Family. Priests assigned as weekend help (and so on) to a parish or deacons assigned to a parish(es) are not part of the Priests *In Solidum* per se, but rather aid the Priests *In Solidum* in their responsibilities. In the same way that these clerics would relate to a Pastor in other circumstances, they will relate to the Priests *In Solidum*, usually with the priest responsible for that parish but always

with the Moderator being able to speak on behalf of the Priests *In Solidum.*

- The laity cooperate in the administration of ecclesiastical goods belonging to the parishes (cf., canon 129§2) but they do not administer those goods in their own name for the parish. They assist the Priests *In Solidum* or One-Pastor in the administration.
- There is an interplay between canon and civil law that creates a need for harmony and consistency.

As a result of this feedback, we made some corrections to our efforts.

We had been using titles for the priests in an *In Solidum* Family which we needed to change. Where we previously had used "Family-Pastor" and "Family-Parochial Vicar," we changed their titles to "Priest *In Solidum.*" We made adjustments to the Playbook and Covenant to reflect this thinking.

We also updated the Playbook to eliminate any wording which might lead one to believe that Mission Support Directors were directly administering the goods of any parish.

These changes were not well received by many of our priests. Some of the Family-Pastors didn't appreciate dropping the word "Pastor" from their title, and many priests felt that calling a former Parochial Vicar the same name as the other priests in the Family was misleading and could cause for confusion.

We also experienced frustration from some of our Moderators in the *In Solidum* Families because their role as a first among equals was hard enough as it was, but now it felt like they had no authority at all.

Even though the overall response from Rome was positive, the changes that we made were not popular. Some of our priests felt like they were deceived, though this clearly was never the intent.

I will say that I sympathize with the concerns that were raised. Even though we did our best to roll things out correctly, the reality is that we were one of the first to make a move to Families, and sometimes being in the lead means more vulnerability to correction.

At the same time, the corrections that we made were relatively minor in the big picture. We were largely affirmed by Rome for our efforts and we have every reason to believe that we have made a pretty solid effort at doing this right.

Wave 2 vs. Wave 1

As of the writing of this book, we're rapidly approaching the launch of our 28 Wave 2 Families. In another year or so, we'll have a much better handle on how that launch has progressed vs. the Wave 1 launch. (Perhaps that means a sequel to this book sometime down the road?) But even today, as we ramp up, there are some very clear differences between Wave 1 and Wave 2 that are worth note.

The single biggest difference is the degree to which Wave 2 priests are accepting the move to Families, which far exceeds the degree to which the Wave 1 priests accepted it. Don't misread this as meaning that they are enjoying the move to Families, but rather that they are much more accepting of it. As we moved toward the launch of Wave 1, many of the priests were unwilling to do much of anything to prepare. They didn't have a lot of energy around Family Gatherings, they didn't start any pre-work on their Covenants, and only a handful of them were meeting as a Family of priests prior to July 1.

How different it's been for Wave 2! Several of the priests in the Families are already meeting with one another, and some of them have already begun discussing their Covenant. My team has received a significant number of requests for us to come to the parishes of the Family and discuss what Families are and why we are making the move. Discussions around Family Gatherings are getting very little pushback. In truth, my team is a bit overloaded trying to keep up with the demand coming from the field. This is quite a change, and it's quite welcome.

But why are we seeing this change? What's different?

The single biggest reason behind the difference is that many priests in Wave 1 simply didn't believe that we were going to follow through with our plans to restructure. They had experienced so many programs coming down from the Curia which were never brought to completion that they were unwilling to put a lot of time and effort into this one unless and until they knew for a fact that it was happening.

Wave 2 priests, on the other hand, are well aware that this is their reality. We're not stopping the move to Families. They've all had discussions with their brethren in Wave 1 parishes and they are quite aware of what's going to be expected of them. To their credit, our priests are very smart and they are very well connected with their brother priests.

What we see today in our Wave 2 activities is a significantly stronger pull for my team's resources, and a significantly higher appreciation for the fact that this is coming and it behooves all of them to get a head start rather than waiting for July 1.

If there is a lesson learned here for other dioceses, it's that your initial launches of Families or Groupings or whatever you call them are going to be rough, and that they will get smoother over time. For this reason, it might be wise to start with a small group of Families in whatever you call your Wave 1. We chose to start with half of our parishes in Wave 1, and that proved to be a rather large group to manage. We got through it, but in hindsight a smaller pilot group might have been a better idea.

Chapter 18 – Advice To Other Dioceses

What worked for us

In my conversations with other dioceses, there are two questions that come up just about every time. These two questions will come as no surprise: what worked and what didn't work. These sound like innocent questions, but in fact they're not. The reason I say this is that something that worked for us may not work in another diocese, and something that failed for us might work well in another diocese. The best way to deal with a particular situation is very much dependent upon the circumstances surrounding the diocese.

However, there are some things I can offer that I believe are somewhat generic enablers to success in restructuring to Families, and I'll list them here.

- **A strong leader at the top.** If the bishop of the diocese is unwilling or unable to be strong in his leadership, there's very little hope of success. The reality is that restructuring is a very difficult thing to do, and if the bishop delegates it and takes a hands-off approach, there's going to be trouble. We were blessed to have a strong leader in Archbishop Vigneron, who made it clear at every turn that restructuring to Families was his decision and that he made it with the firm belief that it was the right long-term solution.

- **A clear mission that goes well beyond restructuring.** No one really wants to restructure, and so moving into a restructuring without an appreciation for an underlying greater mission will be difficult. Our mission in the AOD is clear: We are on the path to becoming a more missionary diocese. Our restructuring to Families of Parishes is not an end; it's a means to an end. We're only doing it so that we can continue on with our mission despite whatever challenges and obstacles we face.

If your mission is just to restructure so that you can cut costs or handle priest attrition, this will be tough to get people to truly support. If that was all that we were doing in the AOD, my Missionaries would have quit a long time ago. What kept them on board was their belief in the mission.

- **A guiding document to provide direction.** Here in the AOD, we had *Unleash the Gospel* as the baseline of our efforts. If ever there was a question about how to proceed, we turned to it for help. Having this document allowed us to rally around something when we developed survey questions, when we decided upon a model for evangelization (Encounter-Grow-Witness is one of the guideposts in *Unleash the Gospel)*, when we structured our Family Gatherings, and so on. We found great value in using it to define our work.

- **Prayer.** We are a people of prayer. If we act without prayer we will ultimately fail. Prayer can't be just an obligation, a check-the-box before a meeting kind of thing. Prayer needs to be meaningful and from the heart. My team has found great value in reading the daily Gospel and reflecting upon it, but we have also varied our approach at times and tried other means of prayer. If a particular style of prayer doesn't work for you and your team, try another. But never lose sight of the great value of prayer.

- **Relationship.** No matter how great a project plan may be, it's the people who will make it succeed or fail. Relationships must be developed and nurtured so that there is a mutual appreciation for one another. Note that a mutual appreciation does not imply similar thinking. I can disagree with what you think but still appreciate the fact that you add value to the conversation. Where there is mutual appreciation, there is the potential to work through difficult issues. Where there is none, the difficult conversations degrade into lowest common denominator solutions which enable a minimization of conflict.

- **Responsiveness.** Being responsive to another is a sign of respect for them as a person. Poor responsiveness is a sign of disrespect. If I don't respond to your email or phone call for several days or if I never respond at all, you will naturally conclude that I don't care. We must be responsive in our communications or relationships will suffer. This can be very difficult, especially for those who have a large volume of communications from others. But it's important enough that there must be some means of handling it appropriately and in a timely fashion or it will ultimately have a negative effect on our ability to make progress and to be more missionary.

- **Significant involvement of the priests.** Without priest involvement in setting up the details, there will be no buy-in. Even when there is priest involvement, there's a struggle to get buy-in. Never let the Curia people define something in a vacuum.

- **Strong, regular, and frequent communication.** At times we were accused of putting out too much information, having too many meetings, and so on. But without question doing so benefited us because we could always say with complete integrity that we tried to be as transparent as we could be. A wise and experienced Communications Director like we had in Edmundo Reyes is very important.

- **A clear project leader.** I'm not by any means trying to pat myself on the back here, but it doesn't take a lot of effort to realize that trying to lead a major project by committee is going to be very difficult. Someone needs to be in charge and make the decisions. I can't even begin to count the number of times that I had to make a decision to keep things moving forward.

That doesn't mean that I ran off without input. But when all the input has been given, someone has to decide what's best given the assessment of the impact to the overall effort, especially when all of the input doesn't align.

- **A committed support team.** I've said it time and again in this book, but I believe that my Coaches and Missionaries were a blessing from the Lord and a critical part of our efforts to move to Families. Their commitment, their collective experience and wisdom, and their willingness to take personal attacks and still take the high road in their response was a thing of beauty. Perhaps you can get such support from a contract organization, or perhaps you may need to find your own Coaches and Missionaries. But either way, hire and use well the best resources you can find to do things right.

- **A clear deliverable from the Family.** In any restructuring, be it a Church or a secular organization, there will be a tendency for the restructured organization to stay with what they know and not come together in the new structure. This is the path of least resistance. If we had just formed our Families and then walked away, they would have most likely done just this. They wouldn't have started truly working together as a Family for many years. But our Family MSPs forced them to come together and start functioning in their new roles as Priests *In Solidum* and as Directors. It forced them to rally around a project that they needed to do to start to understand and work in their new roles. If you're contemplating a restructuring to Families or something like it, it's quite helpful to make it clear that once the restructuring is done, the Family will be required to do something significant as a Family to prime the pump and get things started.

- **A coordinated effort from the Curia.** If the various departments of the Curia are not aligned as to what we are asking of the parishes and priests, it can cause for confusion and anger out in the field. Priests are justifiably frustrated when they receive contradictory information from different people who work in the same building. Find ways to keep your Curia aligned and focused.

If these foundational things are in place, there is potential for success. Not a guarantee of success, but potential for it. Without these things there is a good probability of failure.

Where we struggled

The flip side of what worked for us is a discussion of where we struggled. What things caused us pain, delays, and unproductive disagreement? As was true in the previous discussion about what worked for us, the things I list here may not be problems for other dioceses. But I'll none-the-less offer a few things that we had to fight our way through with the hope that they may help others who choose to restructure as we did.

- **Spiritual warfare.** There are some who either don't believe in spiritual warfare or who downplay it. I say that it's very real and that it can cause any major initiative to fail if it goes unchecked. If the devil sees that we're making progress toward being a better Church, toward bringing more people to the faith, toward being a more missionary diocese, why wouldn't he try to stop it? It only makes sense. But I think that there's a misunderstanding of what it is. Some think of spiritual warfare as things banging in the night, evil spirits making themselves present to us, and so on. While these things can be evidence of spiritual warfare, they are by no means the only methods. In fact, I think that the devil is smart enough to know that if he were to be so obvious about it, we would be much more inclined to fight it. But if its subtle, we just let it go on like the frog in the pot that is slowly brought to a boil. To fight spiritual warfare, be vigilant in prayer, don't hesitate to bless rooms before difficult meetings, go to Mass and adoration as a team, and make St. Michael your friend. We probably didn't do enough in fighting back on this issue, and it was particularly obvious in the early days of our effort.

- **A spirit of confusion.** Whether it's caused by spiritual warfare or just plain poor business skills, I've found that a spirit of confusion was something that we had to fight our way through on several occasions. I saw this in meetings that went on for what seemed like an eternity with no clear purpose, in emails that created confusion about what's being asked, and in complex conversations that led to nowhere. I like to think that there's a Biblical example of this spirit of confusion found in John 7:40-53.

> *Some in the crowd who heard these words said, "This is truly the Prophet." Others said, "This is the Messiah." But others said, "The Messiah will not come from Galilee, will he? Does not scripture say that the Messiah will be of David's family and come from Bethlehem, the village where David lived?" So a division occurred in the crowd because of him. Some of them even wanted to arrest him, but no one laid hands on him. So the guards went to the chief priests and Pharisees, who asked them, "Why did you not bring him?" The guards answered, "Never before has anyone spoken like this one." So the Pharisees answered them, "Have you also been deceived? Have any of the authorities or the Pharisees believed in him? But this crowd, which does not know the law, is accursed." Nicodemus, one of their members who had come to him earlier, said to them, "Does our law condemn a person before it first hears him and finds out what he is doing?" They answered and said to him, "You are not from Galilee also, are you? Look and see*

that no prophet arises from Galilee." Then each went to his own house.

There are only 15 sentences in this passage, but seven of them end with question marks. Only two of the questions are answered, and one is answered with another question. Nothing is resolved. Nothing is finished. And when they were done, they each went to their own house so that there could be no further discussion. This passage is filled with confusion. It almost makes me want to jump into the scene myself and demand clarity about what's being said and what are the next steps that need to be taken.

I found that in my secular career, there was almost always a certain clarity of purpose. If a meeting was moving forward without a clear purpose, someone would ask what we were trying to accomplish. It's very possible that my experience in this regard was shaped by the fact that I worked in manufacturing, where there's simply no time to waste. Sixty trucks an hour off the end of the line was what motivated us, and anything that didn't help achieve that goal was considered superfluous.

This was not the case in the Curia. Perhaps it was out of an abundance of kindness, but a spirit of confusion was all too common. I found that at times I had to just pause, perhaps in the chapel, and clear my head about what it is that we were trying to do and then recalibrate myself to get things moving again.

If you find that you are experiencing a spirit of confusion, don't just accept it. Seek clarity, or perhaps provide clarity if that's your role to play, but don't sit back and accept it.

- **Clearly defined handoffs.** One of the things that we've struggled with more than I would have ever imagined is trying to define when my team is ready to move on and when the mainstream Curia departments are ready to jump in and take ownership for the Families after launch. I confess that I am to this day perplexed as to why this is a point of contention, as it's pretty simple in my mind. But at the same time, I can't deny the fact that there is confusion.

  If you have Coaches and Missionaries, or a consulting firm, or some subset of the Curia set aside to drive a restructuring in your diocese, it will be important that everyone agrees up front on when that team's work is done. For example, is the restructuring team done with a Family when the priests are named and in place? This could wind up being nothing more than a symbolic change if they're named but not yet functioning in their roles. Is it when the next level below the priests is named (in our case, our directors)? This might be a good definition, but some Families will do this very quickly and others may go well beyond the milestone date. You can't have your launch team sticking with a Family for an extended period of time, even if they're struggling to make progress, or the mainstream departments won't be in the picture.

  While the specifics as to how a diocese will define the handoff will vary, it's important to have some agreement up front so that there's no confusion or disagreement down the road. Not doing so will lead to endless and quite frankly wasteful debates about whether the handoff was too soon or too late.

There are countless other things that could cause for struggle, but these are listed here as a few things that we've dealt with in hopes that others can put plans in place up front to avoid them.

Chapter 19 – Final Thoughts

The End, But Perhaps Not

You may be wondering, did I ever find enough rocks to cross the river? The truth is that I don't know. I have a sense that there's more to be done than what I understand today. I may not see the final rock until the Lord hands it to me when we meet face to face.

But what I do know is that I have been blessed beyond what I deserve for the journey that I've been on. For years I had dreamed of leaving my secular job to do something for the Church, and I finally got my chance. It's been incredibly difficult, and it's not what I wanted or dreamed about. But I believe that we were a part of a very difficult restructuring that will pay dividends for years to come. I believe that we're positioning ourselves here in the AOD to go on mission despite the priest shortage that we're facing. I believe that this was a painful path to follow, but that it was the right path to follow.

My team may never see the full impact of the work that we've done. It may take many years to fully come about. But here's the thing about being on a journey of faith: we have to accept the fact that we may never see the result of what we've done in our lives to try to further the kingdom of God.

What's interesting as I write this final chapter is that in about a year, when the Wave 2 Milestones have largely been hit, my team will disband. Our work will be done, and we'll move on to other things. I've already lost one Coach and a few missionaries to other jobs, but most of these moves have been to positions where they can continue on as disciples, utilizing all of the training and experiences that they've had to serve the Lord in other roles. I find great comfort in this. These fine people are going to continue doing good work for the Lord and for his Church for years to come.

It's my fervent hope and prayer that the Archdiocese of Detroit will continue on our path to be more missionary. I pray for it every day at morning and evening prayer. I believe that we've set the stage for this to happen, but only time will tell how it will play out.

I also hope and pray that other dioceses around the United States and around the world will have the courage to be nimble like the early Church. That they'll make the necessary changes – whatever those changes may be based on their circumstances – to do what it takes to expand their efforts to go and make disciples.

The Church is led by the Paraclete that Jesus promised us when he ascended into heaven. We can't and we won't lose the war, but we can lose many battles along the way if we aren't willing to embrace the new evangelization and think seriously about how we can carry out our function as Church more effectively.

I hope you enjoyed the story of our journey and how we're restructuring for Mission. And if you are part of an effort to restructure in your diocese, know that my prayers go with you.

Peace,

Deacon Mike

Made in the USA
Monee, IL
22 July 2022